The Outhouse

Ava,
Thank you for your
support! Hope you enjoy it.

David W. Dodo

978-1-312-57614-8

The Outhouse

David W. Gordon

Claymore 1745 Press

2014

ISBN 978-1-312-57614-8

Third Printing: 2014

ISBN 978-1-312-57614-8

Claymore 1745 Press
New York

Claymore1745@yahoo.com

Ordering Information:

Special discounts are available on quantity purchases by corporations, associations, educators, and others. For details, contact the publisher at the above listed address.

U.S. trade bookstores and wholesalers: Please contact Claymore 1745 Press via email at claymore1745@yahoo.com or by mail at the above address.

For Dad –
Dedicated to a man who lacked a father and became a
great one despite that.

Thank you.

Acknowledgements

I don't know if this analogy has ever been made, but writing a novel is sort of like sending a man into space. It's the astronaut that gets all the credit, but he couldn't have gotten there without a massive team of people. So, when I embarked on the writing of this novel, I thought, I was alone in its creation. I assumed it was an isolated endeavor. I could not have been more wrong.

Just like that astronaut, I had a considerable team of people who supported me. First, the story concept came from a short story my father had written as a child. If that were not enough, the sense of dedication and belief in myself that he, and my amazingly hard working and devoted mother, instilled in me, made all the difference in the world. The time to write was graciously donated to me by my loving wife. She was so understanding and patient that nothing could have happened without her. My sounding board, part time editor, full time cheerleader, and supplier of snacks when I would not stop writing; I owe her everything.

Gracious thanks go out to all of my early readers. JoAnn Bronchilde, for her meticulous eye for detail, Nicholas Oliverio, for his help in seeing some of the major flaws in the early drafts, Christine McNeil, for her passionate support of those same early drafts, Lynn Gilchrist, for her review of my history, Anna and Brian O'Connor, as well as Lisa Napolitano, for their encouragement, and too many others to name. I could not have done it without all of your support. I am truly humbled by all of your efforts. Simply put, no astronaut is ever really alone.

Prologue

Alameda County, California, February 8, 1987

In an idyllic, breezy backyard, an archeologist was busy at his craft. This archeologist was no Indiana Jones. He wore no fedora or faded leather jacket. He came prepared with no weapons, surely not a whip or sidearm. Evidenced by the nearly healed scratches across his head, he sorely lacked the charm and finesse of Dr. Jones when it came to the ladies. He had none of the intellectual prowess and detective skills that made the hero of the silver screen so formidable an opponent. What little they had in common was threefold. Each had a passion for the outdoors, or at the very least, a feeling of being trapped while indoors. Both exhibited the rather strange addiction to dig into the ground and unearth mysteries. Lastly, they both had really cool names. Koda, though, had a far sweeter and more endearing personality than his famous counterpart. He never showed a hint of anger, impatience, or frustration. A more steadfast and loyal friend one could not ask for. Moreover, he wasn't afraid of snakes.

Koda, a burly, wide-chested yellow lab with luminescent green eyes had spent the better part of three days scampering in his new yard. It was a broad swath of old farmland outside Oakland, California, that was neatly wrapped at the outer edges with old post and rail fencing. Punctuated here and there by trees that provided a perfect mix of sun and shade, and a gentle wind that felt like a softened blanket that wrapped around a small pond at the southern edge of the property; the land offered everything a dog could ask for. It was truly a paradise for dog and man alike and Koda had spent his days as a hard core explorer and companion to the children, while his nights slipped away snoring off the exhaustion at the foot of a child's bed.

If a description had to be offered of Koda, he could best be described as over indulged. At one hundred and ten pounds, he was a massive and imposing Labrador who showed all the signs of a much pampered existence. He had two energetic children who romped and played with him on a daily basis. A five year old girl and a six year old boy that played as differently as their sexes could allow, Koda knew just how to interact with each of them. How much rough housing was enough, or just the right quantity of ribbons and bows that would satisfy. Koda could boast the ability to fetch and hold three tennis balls in his mouth at once. A semi-pro at fake wrestling, Koda made losing to the kids look believable despite his size and weight advantage. Nothing the children had ever torn through and unwrapped on Christmas morn before or since could compare to him. The ultimate in play things, he was a wellspring of effortless joy to them as they were to him.

The children, too, were a constant source of all manner of edible goodies that came to him without effort. There was never a need to beg for attention, nor food. A nudge of his nose or the resting of his massive snout on a lap and food simply flowed. Koda had everything handed to him in life and he knew no other way. His newly constructed house and massive fenced in yard were simply the next step in the natural progression of the charmed life he led. There was no reason today would be any different.

Koda had decided to explore the northern edge of the property today. Whether it was thought out or mere whim, a scent on the wind or the quick motions of a snake that caught his attention one could not say. He sniffed the newly grown bright green grass and nudged small rocks with his nose. Occasionally, he would pause to relieve himself here or there, or scratch his backside rhythmically on a tree. A bird landed to his right and he immediately gave chase only to be foiled at the last minute as it took flight. Undaunted, he returned to his previous course and meandered along towards the fence line. The trek was suddenly interrupted again as Koda made a quick left and buried his nose to the ground. He headed towards the area where the father had been grading the land in preparation for a shed. His pace quickened and soon went from a cantor to a full gallop while his nose remained pressed firmly to the ground. He went some thirty feet before seemingly striking an invisible wall, his backside coming up off the ground as his front paws dug into the earth sending the rest of his body into a skid. He did a quick circular motion around the area that looked much like a native rain dance. Then, he started digging.

Clouds of dirt and uprooted grass flew out from behind him at a rampant pace. The property of 14 Par Court seemed as if it were once again under construction again. The dust storm he created lacked only the steady beep-beep of construction equipment going to and fro. Then, as suddenly as it had begun, the digging stopped. The dirty fog began to clear and Koda's white fur could be seen like the sun peeking through the clouds, as he toiled and worried at the hole he had made. His furry frame lurched backwards as he yanked something shiny out of the ground. The flurry of digging began anew before the old beer can had even hit the ground. Koda had found a treasure trove of construction garbage and discarded lunches and he was not about to stop at the first piece of gold. Small scraps of discarded lumber, what looked like the remains of a glove and even a small ball of tinfoil that had once held a tantalizing sandwich were all excavated within a few short minutes. Yet, none of these items held Koda's fancy for more than a moment. He had caught the scent of something more exciting.

Koda spent the better part of an hour gnawing away at his discovery before he was called for. The squeaky notes of a little girl's voice could be heard on the wind over his grating teeth. "Hear Koda!" seemed to echo in the dog's ears, but he did little more than look up. When he saw that there was no need for an urgent reply, he went back to enjoying the bounty he had worked so diligently to exhume. As he worked the marrow out of the bone that he held in his paws, the drool and slobber flowed freely down upon his work. He heard his name again, stronger and closer this time. He did not pause, rather instead, quickening his pace like a starving man trying to gain the bottom of a pot of soup. It seemed nothing could pull him away. When the screaming started he jerked his head upward so quickly that a string of drool went sailing into the air and landed with a splash right between his eyes. The screaming of the little girl and the unexpected bomb of slobber left Koda disoriented. Though he could not have been as stunned as the little girl was. Koda abandoned his bone and darted toward her. Seeing him coming she turned and ran, her pig tails splaying out behind her with her screams muffled by the air rushing past as she fled. Koda knew this game and quickened his pace. Soon he was in position and stuck his head between her legs sending her stumbling to the ground. He mounted her and sloshed his tongue over and over across her face as he had done a hundred times in the past. She squirmed and attempted escape, screaming as he nudged her from side to side with his head. The game would end when she told him to stop. All she needed to do was give a gentle tug on his ears but she never did.

The girl's screams had reached the ears of her parents and they had come running. The mother, a petite woman in her mid-thirties with a loose fitting pink shirt and completely mismatched yellow sweatpants, arrived holding a pristine unused lawn rake in hand. The father, a stout, serious looking fellow in a tight t-shirt and jeans had turned up empty handed, but ready to fight. On his hands, he wore large lawn gloves spotted with dirt. Koda had no idea they had arrived. He could not hear their shouts over the girl's screams. He had no idea the father had jerked the rake from the mother's hands. The smell of urine reached his snout as the girl's bladder gave way. It was in that moment that he took the very first hit of his life. The man had sent the shaft of the rake into his side with a powerful slap. Tumbling, Koda's eyes went wide and the sun seemed to blink in and out of existence. When the rolling stopped his side ached and it hurt when he tried to stand. He collapsed onto his haunches and tried to piece together what had happened. Mother held daughter in her arms. Father rested the rake on his shoulder. All seemed to stare blankly at his treasure trove of bones. It was a collection that clearly included the skull and rib cage of a long dead person.

Chapter I

Sangreal
September 13, 1987

I never knew my grandfather. That's not for dramatic effect or anything, it's true. I never met the man. My father never really spoke about him either. He was the most mysterious figure in my family. A shroud of silence enveloped my father any time a question arose that centered on this elusive individual. My mother, usually the demure and soft-spoken housewife in furry pink slippers and some variation of a horrible flower printed housedress, would always quickly intercede on my father's behalf anytime my elder brother and I risked a probing question, "Jeffrey! Jason! He got on a bus one day and left. Never came back. Left your father and his brothers with nothing but a brokenhearted mother. Go play!" Storm clouds would seem to gather in the house. The words would rumble like thunder warning a lightning strike was imminent. A stern, serious expression would slice across her narrow face, removing her natural beauty and replacing it with an awful scowl. Her short, incomplete sentences were uttered with a quickness and sharpness of tone that belayed a deeper warning. This was one of the few topics that brought out a hidden strength in her. A protective side, the mother bear buried deep inside her seen only when a loved one was threatened. That seemed to be how she always reacted to our questions, like they were a threat.

Of course, that left my brother and me yearning for information. Jason was a year and a half my senior. Not quite Irish twins, but close enough in age to be heated rivals; we had a penchant for beating one another to a pulp, with Jason often the beater, and me the pulp. We looked nothing alike. Jason, the image of my mother's side and me, my father's. We had different interests and saw the world in very different terms. If my parents were asked, they would describe us as oil and water; two things impossible to mix, destined never to get along. Yet, there was one thing that united us like no other, our parents. If there was a mission to gain advantage within the household over them, we worked together like a well-oiled machine. Any time a family event occurred, our sonar was actively pinging for opportunity. We would circle my relatives like sharks, chumming the water with comments about fathers, grandfathers, marriage, buses, anything we could think of in an attempt to get even a single nibble. Sometimes, one would press while the other backed off, but the hunt was always a team effort. Once, we even plied my father with his typical seven and seven drink, offering to make it for him since Mom was out with her lady friends for the evening. Taller than me by almost a full foot, Jason climbed atop the kitchen counter and gathered the necessary items and dropped them into my eager arms. He slithered off the counter and we focused intently on the task at hand. Jason and I smirked at each other as he poured in more of the liquid from the dark Seagram's bottle than was safe for an elephant to drink. He added a bit of soda and I stirred, the sound of the ice clanking in the whirlpool my finger created. In a massive half-gallon carnival-style glass that took two hands to carry, we delivered it to a father who drank it solely because his sons had made it. It was better than a mud pie, at least. We waited patiently as it took effect. We lay in wait, ready to pounce at any perceived weakness, but every question we used in an attempt to scratch the surface met with skillful avoidance. The man was a gazelle and no matter how tall the grass was or how quickly and skillfully we tried to sink our teeth into him, we would be left with an insatiable hunger. The mystery of our unknown grandfather was the rare case where our team efforts had yielded no success whatsoever. It was like a Christmas present you could perpetually shake, but never unwrap. The story of my grandfather became our white whale. For my brother and me, we sought the story out with a fervor that rivaled a grail quest. Success in our endeavor seemed just as unlikely.

My uncle and father's eldest and only surviving brother had passed away a week earlier in the beginning of September 1987. I was left with one surviving "uncle" so to speak, John, a great burly man whose hands swallowed mine whole when we would greet each other. He was my father's best friend, who just so happened to be married to my mother's sister. My father had been taking the death of my uncle hard, despite the fact that he had always seemed far closer to John than his own brother. Dad was sullen and silent. He seemed to brood more than grieve the loss of his brother.

I was in the small study off to the side of the house when the doorbell rang. My wife was kind enough to sacrifice a formal living room to my burgeoning career in journalism and freelance writing. I had grand dreams and she always played the role of the supportive wife. We walled the room off and I quickly finished it by overstuffing the room with a massive, dark stained oak desk, two odd recliners, salvaged from previous living room sets that had seen better days, and a plethora of eclectic books that cut across every genre and age.

The front door creaked open and my wife greeted my father warmly at the threshold. Dressed in an elegant navy dress that accentuated her petite figure, she invited him in. I listened attentively, though I did not rise to leave the study. They exchanged a hug and Lisa offered her condolences again. "Hello Paul. I'm sorry about Jack. Please let me know if there is anything you need," the words were inadequate, full of all the fruitlessness that grief bears. Yet, her voice was sweet and immediately endearing, one that put everyone and everything at ease. When we had first met, I heard her before I saw her. If it was possible to fall in love at first hearing, I did. Her voice invoked in me images of Homer's Odyssey and the Sirens of legend, those enchanting lyrical voices that dragged sailors towards the rocks. We met at a Delta Phi mixer at NYU. I heard her alluring voice and maneuvered to meet her. Unfortunately, I took a pretty rough and utterly embarrassing tumble over an end table and wound up planting my face into the floor. I turned over, more humiliation than hurt stretching across my face, to be greeted by her whimsical smile and a small, soft hand reaching out to me.

It was that same touch that gently escorted my father into the study. As I watched her hand drift away from him, I took stock of the man who had raised me. Lisa was a diminutive woman with a small, but athletic frame who was dwarfed by the man next to her. He was broad-framed and heavy-set with thick, powerful arms. His belly had expanded over the years. "The six pack is now a keg, eh?" he was fond of saying as his hand smacked into his portly midsection. At 64 years of age, he was tired and haggard; though one would not know it by the amount of work he did each day. A life of arduous physical labor had taken two of his fingers and more than that from his height as his hunched frame aged faster than any of us would have cared to admit. He and I were polar opposites in this regard. Though fit and muscular, I possessed none of the worn qualities my father exhibited after more than thirty-five years running a construction company. A childhood spent heeding the commands that I not make my living with my hands as he had done, ensured that my body did not suffer the ravages of excessive wear and tear. Instead, the evidence of my work, I wore on my head. Here, I matched my father with ease. Though 26 years his junior, my hair, too, was thinning and gray, though far better organized and more neatly trimmed than his. His hair was always disheveled from multiple swipes of his hand moving up and down his face. He would bring his hand up to his chin and send it careening up through his hair in direct correlation to his stress level. It was a motion I had inherited and exhibited only when I was feeling overwhelmed. When a deadline loomed or I struggled to find the right words for a piece I was working on, my wife would know as soon as she saw the tell, the same tell my father had. It was that very same mannerism that allowed my friends to fleece me at the poker table on a regular basis. More than once in our lifetimes when my father's hand headed upward towards his hair, did that motion cause my brother and I to dash from the room before our father's calloused hands flew at us.

Today, that motion brought no fear, only sadness. His eyes drooped heavily from lack of sleep and his voice quivered as he slid a newspaper across the table to me. The paper was folded neatly. Pages had been tucked together to ensure that a single article would remain visible. A thick headline was supported by a single large photograph of a yellow lab decked out in a blue ribbon. The dog looked as if he had one first prize at a county fair. The headline, however, told a different tale. This was the dog that had discovered the mass grave in California. I tried to read the article, but it had been a victim of Chinese water torture. Dots of water had smeared the ink and the article was all but illegible now. Holding the paper in hand, I looked quizzically at my father.

His eyes were locked on me, searching, drilling even. He was trying to see if the article meant something to me.

"I heard about this," I said flatly. My answer apparently satisfied him and the mining operation that was his eyes stopped cold.

His eyes began to search upwards. The loose skin of his neck became taut and it eerily altered his voice as he spoke, "Would you write something for me?"

Here was my most outspoken critic asking for my services? I had always known that his harsh words and demanding nature were a challenge to me. "You're better than this," he'd admonish. That mentality permeated every comment; every look, and it drove me. It was always sitting atop the nest egg of my insecurities, helping to keep them warm and ready to hatch at the worst possible moments. This request was nothing short of shocking to me. It took a moment for me to regain my composure before the words fell from my lips, "Sure, Dad. Anything you need."

The offer was an earnest one, meant to repay a lifetime of debt I owed the man. I would have done anything for him. Sons often love their fathers. They often idolize them and make them legends in their own minds. It wasn't difficult to find reasons to love the man. My father was someone who was as self-sacrificing as I had ever known. I had never seen him put his own needs before the needs of another my whole life. Though he never attended church with the family when I was young he had always seemed the most Christian man I had ever encountered. I never understood why he got to stay home while Mom dragged the rest of us out of the house every Sunday. In my own household, Lisa made church attendance a tacit requirement. She employed that voice of hers that I had realized many years ago I could not say no to. Though I despised any organized religion, I was a regular attendee every Sunday at Saint John's Cathedral. It was a small price to pay to make her happy.

During my time in the military, I had learned the ability to be physically in one place and mentally in another; a survival tool required of all soldiers. One of the many odd skills acquired during my service that found a pragmatic civilian use was when I sat physically in a pew while my mind blissfully spent time elsewhere. When we were dismissed, I would often smile as aggressive parishioners would attempt to run each other down instead of allowing a car in front of them to leave the church parking lot before them. I could not help but reflect on what my father would have said. "One and one and everybody moves," he would utter in a soft frustration speaking to the air in the hopes that the wind might carry some sanity to others. I found myself mirroring him on more than one occasion in this regard. I didn't worship the man I thought my father could be or might be. I idolized the reality of the man and all that he was. Simple, kind, benevolent and giving. He had been determined to be the father that he never had. This he had done in spades and asked nothing in return for it. As with all things in his life, what he determined to achieve he did regardless of the personal cost to himself. The man could ask anything of me and I would give it willingly without question.

His heavy frame sunk slowly into the worn, brown armchair at my side and his head seemed to burrow its way into his chest. Resting on his lap was a weathered family photo album. It had aged creased lines running intermittently across the rather ugly green cover. Punctuated with various stains, the cover offered its center up to an old family photo. A black and white photo of a large family remained a timeless centerpiece that invited viewers into a bygone era. The faces were unknown to me, yet felt somehow familiar and welcoming despite the stern countenances they wore. The clothing was simple and showed signs of farm life. The background was dominated by a large two story house surrounded by an expansive porch. It was instantly nostalgic, giving a feeling of Americana, like an old movie. No, more like Wood's famous American Gothic painting with the pitchfork and its two stoic figures staring blankly at the viewer. It was both eerie and comforting.

I felt the lump form in my throat and I choked back the first stages of the tears that were welling up from within, not for my deceased uncle, but for the shell of a man my father had become. His wrinkled hands shook as he placed the book reverently onto the coffee table before us. We both sat in silence for a few moments. I waited respectfully and rather uncomfortably for him to elaborate on his request.

He adjusted in his seat several times, apparently seeking comfortable footing from which to launch his purpose. He spoke without raising his head, "It's time for a history lesson." Having no idea what was about to transpire, I again waited while the silence hung heavily in the room. "Your grandfather," he began the sentence with a whisper, but it might as well have been a catastrophic explosion as my body tensed into a solid block of muscle and sinew as the anticipation flooded my heart.

The white whale would meet its end today. The grail, discovered! The fountain of youth finally placed upon the map. I was in shock. I was paralyzed with apprehension for fear that I might do something that would cause him to retreat before I could discover the secret. Realizing I was holding my breath, I brought myself under control and forced the air from my lungs. My mind quickly dashed to how much I would enjoy rubbing this most secret discovery into Jason's face. How I would toy with him and offer dribs and drabs of the story as he salivated for more. Oh, how I would enjoy this! I had to forcibly stamp down those thoughts. In my mind, I placed a heavy anvil on them using the images of the cartoons my brother and I loved so much, even including the little Acme insignia in my vision. The anvil could be pushed off, unveiled when the time was right, so I could savor the moment at a later date.

"Your grandfather," he said again, louder this time, but still not in the strong deep bass I had come to expect from him. "my father was a good provider, a good father to us boys. He would have liked you." Unsure what quality or qualities my father was alluding to, I sat stoically and silently, and let him continue. My father once said that he loved that I always seemed to know when to speak and when silence could do the speaking for me. "He never got on a bus."

Imagine it. The one piece of information my brother and I had ever known about the man and it was a lie. If curiosity killed the cat, I was willing to die nine times over now. My appetite for the story was insatiable and growing exponentially. His head began a slow ascent, his neck craned upward at a crawl and his hazel eyes gained a parallel plane to my own before he spoke again. When he did, I could not have been more stunned. "I killed him."

Chapter 2

Genealogy
March 29, 1987

On the TV a chubby, slightly balding Caucasian man in a stiff brown suit stood at the front of a large modern house with cedar shake siding waiting for his queue. The wardrobe choice was a poor one that blended in with his background and made his head look like a free floating dismembered Scooby-Doo ghost in front of the house. When the queue finally came, his saggy face tightened and a serious expression replaced the rather dopy look that had previously occupied his jowls. Clearly, he was a TV reporter who had a face for radio and a voice for it, too. His deep smoker's baritone resonated through the air as he began his report, "On March 28th a Labrador Retriever received a commendation from the Alameda Sheriff's Department."

The reporter began a slow stroll that seemed a labor for him even at such a simple pace. He leaned down and the dark brown spotted tie wrapped around his neck sunk towards the ground and tickled the head of a large yellow lab. Koda gave him a quick glance, using his snout to toss the tie to the side. Koda wore the bright blue ribbon he had received the previous day. The reporter cradled the ribbon in his hand and his heavy belly crashed like a wave over his belt and made his heavy breathing seem all the more certain to lead to an imminent heart attack. "Without Koda here," the reporter pushed the words out, but ran out of air and had to force a deep breath into his lungs before he continued, "the victims of the *Outhouse Murders* would have gone undiscovered." The dramatic effect he attempted to inject into the statement fell flat and he sucked in a few more quick puffs of air as he took a knee next to Koda and continued, "On a quiet afternoon in Alameda County, California, a portly young Labrador Retriever named Koda made a startling discovery. Koda, a 1 year old golden lab, had only lived at 14 Par Court for a few days."

The reporter now seemed to have hit his stride or at least the ability to string more than a single sentence together. "His family had just moved to the neighborhood and he had not even begun to explore all it had to offer. The dog spent his time playing, exploring and causing all sorts of mischief." The man rubbed Koda's head awkwardly as he carried on. "Then, while exploring in the back yard, Koda decided to dig himself yet another fine hole to the chagrin of his owners. However, this new gap in the lawn was a bit different. Instead of burying a bone in the hole, the pup pulled some up." Pride flashed across the reporter's face at that remark. A slow start, but now he felt he controlled his audience.

He rose from his knee and walked towards the front door of the home. A large carved sign inscribed with the family name could be seen just below the brass door knocker. He pointed to it as he spoke, "The Brophy family had only recently moved into their newly built dream home. Koda was lucky enough to find himself the proud new owner of a fenced in back yard. It was his dream home, too." A little smirk cut across his face. He moved off the porch and into the expansive yard; his camera man following in stride. A few beads of perspiration formed at the thinning widow's peak on his head. "The property, constructed by the Conklin Brothers Development Corporation based in San Francisco, is situated on land owned for generations by the Miller family. It was sold for development in 1975. Mired in zoning battles and environmental concerns the land was untouched for almost ten years." A little twig caused an almost imperceptible stumble. The droning baritone of his voice edged higher; but only for a moment. "Beginning in 1984, a series of charming homes with every modern amenity one could hope for began to bloom where vegetables once grew. The property, like those that surround it, was built by architects and laborers who turned the area into a luxury community and nine hole golf course completed in 1986." At this statement the camera man panned to give the viewing audience a look at the course and the sparse number of people currently playing on it. When the camera returned to him the reporter had wiped the sweat away and straightened his tie. "It was one of almost a dozen houses carved into the old Miller farm offering middle class families a gorgeous neighborhood with a large pond and views of the small, well-groomed golf course."

A few steps brought the reporter to a wooden swing bench capped by an elaborate gazebo and a man and woman seated together. "For the Brophy's it was a dream home." The reporter took a seat next to them on the bench. Mrs. Brophy was petite, well groomed and rather stunning in a simple black dress. Mr. Brophy was athletic and exuded confidence in a tailored pair of dress pants and a dark blue golf shirt. The three made an odd pairing and the reporter looked more than a little out of place in this setting. He pressed on despite it all, "It was a day like any other in the idyllic suburb of East Oakland. The family had been enjoying the cool breeze and soft autumn sun. Mr. Brophy was doing some weeding while the missus watered her new flowers and Koda scampered playfully in the back yard." It was clearly a struggle for the reporter to allow anyone else to occupy his limited air time.

After asking Mr. Brophy to recount what had occurred that day, the microphone moved in slow motion towards the homeowner. Mr. Brophy leaned forward, his sinewy arms bulged as they took position on his thick thighs, "I was in the front pulling some weeds. We were going to have a neighborhood party and Kristen wanted things to look their best." He paused for a moment and gave his wife a smile. "Next thing I knew our daughter was screaming. Kristen had gotten to her first and when I had arrived I saw the dog on top of her." The smile had been replaced with a serious expression, one that made the man look more than a little scary. "I took the rake from my wife and knocked him off her and that's when we all saw it." The couple's hands seemed to intertwine almost simultaneously, taking strength from one another.

The reporter rose from the bench leaving the couple and continued to head deeper into the yard as he spoke, "The recent construction, coupled with the grading of the property, and aided by Koda's energetic paws, had unearthed a shallow grave. Mr. Brophy called the sheriff's department and explained what had transpired. The first deputy arrived within fifteen minutes and was followed by an endless stream of officers and equipment that swarmed the property." His stumpy fingers pointed to various bits of the remaining evidence of police activity as he spoke. Tracks from backhoes had scratched deeply into the yard. Police tape fluttered in the gentle breeze and the lawn was pot-marked by holes with one large crater roped off with police tape and makeshift sticks stabbing into the earth to hold it in place. "Mrs. Brophy, already distraught over the discovery, tried to control the flood of people and machinery pushing into her backyard. The excavation had begun and Mrs. Brophy watched in silence as her beautiful lawn was torn up. The neighborhood party would have to wait."

Carl Erzt returned now to the bench and reoccupied his previous seat. "Were you surprised by the response from local authorities?" he asked, poorly transitioning from one segment to the next of his lengthy report.

This time it was Mrs. Brophy who responded, "We were stunned by the size and speed of the response. Steve and I wondered if the Sheriff's Department had already known what they would find."

The reporter flashed a huge smile as Mrs. Brophy had responded just as he had coached her to. He quickly took over the narrative. "Over the course of the next three weeks law enforcement personnel exhumed the remains of 38 bodies from a single corner in the backyard of the Brophy home." His voice quickened as he moved on. This was his glorious moment. The segment that was going to make his career! "The bodies were dismembered and decomposed with little more than bone remaining." He rose from his seat and moved slowly towards the camera giving an almost 3-D effect, "Yet, something always struck the Brophy's as strange because the detectives never really asked them any questions."

Now was the moment of the big reveal, the information that no other news agency had. It was the little tidbit that came to him via his friendly connections with the Sheriff's Department, particularly the sheriff's secretary who just so happened to be his sister-in-law. "What Mr. Brophy and his wife did not know was the Sheriff's Department had tried to search the area almost two months ago, but had not been allowed to do so." "Bam!" he thought. There it was. Take that world!

He continued straining for perfection with every word, "In December of 1986, three months earlier, the police received an anonymous tip that a mass grave could be found at the home. Initially, the tip was dismissed as the ranting of some lunatic, but the calls kept coming. In fact, sources close to the investigation say the informant was persistent and patient." The gleam could no longer be hidden as he recounted what he was given, "The informant offered specific details about the site but never gave a name. The caller even referenced some unsolved missing persons cases in the region. My sources said he either did his homework, or he knew something. Law enforcement agencies knew they couldn't get a warrant on an anonymous tip, so they contacted the Conklin Development Corporation to see if they could look around the site. When they told them what they wanted to look for, the Conklin Corp refused to allow a search."

Oh, it was pure gold what he had. It was the very currency that he had used to parley with his bosses to get this assignment. "The Conklin Development Corporation could not be reached for comment at press time, but sources close to them have stated that the company was concerned it could face significant economic loss if the new development had faced allegations of being a mass grave. The Conklin Brother's didn't account for a spunky young lab, though. Koda's discovery became the focus of a massive police investigation and has fixated the nation, stunned by the barbarity of the discovery and wondering how and why it all happened. Local law enforcement agencies have offered a final gruesome tally in what has been dubbed the *Outhouse Murders*. The dismembered remains of thirty eight victims have been disentangled and removed from the site where the Miller family outhouse once stood."

He paused and a series of historical images flashed across the screen as he spoke, "A local farm throughout the Depression and through the late fifties, the Miller residence passed through at least three generations of the family according to local records before being sold for development as a residential community. Police have confirmed that a member or members of the Miller family are the prime suspects for the murders. Details are emerging as to who the Miller family was, and conjecture is running rampant as to who would commit such heinous acts and why. Police efforts to investigate these grisly murders have been hampered by, and I quote, ". . . the passage of time and the limited records we have to go on." Clues as to what may have happened on the farm some thirty years ago are scant. Until the name of the informant is discovered or the police track down the family, the truth behind the *Outhouse Murders* will remain buried." Yet, even as he said it, he knew it wasn't true. Thanks to his sister-in-law, he would be the one to reveal that to the world, too. "Not yet though," he thought. "Always leave them wanting more." He paused briefly before signing off, trying to suppress a coy smile as he did. "This has been Carl Erzt reporting."

Chapter 3

Revelations

I knew I heard him say it. It was as clear as day. My father had said he killed his own dad. I do not know what abject terror or shock my face betrayed. I have no idea how I must have looked to him as he delivered this revelation. I only know that, whatever my reaction was, it constituted the culmination of his greatest fear. I watched as the oppressive silence was shattered; as the man I aspired to be crumbled into a mass of sobs and tears. All I could do was sit there and stare as his head bounced in his hands, while his back rose and fell as his lungs fought through the sobs. I had only seen the man cry once in my life before.

It happened when I was in that awkward stage of not being a boy, but not yet really a teenager either. I had dreamed of being an astronaut and had taken on a paper route to fund a trip to Florida to see a launch. It was a boyish dream, but one that I had perseverated on and persevered through challenges great and small to achieve. Four-thirty AM trips around the neighborhood on my bike delivering papers, substituting schoolwork when other kids my age were playing and raking leaves around the neighborhood instead of playing baseball, I was determined to see the dream into a reality. My dedication and resolve made the man proud and I knew it. His pride fueled my drive.

Then, it happened. The fire on Apollo One. Three dead astronauts, Grissom, White, Chauffey and with them the resolve of a child. I packed up the models, the toys, and my hopes, and tried in vain to push the heavy box into the attic. In tears, I asked my dad for help. He nodded his assent and walked quietly with me to the foot of the rickety fold-out stairs. He picked up the box and walked up the stairs, never saying a single word to me. I watched at the foot of the stairs, tears streaming down my cheeks as he place that box in the back corner of the attic with the same level of gentle care he had given our dog Sheba when she had died. His hands placed it down softly and he paused over the box for a moment as if in prayer. I waited at the bottom of the pull-down stairs for his return, but it did not come. I shifted to the side of the stairs to see what was delaying him when I saw the unmistakable signs of tears falling from my father's eyes! I never told him I saw. I did not understand it then, but I grew to understand it when my own children were born. It killed him to watch my dream die. To him, it was as if someone had killed a part of his son and he was powerless to respond. I watched as he wiped the tears away and came down the stairs. A quick rub of my head and off he went. Those were the only tears I had ever seen from him until now.

"Dad," I stammered, concerned no longer about the long lost grandfather quest, but the man in front of me, "I don't understand." Finding my feet I grabbed him a tissue and began rubbing his back, his flannel shirt scratching at my hand as I did so. "You can't blame yourself." I had every faith that his words were claiming a greater share of responsibility than he deserved. His were broad shoulders, used to taking on the weight of the world. If he were a Greek God he would be Atlas for certain. Any organization he was involved in would inevitably find him leading it. At work, he never asked a man to do something he was unwilling to do. That strict philosophical approach to accountability and effort was imbued into his sons as well. When I was sixteen, working at the hardware store, I had been promoted due in no small part to the work ethic he had instilled in me. It was the first time I would be in a true leadership position, responsible for men twice my age. My father did not congratulate me. There were no accolades, no celebration of my triumph. He merely placed his hand on my shoulder, looked me square in the eye and said, "A leader always takes a little more of his share of the blame and a little less than his share of the credit." A motto he lived by and I strove to honor. He wiped only a portion of the tears from his face and he brushed off my pitiable attempt at consolation.

"I killed my own father." The words hung in the air as if they did not know which direction would offer cover for them. The armchair creaked with age and the strain of my father's weight as he shifted uncomfortably in it. His fists clenched, he raised his right arm and pounded his chest, "I killed him. I did it on purpose, and I meant it." His deep sadness had turned quickly to seething rage as he spoke. His face had taken on a shade of deep crimson and the tears now looked as if they were streams of lava spewing from a volcano.

For my part, I sat in stunned silence as everything I once knew was being decimated by my father's apparent confession. "He was a lying bastard! A son of a bitch that deserved everything that I did!" Spit flew from his mouth as he spat the words. Suddenly cognizant of his own language and the volume of his voice, as well as, the attention it might attract, he quickly brought his growling under control again. "Why did he have to do this to us?" he said. The words were tinged with hatred and regret and confusion. They were a murky recipe of animosity and veneration. Quickly, my father's head fell again to his chest and the tears fell freely.

With one hand on his knee and another rubbing his back I stammered, "It's okay, Dad. Everything is going to be okay."

For a man who made his living in words, I had none to give him when his elder brother had died and I had fewer still to give him now.

Slowly, the heaving of my father's chest subsided and his breathing slowed. He wiped his face and brought his head high. He stiffened his back and released the pressure in his fists. For a moment, he looked the part of a soldier preparing for inspection. "Sit, please." He pushed the words out trying to bring a level of composure to his frame that had been lacking since the start of our conversation.

I did as he asked. I took a seat in the smaller rocker that my wife often sat in while I wrote. It was an old wicker chair with an orange cushion that looked tragically out of place in the study. She would often sit reading a book while I pounded away on the typewriter. Occasionally, I would look up and see her smiling sweetly at me. I would return the smile, and she would simply return to her reading. I never really did understand why she sat with me. I argued with her about it sometimes, feeling like she should not have to endure it. Secretly, I loved that she did it. I loved the rocking chair because it was the place that her smiles emanated from. I only hoped that I could bring him the same level of comfort Lisa gave me.

I waited for him to go on with the confession for lack of a better word. He stared at me with the same dogged determination I had seen in his eyes when I told him I was joining the Marines. We had been in the back yard chopping firewood for the coming season when I had worked up the courage to tell him that I was doing as he once did, enlisting. For a man who had worked so hard to ensure that his son did not follow in his footsteps, I doubted he would take the news very well. I don't remember exactly how I had said it, but he got the message and paused the heavy, eight-pound splitting maul in mid-chop. I remember the axe falling back onto his shoulder resting on one of the many flannel shirts that had become a sort of self-imposed uniform for him. His hazel eyes met mine and they looked as they did now; strong, defiant, and brave, with flecks of anger spread throughout. How I wish I had those eyes, that courage, but that was one gift I never felt I had fully inherited from him. At this moment, just as I had done then, I stood frozen, waiting to see what those eyes would bring forth. Would it be a great tempest of frustration over my supposed lack of judgment or serene and stoic lecture? "Semper Fi." he said flatly. "Your mother isn't gonna be very happy, you know." The great eight-pound maul slid from his shoulder and pummeled a large piece of wood splitting it in two. I leaned over and reset one of the remaining sides onto the block to be split again. Without a word he struck again, and we were back in the groove.

I had expected a fight and none had come. I had expected a stern reproach at the very least and even that was not forthcoming. I had known he was not happy with my plans to join the military, much less the Marines. His response shocked me not so much for his lack of argument but for the show of respect he had given to me at that moment. He did not try to persuade me or discount my decision. He backed my play. He supported me despite his own feelings and at that moment I loved him all the more. It was the first time I felt like a man in his eyes. We worked the rest of the day and did so in silence. The rhythm of our labor remained unbroken, splitting, setting, stacking, splitting. I did not break the silence then. I would not break it today and so I waited for him to continue.

There was no thudding of the maul in the study, no shredding of maple or oak or pine to help assuage the oppressive quiet. Thankfully, I did not have to break the silence that pervaded the room that had become my father's makeshift confessional and I, its unwilling priest.

Still staring at me he gave the first clue to his intentions, "I want you to write our history. I want you to tell the story of our family as you have done so well for others."

I accepted the compliment graciously, "Thanks, Dad." I rose with purpose and gathered my notepad and pencil from my desk. Pulling the thin drawer open, I grabbed the sharpener and gave it a few turns before tossing it back in. I looked around a moment for my tape recorder which was never the last place I left it. My wife, ever helpful in organizing my things, had moved it to an unknown location. As always, my work began with a search. It was ironic that the greatest mystery of my brother's and my life was about to be solved, but the mystery of where my tape recorder was what took precedence! Moving a few stacks of paper, tearing open each of the drawers and finally discovering the recorder in the last place I looked, on a shelf with the latest fiction additions to the library.

My father had sat and watched me as I had searched and a half smile cut across his face. "She's just like Mom, you know." I answered with a forced smile not letting my frustration get the best of me. Internally, I promised to get a lock for the study and ban her from her organizational missions. I envisioned a big one, a medieval sized bolt-lock, maybe even a moat! It was ridiculous but the thought made me smile.

"Sorry about that. She does that to me all the time," I said quickly trying to get our conversation back on track.

The wrinkles on his faced creased and he said, "You know, you won't ever win. Just do as she tells you. It's easier that way." His face wore a familiar expression. These words of wisdom were not the first he had imparted to me. Nor would they be the first I ignored despite how right he was.

"Lisa and Mom cannot stand to see anything left out for too long. Remember when Mom used to clean up the tools when we were still working? I still remember when you fell over her as she was cleaning up under the ladder!" The reminiscence was off topic but I could not help it. My father beamed with happiness at the memory, though the day it happened he was anything but pleased. There were numerous "Damns!" and "What the hell's?" and "Jesus H. Christs!" fired off at Mom that day. Once the tirade ended, and we returned to installing the ceiling fan, it took a solid two hours before he changed the subject to something other than Mom's cleaning addiction. Despite the momentary frustration and the foibles present in all good relationships, the two adored and respected one another tremendously. Their marriage was the envy of all who knew them. The smile on my father's face held tight to the memory for a few moments before falling into a cavernous frown. "She's the reason I did it," he whispered. I nodded agreement to a statement I could not fully grasp. "He was going to kill her right before my eyes. I had to make a choice."

Then, my father began his story.

Chapter 4

Family Matters
Alameda County, California, 1932

I grew up on a farm in California, outside of Oakland. I was seven in 1929 when Wall Street crashed and took the nation down the toilet with it, though my family was lucky and had escaped the worst the Depression had dumped on the country. Later on, while other families competed for work against the Okie's migrating into the state, my family seemed unaffected by the economic realities of the Great Depression. We lived outside Oakland where, as the number of homeless in the state swelled to enormous proportions, the winter of 1932 gave birth to Pipe City. The people who lived in those six foot long concrete sewer pipes called the encampment Miseryville. The pipes, stored above ground by the American Steel and Concrete Pipe Company, were unused save for those that made makeshift homes from them. Each pipe offered the resident space enough to slide in and make a bed for themselves. Taken as a whole, the area looked like the entire city had hung out their laundry to dry just as a tornado struck. The pipes were capped with shirts, trousers, and blankets of various colors and qualities. Dotting the landscape, scavenged pots and pans were strewn about in front of the pipes. My father would often take Jack and me into the city on business and we would pass Pipe City, as the press called it. We sold vegetables to the grocery wholesalers in the city. My father would negotiate prices with the wholesalers while Jack and I sat in the Fageol truck my pa had bought right there in Oakland. Staring out at the triangular shaped hood we waited for his return. My pa was proud to own a two-ton Bear, not the smaller Cub version most of the local farmers had bought on installment. It was a badge of honor for my pa that he owned the truck outright and had not bought it on time. At least three times a day Jack and I would hear some variation of, "Damn fools is what they are, damn fools. What kinda person buys somtin' they can't afford? Fools, I tell ya." He loved that truck and would not hear a bad word spoken about it no matter how old or beaten down it had become.

I remember one day my father returned to the truck looking downtrodden and broken.

"Pa, what's wrong?" Jack asked.

"Let's get home, boys," he muttered trying to avoid Jack's and my gaze.

Jack was my older brother in age and size only. At thirteen, he was the image of a brawny young farmer and the spitting image of our father. Broad shoulders, strong arms, and the hint of facial hair that made him look eighteen when he was a ways off of that mark. What he had on me in strength and speed he sorely lacked in brains and logic. Two years his junior and far more than that in size and weight that had not yet come, I was smart enough to know not to go down the path he was headed.

"How much did we get, Pa?" Jack issued a more pointed question knowing the probable source of Pa's frustration.

"Not enough." Pa spat as he fought with the engine to get it to turn over.

Without warning, Jack threw the metal truck door open and leapt down from the cab. Jack charged through the grocer's door with clenched fists. Pa froze for just a moment before he tore out of the truck in pursuit. I never knew what happened in there, but I witnessed the consequences of it sure enough. Jack got the worst lashing with a belt I had ever seen. Pa was relentless until Ma called everyone to dinner. The lesson was apparently taken to heart and Jack never interceded on Pa's behalf again.

I always loved our trips into Oakland. My father would negotiate with grocery wholesalers for the purchase of our vegetables and Jack and I would wait in the truck. If negotiations went well, Jack and I were rewarded with a piece of candy from the small shop down the street. No words were ever exchanged regarding this system the family had in place. It was simply an unspoken and accepted practice. My father would get in the truck, the engine would roar and we began our slow move down the street. The cherry-red Davidson's Five and Dime sign etched with dirty white lettering grew large on approach, dwarfed only by our anticipation. We would both listen intently, hoping to hear the engine downshifting, anything that would give off a sign that the truck intended on stopping. The door would fly open before the rubber of the tires had a chance to settle, and Jack and I would bound into the store like rabbits. I still can't eat a piece of strawberry liquorice today without thinking of those days. Just the smell of it makes me young again. However, if negotiations went poorly, we did not get candy though we still got to do something I came to love.

My father would take us to Pipe City and let us drop off a crate of vegetables to the homeless, downtrodden inhabitants. As we parked the truck in front of the massive concrete pipes with their cardboard curtains and burlap drapes, Jack and I would hop out and wait for the first sight of the denizens of Pipe City to emerge. Slowly, the burlap would begin to sway to one side or another and the residents of each pipe would appear. Often dirty and unkempt, sometimes lacking shoes, they would walk slowly towards us knowing our purpose. Many times before, we had arrived with a crate or two of vegetables. My mother described it as "Christian charity", but she never came to make the delivery. It was as if she needed to do it but didn't want to face the stern reality of the life these people endured. In my heart, I think she feared them because we were not one of them. Not yet at least. The folks here subsisted on Mulligan stew, mostly water with a scavenged, half rotten vegetable or two if they could forage for it.

A tall thin man in his mid-forties always spoke for the group, acting as a sort of mayor.

"Mr. Miller," he said in greeting.

"Howdy, John," my father replied without even a hint of pity.

We had learned long ago that pity was not a welcome sentiment in Miseryville. The deeply ingrained sense of rugged individualism that coursed through the American spirit did not allow for it. No matter how bad things were, one thing was never acceptable; pity.

"Paul, you doing well in school, son?" he would ask.

I would nod and answer, "Yes, sir."

"How 'bout you, Jack?" Jack would nod as well and reply as I had.

However, Jack's answer held far less truth than mine. The man would smile and offer his appreciation.

"We all thank you sir. My wife and daughter pray for your family every night, Mr. Miller."

Family. His was one of the few families that resided in Pipe City. Mostly men filled the ranks. They waited for work. They, like the Okies, desperate migrant farmers from Oklahoma and the rest of the Midwest, who would soon flood California, waited for something that would not appear. Yet, these folks were not as beaten down as the Okies who found that there were no jobs to be had in California. The denizens of Pipe City had not endured the Dust Bowl, not waited for the rain that would never come. In them, the glimmers of hope still flickered, however faintly.

The tall thin man was fascinating to me. He struck me as half ghost, half real. It was as if he was the walking dead in a way. An apparition sent to haunt those who ignored the want and hunger of the world. I did pity him, even though, I tried not to show it. My father often spoke to us about the ragtag community. Neighborhood donations and money from odd jobs performed by individuals within the community helped sustain the group.

"The mayor makes sure everything from donations to food gets shared with everyone," Pa explained.

I never knew that much about the man other than his first name. To me, he was always just, the mayor, the most important guy I had ever met in person.

The best part of leaving home was coming back. Our trips into Oakland would often last the better part of a day. The excitement that welled within us in the earlier parts of the day surely waned as the hours dragged on. Typical of youthful exuberance, Jack and I bolted out of bed and raced through morning chores just for the hopes of earning a seat in the truck. A seat that lacked all the amenities of a modern vehicle and offered a level of comfort that was more akin to the Spanish Inquisition then it was to a sofa. Yet, we wanted to go with all our hearts. On the days where success equated to candy, the ride home was more bearable though not any less uncomfortable. My father would joke with us and tell us stories of his days in France as a soldier in the American Expeditionary Force. His stories often recounted the practical jokes played between bored soldiers and the ridiculous attempts to obtain food from various sources that stretched even a child's imagination to its limits.

Most began with, "I ever tell you boys about the time . . .?" and ended with a "Heh, wouldn't wanna do that again." Those stories are my fondest memory of him. A time when he was not burdened by the pressures of farm life, the relentless onslaught of financial pressures that hung upon him like that of Marley's chains. He was never jovial, never really relaxed in the truest sense of the word. Yet, it was in those long drives with bumps and potholes that would send one's head careening towards the top of the cab wondering if a broken neck would be your undoing that I found myself closest to him. I knew I could never equal him in his knowledge or ability, but I wanted to emulate him, to make him proud.   It was in those long trips home that Jack would stare quietly out the window while I stared at Pa. His face, potted from pox in childhood, stained red from the sun and squinting to see the road before us, was for me, a thing to be studied.

The trips home were quite another thing when negotiations went poorly with the wholesalers. Disheartened and seething with rage, we would know before he entered the truck not to utter a word. The door would slam shut, sometimes bouncing back open from the sheer force he applied. He would drive hunched over the wheel, huffing and sighing, never looking over at us despite our concerned stares. Jack would occasionally poke me in the side trying to prod me into breaking the silence but my father's sullen mood would hold an iron grip of fear over me. The muscles in his arms never relaxed as he gripped the wheel and squeezed it as if he were ringing the life out of one of those wholesalers. The veins pulsed and his entire body held a statuesque pose. So, too, did I. It had been just over a year since we had made a stop at Davidson's Five and Dime. More than a year without liquorice.   Still, Jack and I abandoned home every opportunity we got and clung to hope. We always had hope.

Arriving home felt like a reprieve from the hangman on those days. Pipe City was on 19th Avenue and the distance to our farm could be covered in about ninety minutes in the truck. To a kid that was an eternity of oppressive silence to endure. The thoughts in my head would steadily appear with no outlet like a thousand horses stampeding towards a shuttered barn door. As we approached home I would stiffen in my seat and begin looking for signs of hope. It was the proverbial light at the end of the tunnel. Thankfully, she never failed to appear.

My sister, Anne, would take our little brother Billy to the edge of the farm to wait for our return. She treated our return like a holiday and would come outfitted in a little yellow frock dress that beamed over the horizon like sunrise pushing through the blight and darkness that loomed over the truck. She was a few months shy of twelve, slight in frame, with narrow shoulders and a thin face. The first glimmers of her would trigger the break in silence.

"There!" I would yell and my father's head would snap in the direction of my finger. He would pull the truck to the side of the road while Anne and I hopped in the back and little Billy joined Jack in the cab for the last leg of our journey home. For as long as she was a part of our lives it was always that way.

Chapter 5

The Sweet Spot
1932

As we headed for home my father knew the ritual and no words were required to get him to slow the truck down so Anne and I could hop out. As the truck ground to a halt our feet would hit the ground running.

"You two be on time for dinner, ya hear?" He'd say as if we would ever be late.

Jack and Billy would head home with Pa while Anne and I headed west. On the edge of our property there was a gnarly old tree with a massive canopy that seemed to scrape the bottom of the clouds as they floated by. Many of the larger branches jutted out over a small pond that spread lazily across the horizon. It had dozens of sturdy branches that sprawled outward in every direction making it the ultimate climbing tree. On the rare day when the heat became oppressive, we climbed the limbs as high as our weight would allow and leaped into the pond shattering the shimmering surface with a loud crack! For two kids it was the perfect location to play. On sunny days the pond twinkled like a thousand tiny stars, and the wind would drift across the pond and caress our cheeks as if it was the gentle hand of God himself. We would walk silently to the tree and sit under its ample shade looking across the glistening water. It was no wonder that Anne always called it the *Sweet Spot*.

It's amazing how a thing can become so important to a person. It was just a tree near a little pond, really. Yet, the *Sweet Spot* was Anne's and my place. It was ours. Something we shared, just the two of us and it was special to me beyond words. It seemed the wellspring of every happy memory we had together.

Anne would often bring a treat for me. Of late, the little nuggets she delivered helped to relieve the depression that set in when we passed Davidson's without the brake pads screeching and signaling a candy stop. The delicacy was always concealed on her person, rolled in her dress or hidden in her sweater, and I would impatiently wait for her to disclose it.

Toying with me, she would act as if there was nothing or that she forgot, "Oh, I don't have anything at all." Anne would sneak a piece of fruit or a hunk of freshly baked bread and even, on rare occasion, a small sliver of apple pie wrapped in a cloth that she would sneak from the kitchen. It didn't matter what she had brought, I loved her for it. One day, after a particularly miserable trip home from the city, Anne had brought me a small piece of cake. She unwrapped it with great pride as she told of her efforts, of how successful a smuggler she had been despite Ma's ever watchful eyes.

"She was sittin right there, I tell ya, right there and I slipped it out unda' her nose." Handing it off, Anne collapsed back into a small notch at the base of the tree trunk and watched me as I cupped the piece of cake in both hands. I raised the cake to my mouth and took an enormous bite. The vast gap between my lips as I shoveled more cake in could only be matched by the size of Anne's satisfied smile. The gentle curls of her shoulder length hair bobbed up and down like a fishing lure as she giggled, eying my efforts to ensure that not one ounce of cake be allowed to escape my lips. For her, these little gifts were a game. To me, they were a tradition.

We played all sorts of games together. We would exhaust every shape and color of the tiniest items on the horizon as we played "I Spy." Various leaves, pieces of fence and all sizes and shapes of clouds became our toy box. Anne would look for anything yellow she could find, and so I often started our games seeking out her favorite color to gain an unfair advantage over her. If it was yellow, she loved it no matter how useless a thing it might be. In fact, "Lemonade What

Was Your Trade" was her favorite game simply because of the color! Though I didn't care much for it, I never complained when she asked to play it.

She would call out, "What's your trade?" and I would answer, "Lemonade!" Anne would beam with joy at the fact that we were now playing the game she adored and would answer, "Well, show us some if you're not afraid!" Then, I would start acting like a lion tamer or a doctor or soldier. When she guessed correctly, I would dash to the fence line, our home base, trying to outrun her before she caught me. Whole afternoons would melt away under the soft yellow sun as we played together.

As the sun faded to a red hue, warning us it was time to head home, we would grow somber. The day was drawing to a close and the mornings that followed would bring chores, school and work. The days would bring the typical infighting that comes with family. Jack would needle me until I swung at him, "Ma! Paul done gone and took a swing at me!" he'd call out for attention. Sometimes, he would try to get me in trouble; other times, he used the wild haymaker as the excuse for a thrashing. I looked up to Jack; but I hated him, too. I wanted to be him and I wanted to beat him so badly that sometimes I didn't know which I wanted more. Even if it wasn't me or Jack, Pa would grow angry at something or other. A tool would be thrown or something would get kicked. He had grown progressively angrier those days. Things weighed on him more; little things brought him to lash out like never before. We saw no evidence of it then that the Depression was starting to encroach on our family. Pa knew it then but none of us could see it. Only he felt the unmistakable tug of being pulled under. For the two of us, the sinking sun would tug us down with it, too. The huffs and puffs of our simple, daily lives seemed to encroach on our fun and we resented the setting sun for bringing them on.

We would walk slowly back to the house. Dragged by the weight of the setting sun, we would tug at it, trying to keep it from sinking, holding it aloft a few precious minutes more. As we made our way down the road, Anne and I would try to bump into each other, knocking each other off balance. Success was measured by how far we could send one another careening off the road and into the grass. Other times we would playfully try and trip one another throwing our legs into each other's path. We would lag behind, tugging at each other. Anne would feign a pebble in her shoe and then tug my sandy brown hair. I would stop to tie my shoe and then dash forward and yank at her curls. We simply found any excuse to slow the trip home. Our time together was precious, and though we never spoke of it, we knew it even then.

Anne and I had a special relationship. In a way, being the middle kids made us a pair. I looked up to Jack, the eldest, and attempted to emulate him in all his physical prowess. I envied Billy, the youngest of us, for being the exception to every rule. But Anne was the one I loved simply for being her. That's why what happened was so hard to endure.

It was about a week after my tenth birthday when it happened. Anne was feeding the chickens with Billy scampering around the coop like a puppy nipping at her heels. Jack and I were carrying seed bags into the barn while my father fidgeted with the tractor.

"Come on Paul, you take too long," Jack complained.

The bags were heavy for me, but he seemed to toss them around with ease. Huffing, I replied, "You got someplace else to be?" my tone was sarcastic. I often tried to bait him though it never ended well for me.

"Some farmer you make," he'd said dryly. "Can't eat books ya know," he added as an afterthought.

I desperately looked forward to the day when I could match him in size and strength for I had years of torment to make up for. "Least

I can read 'em," I shot back at him as I dropped a bag on the stack in the barn, secure in the knowledge that he was already half way back to the truck and a minimum safe distance had been established between us. That's when I heard him scream.

Chapter 6

Pain
1932

"Pa! Pa! Quick!" Jack was yelling, an unmistakable urgency in his voice.

I ran out of the barn and nearly got flattened by my father as he came from working on the tractor. Jack had vaulted over the fence into the chicken coop where Anne was lying face down in the dirt. Billy was sitting on her back, riding her like a horse and whooping loudly. Jack tossed him to the side and he hit the ground hard and immediately started to cry. Pa and I didn't pay the slightest attention to him, though. Jack had turned Anne over and was brushing the dirt from her face. He used his forefinger to scrape the mud from her lower lip. Suddenly, she was lofted into the air, a pair of strong arms taking her away from us with stunning speed. Pa had scooped her up in his arms and was three steps towards the house before Jack and I knew what had happened.

We ran to the house and almost tore the storm door from its hinges as we entered. Pa had laid Anne on the kitchen table and Ma had already stuffed several dish towels under her head. Jack and I both stood waiting, not knowing what to do. Ma rubbed Anne's cheeks and called to her, "Anne. Anne, dear, can you hear me?" Pa had stood back and joined us in our useless vigil. Ma ran her hand along Anne's head and shot a look at Pa. "She's burning," Ma murmured almost inaudibly.

Pa was already walking towards the front door as he said, "I'm gonna go for the doc." He grabbed his hat as he passed out of the house, and the wait began.

The Outhouse

When we heard the truck coming down the path to the house, Jack ran to the window. "Ma! Here he comes!" Jack dashed to the front door to open it as if that would somehow speed Pa into the house. I was standing in the kitchen holding a cold towel over Anne's head. She had awoken for only a minute while Pa was gone. She mumbled something imperceptible and then fainted again. Ma had me run to the well with a bucket to fetch some water for her, and now I stood holding the wet towel in place while she paced to and fro. Pa charged through the front door without acknowledging Jack's efforts at holding it and the doc followed close behind. The two came into the kitchen, and the sense of urgency in Pa's face made me nervous beyond words.

The doctor was a curmudgeonly old man with a bushy white mustache, leathery lips, and narrow eyes partially hidden behind his thick glasses. He was tall and thin, with gangly fingers and well-groomed fingernails. No one could ever mistake him for a farmer or a laborer. He held his old leather bag in his right hand and seemed to lean in that direction. If the wind blew, he would probably be sent careening fifty feet before he landed and shattered into a thousand pieces.

The doc went to work right away shuffling across the floor towards Anne. He placed his bag on the table and opened it, removing a few items as he surveyed the scene. He pushed me aside with a flick of his wrist and began to check Anne's temperature. Next, he listened to her heart. He lifted her shirt and pushed on her belly a bit.

"She been coughin' or complainin' of a headache lately?" his hands now feeling around Anne's neck.

Ma nodded her head and then realized that the doc couldn't see her, "Yes." His hands slid back down to her belly poking and prodding.

"Was the cough like a bark?" He made an imitation whooping cough sound.

"No," Ma said flatly, her nerves starting to overcome her.

"Hhmm," he muttered to himself leaving the rest of us to wonder.

I hated him. I blamed him for the big scar on my left arm and the pain of the stitches both going in and coming out. I had suffered a large and deep gash in my forearm when Jack and I decided it would be a good idea to surprise Pa and build a new shed. Like any plan from a six and nine year old mind it was better in thought than in reality. An hour into our endeavor with jagged wood and sharp saws it was a nail that did me in. We had driven a dozen or so nails into one board in the hopes of getting the shed to come together. Every one of them stuck out the far side giving the wood the look of a terrified porcupine with quills ready to strike. I walked past it without looking and scraped along as it tore a hole into my arm. Ma couldn't stop the bleeding and so it was time for the doc. "Stop fidgeting," he kept repeating as he sewed my arm up while I cried. "Quit your griping, child," his cigarette bouncing in his mouth as he issued his commands with puffs of smoke floating into my face. The man was inhumane, uncaring and I never could breathe around him.

He turned away from Anne almost as fast as he had arrived and dug his hand into his shirt pocket. A quick flick lit the match, and he was puffing away on his cigarette as he began to speak.

"Typhoid be my guess," he said in an all too matter of fact tone. "We can do some blood or stool tests, but that ain't gonna matter none right now." Taking a long drag from his cigarette and letting the smoke fill his lungs he said, "Try and keep the kids away. Keep her hydrated best you can. I'll be back in a week to check on her." He lifted his bag and shuffled to the door. Pa walked him out and paid him for his time.

The days dragged on. Anne had risen from bed only with help and only to use the outhouse. Sometimes, she would make it and other times Ma would clean up the putrid green slime she would inadvertently leave behind. I got caught sneaking into her room four times in a single day before Ma conceded and assigned me some of Anne's care. I helped keep her lips moist as she breathed with her mouth open as she lay in bed. Ma said I needed to squeeze some water into her mouth every hour so; I did exactly as I was told. I even volunteered to help Ma clean the soiled linens, but Pa yelled at me, "Whose doin' your chores when you're doin' all this?" By the time the doc came back Anne's fever was worse and we were all exhausted. He had nothing new to offer but didn't mind getting paid all the same. He suggested sending Anne to the hospital but knew we could never afford it.

Two days later I entered her room alone. It smelled funny, not like usual. The air in the room was dank and stale, taking on the smell of the barn in the middle of summer. "When Anne got well she would beg Ma for lemons to make the room smell better," I thought. For now, Anne seemed not to notice the stench nor my arrival. She lay still in her bed, the quilt my grandmother made for Jack when he was born neatly pressed around her sides. She lay on her back, her eyes closed and her body still. Her face was thinner now, gaunt and sallow. I stared at her from the doorway for a moment trying to not think the worst. It was so hard not to think those thoughts. Everything I saw looked the part of death. I had seen enough living things die on the farm to know the signs.

"Keep up hope and don't you dare show her you're scared, hear me?" Ma scolded. Her look was falsely stern, poorly hiding her red, swollen eyes and sullen feeling of despair. The sight of Anne looking so ashen was more than we could bear. She was normally so bright, so vibrant, and alive. Looking at her still and silent in her bed reminded me of a party bonfire, the center of all activity, warmth and fun the night before, now cold and silent. Tears began to fall unabashedly from my eyes as I walked to her bedside.

I took up a post next to her bed, sitting on a small wooden stool next to her. I stared at her. Her body was unnaturally still. The silence in the room was oppressive and I felt I could hear the tears rumbling down my cheeks. Anne's breathing was so shallow that I brought my head to her chest. Her heart beat meekly, and her chest raised and lowered almost imperceptibly under the weight of the heavy quilt. I gently rubbed the tips of my fingers over the skin of her forearm. The soft caress elicited no response but I continued it anyway. For several moments I rubbed her arm before I spoke to her. "Billy misses you. He bit Ma today. Right on the hand as she was trying to dress him." I knew that would make Anne smile. Pa was always saying that he thought Billy mixed up who his mom really was. "That boy don't recognize you, Ma. Little Anne sure be the one for him. It's like watching a kitten tryin' to nurse off a sow, I tell ya." Anne didn't smile, though. She offered no response to my touch or my words.

"Ma said I should come read to you," I whispered. I got up and walked across the room to her bookshelf. It took only a moment for me to find the book I was looking for. We had about twenty books as a family, one of the many gifts left to us from our grandfather, and most were stored on the shelf in Anne's room. I looked for a volume with an off white binding and green trim. When I found it, I pulled it from the shelf and looked at the funny lion on the cover. He wore glasses and had a deep orange mane, on a green backdrop. The title was a mix of both green and orange text. Holding the volume in my hands, I scurried across the room taking a seat back on the stool. "*The Wonderful Wizard of Oz*, by L. Frank Baum," I said as I flipped through the first few chapters. I wanted to read her favorite chapter where Dorothy Gale started down the yellow brick road. "Chapter Three, How Dorothy Saved the Scarecrow," I began.

"When Dorothy was left alone she began to feel hungry. So she went to the cupboard and cut herself some bread, which she spread

with butter. *She gave some to Toto, and taking a pail from the shelf she carried it down to the little brook and filled it with clear, sparkling water. Toto ran over to the trees and began to bark at the birds sitting there. Dorothy went to get him, and saw such delicious fruit hanging from the branches that she gathered some of it, finding it just what she wanted to help out her breakfast.*

Then she went back to the house, and having helped herself and Toto to a good drink of the cool, clear water, she set about making ready for the journey to the City of Emeralds.

Dorothy had only one other dress, but that happened to be clean and was hanging on a peg beside her bed. It was gingham, with checks of white and blue; and although the blue was somewhat faded with many washings, it was still a pretty frock. The girl washed herself carefully, dressed herself in the clean gingham, and tied her pink sunbonnet on her head. She took a little basket and filled it with bread from the cupboard, laying a white cloth over the top. Then she looked down at her feet and noticed how old and worn her shoes were.

"They surely will never do for a long journey, Toto," she said. And Toto looked up into her face with his little black eyes and wagged his tail to show he knew what she meant.

At that moment Dorothy saw lying on the table the silver shoes that had belonged to the Witch of the East.

"I wonder if they will fit me," she said to Toto. "They would be just the thing to take a long walk in, for they could not wear out."

She took off her old leather shoes and tried on the silver ones, which fitted her as well as if they had been made for her.

Finally she picked up her basket.

"Come along Toto," she said. "We will go to the Emerald City and ask the Great Oz how to get back to Kansas again."

She closed the door, locked it, and put the key carefully in the pocket of her dress. And so, with Toto trotting along soberly behind her, she started on her journey.

There were several roads nearby, but it did not take her long to find the one paved with yellow bricks. Within a short time she was walking briskly toward the Emerald City, her silver shoes tinkling merrily on the hard, yellow road-bed. The sun shone bright and the birds sang sweetly, and Dorothy did not feel nearly so bad as you might think a little girl would who had been suddenly whisked away from her own country and set down in the midst of a strange land."

I looked up at Anne's face and saw that her eyes were now open. "Hello," I said beaming brightly. When she did not respond I took her hand in mine, "Anne, do you want me to keep reading to you?" She did not answer. She did not move and I now saw that she did not breathe. Dropping the book I added a second hand to hers. "Anne! Anne! Stop it. Please. It's not fair. It's not fair. Please don't do this." I tugged at her hand, jostling it as if to force movement into her. Her fingers were cold and did not return the squeeze I applied. I started to yell louder at her, angry now at what she was doing. "Don't you give up! Don't you leave me!" Nothing. No movement, no life and no warmth. I bent over and lifted the top half of her feeble frame, taking her into my arms. I hugged her so tightly, trying to keep her warm. I held her, rocking her in my arms as I cried, not ready to say goodbye. Anne was dead.

I held her in my arms and dreamed she had just been deposited in that strange land. That she would meet wonderful friends that would care for her and protect her, that the bright yellow bricked road would rise to meet her and guide her to the gates of the Emerald City. I saw her in her bright yellow dress, walking along the path, smiling as she took in the wonders of the world. She carried her basket covered in cloth. I imagined the goodies she had hidden and wondered what she might bring me. I wondered when the Great Oz would see fit to send her back to me. I wondered when we might meet next at the Sweet Spot, that wonderful place; a place I no longer believed existed.

Chapter 7

Depression
1932

The days that followed were filled with funeral preparations and visits from neighbors. Condolences were offered, hugs exchanged, an assortment of ornately prepared dishes appeared despite the hardship, enough to feed a small army but nobody was hungry; nothing would change what had happened. Anne was gone. Dead. Never coming back. No more visits to the Sweet Spot for picnics. No more yellow dress to welcome us home. No more. Nothing. No Anne. It wasn't fair. Pa had come into Jack's and my room the day before the funeral and sat on Jack's bed. His eyes were swollen and dark and his hair was disheveled. He looked down at the floor and swept his right hand into his hair, rubbing his head. Bringing his arm down he patted the bed indicating for me to come sit next to him. I rose from my bed slowly and wordlessly, padded across the small bedroom and sat next to him. He smelled slightly as if he had not bathed in days. "Me and Ma want to bury her near the tree," he said without raising his head. "Near the pond," he added as if I had not discerned his meaning. "She always loved that spot," the words lingered, taking too long to come out. He struggled with them and it was clear to me how hard he was taking her death.

I had been crying before he came in and the news he brought offered no respite. I brought my hand to his shoulder and let it fall. Pa turned and looked me in the eyes. His face contorted with anguish he sputtered, "It shoulda never happened." The dam broke and the tears gave way. He rose quickly and walked from the room without ever looking back.

The Outhouse

The family was off. Everyone seemed unlike themselves. Jack had not instigated a fight with me since Anne left us. He had not punched me, pushed me or even tripped me. I swear he actually tried to hug me once at the bottom of the stairs. The day after Anne died we had come in from working in the barn. We both reached the foot of the stairs simultaneously and paused to see who would fight to gain advantage for position. Neither of us bothered to try. Who went up the stairs first didn't seem to matter as much now as it once did. Jack looked at me with a quizzical gaze. I stared at him. It was like looking at my father in a slightly reduced form. I waited for him to speak and when he didn't I turned to go up the stairs. I saw his arms reach out for me and I recoiled thinking his attack was imminent. When I receded from his grasp and turned to face him once again, he looked at me with an odd expression and then headed up the stairs without saying a word.

Late that afternoon I walked the farm in a haze. There was a dull thudding emanating from the barn, and I found myself drawn to investigate the noise. The faded crimson door to the barn hung loosely on its hinges and I pushed it to the side as I entered. My father was dragging a long piece of pine across the ground and my eyes instinctively followed him and then passed him to glance in the direction he was headed. A small wooden box was taking shape amidst hay and scrap lumber. It was clear what he was building. Pa never even looked up at me. I stood watching him work for a few minutes. The weight of realization was tremendously heavy. I had waded in sorrow not realizing everything that needed to be prepared.

Without thinking I stammered, "Ne . . Ne . . . Need a hand?" I was surprised by my own offer. Pa stiffened, as if he was shocked by my presence or maybe by the offer I had just made.

His eyes locked on me and he hesitated for a moment before he spoke. "Love one," he said as he held out the hammer offering the handle to me.

I shuffled forward and took the tool from his hand. The thudding and thumping carried on throughout the afternoon and had even drawn in Jack to lend a hand. When the coffin was complete I uttered, "I'll be back in a jiff."

I reappeared a few minutes later with a few paint brushes and an assortment of paint pulled tightly to my chest. Jack ran towards me and took a few cans from my hand as they started to slip out like so many snakes. Pa didn't smile, but his rigid countenance seemed to ease a bit as we spread out and went to work. "I'm proud of you boys; ya know that, don't ya?" Jack and I paused and looked at him. "It's a hard thing ya done here. Nobody should have to do this, especially kids." His eyes welled up but he held it all in. "You boys showed strength here today and that makes me real proud of ya. Lots of people just avoid the hard things in life. Ya faced 'em head on like men."

He motioned as if he was going to take us into his arms and hug us, but he didn't. He stopped short of it and then turned away. Jack and I silently, but proudly, added the finishing touches while Pa tidied up the tools, avoiding our gaze for the remainder of the day.

The morning of Anne's funeral was born bright and crisp. The sun swaddled the farm in a warm blanket of yellow rays and clouds puffed across the sky like soft pillows. A mild breeze slipped across the pond and offered fresh air as the leaves gently swayed to and fro, giving life to the day. It was a perfect day; the very worst day of my life. I lay in bed, getting out would mean accepting the day had arrived, and I was unwilling to admit to that. Rolling onto my side I looked over at Jack who was splayed across his bed, one arm falling limply to the floor. I watched him sleep for a few minutes, wishing I could feel half as peaceful. I wished the fatigue I felt would conquer my mind. I heard rustling downstairs and forced myself to rise. I dressed in my best hesitating at every turn. Quietly, I crept from the room and slipped down the stairs. The aroma of bacon and eggs wafted from the kitchen. My stomach ached with need for sustenance as Ma's special breakfast, meant to fortify the family, sizzled in the kitchen. But the heart was stronger than the stomach. I was not ready to face anyone just yet, and so I skipped breakfast.

The day became a haze of hand shaking, hugs, and kisses. I still could feel nothing, but a seething sense of anger. I was mad at everyone who came that day. Mr. and Mrs. Gruber arrived with sullen faces followed by their obnoxious sons that no one liked. The Shea family flitted about the farm constantly asking Ma if she needed anything. If I heard it once I heard it a thousand times from them, "You just let us know if you need a thing, ya hear?" Our giant neighbor, Mr. Schultz arrived next with his daughters in tow. In many respects he reminded me of a slightly younger and taller version of Santa Claus. He was big and plump and jolly but had not turned white of hair yet. He had a booming voice and a laugh that shook the walls. He was fond of slapping Pa on the back and offering encouragement or satisfaction with a particular statement. Pa usually looked pained afterwards, but it never seemed to interfere with their friendship. Mr. Schultz lingered near Pa, dwarfing him in stature, while his girls sat on the porch and waited, fiddling with the muted yellow ribbons in their hair. I smiled at them in appreciation of the gesture, but I couldn't really be happy to see them since every person's arrival was another nail in the coffin. A coffin I had helped to build. I wanted them to go home. I wanted the priest to shut up. He droned on about God, about salvation and angels. He promised Anne was needed somewhere else more than we needed her here with us. He was wrong. When he was done it was my turn.

Ma had asked me if I would read one of Anne's poems. "I would ask Jack, but I don't know if he could do it," she joked trying to lighten my mood. It didn't work. I reluctantly agreed and did so only because I thought Anne would be happy if I did it. Now that it was time to do it, I wished I had said no. With my eyes swollen and my heart weighed down by stone I began;

God how I love the sun,
How it brings with it so much fun.
God how I love the breeze,
How it always makes me feel at ease.
God how I love the rain,
How it seems to wash away my pain.
God how I love the puffy cloud,
How it makes me dance and sing aloud.
God how I love to be alive!

As I finished the final line, my head bowed low, the tears began to rend the paper, weakening it. It was as if age, wear, and use would slowly disintegrate that tiny sheet of paper. It would cease to exist and with it my memory of her. I swore I would never forget her, her poem, how she looked and smelled. I swore to God, and I prayed that I would always be able to see her in my mind. It was the vision of her face, her cute little smile that remained bright in my mind.

It was ending now. Pa, Jack and I, along with our neighbor, Mr. Shultz lowered her into the grave. Mr. Schultz's middle daughter, Sarah, burst into tears and held her hand over her mouth. She was a petite blonde girl with eyes as deep and as blue as the Pacific. One of the little ribbons she wore in her hair had loosened and hung limply down the side of her face. She looked so miserable and disheveled, her eyes puffy and growing redder by the moment. As I looked at her a hint of a smile cut across my face. I was happy she was crying. Not because I enjoyed her pain but rather that someone else felt so uncontrollably sad. In her, I had found a kindred spirit if only for the briefest of moments.

The casket we had built Anne was adorned with both real and painted flowers that Jack and I added as well as a small yellow moon I painted on the top in honor of her favorite color. Each of the attendees passed by the hole and dropped some soil atop her coffin, slowly covering over the flowers and leaving just a bit of the moon to peak out amongst the dark clouds of dirt. I couldn't look anymore. I turned and found myself wrapped in my father's arms. It was the first and last hug I ever remember him giving me, and I soaked up all the love and comfort I could. "I'm so sorry, Paul," his words were firm, filled with strength and power just as his hands pulled me tight to him. It felt like he was protecting me from falling, collapsing into her grave and going with her into oblivion. Even when I released my grasp his stayed and it was not until only our family remained that he finally released me.

Ma tried to take Jack and me back to the house with Billy, but we couldn't. "Come, boys," she ordered. We did not openly defy her, rather just numbly ignored her command. Pa looked at her and told her it was okay not with words but with his eyes. She turned and taking Billy by the hand walked away from the Sweet Spot never to return again. In all the years we lived there I never saw Ma visit her grave. Without words we picked up our shovels, Pa first, then Jack, and finally me. We dug the spades into the soft mound of dirt. I worked with my eyes half closed as the moon was eclipsed in darkness and the casket disappeared from view. When we had finished we walked home in silence and spent many of the days after in the same depressed state.

Four days after Anne's funeral it was time to head back to Oakland for negotiations again. My father was sullen and silent. Jack and I did not jump in the truck as usual. For my part, I still had not accepted what had happened. The reality of it had not yet set in, or maybe I simply refused to believe it. Mother had spoken only a few words to us as a family since I screamed from Anne's room not willing to let her go. We were all together and yet miles apart. The thread that had connected us had unraveled.

On Sunday morning I arose early. I was tired, but getting out of bed was better than waiting for the nightmares to return. I moved quietly to the door trying not to disturb Jack from his deep slumber. My feet shuffled across the wooden floor, and I gently opened the door and closed it behind me. I tugged at my pajama pants and let my feet drift down the stairs, my eyes barely open. I could hear the unmistakable sounds of someone in the kitchen. As I rounded the corner, rubbing the sleep from my eyes, I saw a thick piece of cake sitting on the table and my mother on her haunches with her head buried in the lower cabinets. It struck me as odd that she intended on eating a piece of cake for breakfast, and I stood somewhat dumbstruck as I stared at her. When she withdrew her head as well as a thick frying pan from the cabinet she let out an astonished squeal.

"Paul! What are you doing up at this hour?" I didn't respond but I sat at the table far from the tempting piece of cake that sat at the far end of the table. Ma didn't scold me for ignoring her. She walked quickly to the table and took me in her arms. She smelled sweet, like honey and fresh bread. Her thick brown hair tickled my face and her chin dug somewhat uncomfortably into my shoulder. Exhausted and depressed, I let everything out. I sobbed and let the tears run dry as she joined with me in a cacophony of sorrow. When the embrace finally came to an end, we both wiped our tears and looked at each other awkwardly. Ma turned without a word and fidgeted with kitchen utensils feigning the need for work. I sat foggy and stared at her.

"That's your cake, you know," she whispered.

I responded with a confused, "Huh?"

"That's your cake," she said again only stronger and with a bit more composure.

"Why?" I didn't understand.

Ma turned to face me and smiled sweetly as she did. "Now, you didn't really think she smuggled all those snacks to you without me knowin' did ya?"

My face must have looked strange indeed because Ma laughed a short chortle.

"Paul, dear, Anne never took anything without me knowin' it. She usually just saved her share for you and brought it to you at the tree. She liked to make you smile." It was the last words that brought a return of the tears in her. "Eat your cake," she choked out amidst the snuffles.

I sat and stared at the cake wishing I could talk to Anne again. I wanted to thank her. I wanted to give it all back. My stomach soured. I ached at my core. I wanted to die.

In time, I gave up looking at the cake and left the table. I headed up the stairs, blindly following the Sunday morning routine, trying not to think about Anne. I bumped into Jack coming down the stairs, but neither of us acknowledged each other. I dressed slowly for church and when I had finished buttoning my shirt I exited our bedroom. I hesitated before the stairs and then turned around. I don't know why I went into her room or what I expected to find, but I did. Anne's room was shadowed. Half of the room was bathed in the yellowish orange glow of the early morning sun while the other half was dark. I stood at the door and looked at the room. Sparsely furnished with a dresser, bed and two shelves the room was empty in more ways than one. Silently, I approached the shelf and drew a book from the shelf. I walked to her bed and sat gently on the edge of it. Opening the book I stared at the words but could not read them. Instead, I let the rays of sun beat on my face. I basked in their warmth and leaned back onto Anne's bed as I let the warm rays pass over me. I stayed there with my eyes closed until I heard Ma call for us. It was time to go to church.

The trip to church was only about fifteen minutes and the family took it in complete silence. Even little Billy seemed to get that this was not the time for his usual antics. As we arrived at the little white church we filed through the tall curved oak doors in a single line, Jack, Billy and me with Ma, my father bringing up the rear. We sat together in a pew, dressed in our best, towards the back of the small church. I found myself looking over at my father. His face was sagging, and his hair seemed a little grayer. His gaze was fixed on the image of Christ on the cross and I doubt he even blinked. As the service began and the dance of sitting, standing, and kneeling spread throughout the sermon my father sat motionless. Never standing or kneeling, just sitting and staring. He seemed unresponsive, statuesque. As the priest droned on about God's mercy and the Faithfull's place in Heaven, I noticed my father's hands. His fists were taut and his knuckles were white. It looked as if his hands would turn inside out as his fingers dug into his palms and his knuckles protruded from the tips of his fists. I looked down at my own hands and found that they mirrored his. We were angry at Him. At God. At how he made her suffer and then took her from us. I realized that I didn't believe in God anymore and neither did he. He had abandoned us, our family, and we returned His actions in kind. He was no longer welcome in our house.

Chapter 8

The Visitor
1932

Our house had been custom built by my grandfather on my father's side. He had come to Oakland through General Motors. He had successfully managed plants back East, and they had asked him to open and manage the new Chevrolet plant in Oakland that GM had begun construction on. He had no family then and so agreed to the lucrative deal. Since the plant was located in the eastern section of Oakland and afforded him the opportunity to escape the city easily, Oakland was good for him. It enriched both his pockets and his life as he married a few years after coming to the city. He had three sons of which my father was the only one who had returned from the Great War. The house had been built on a farm he had purchased. He intended on becoming a simple farmer in his twilight years. When he passed away, my father inherited the house and a small amount of GM stock. It was that stock that helped to expand the farm, the number of farm hands and the success of our family.

During the twenties, GM, like many stocks, had benefitted from the abundant profits of the bull market on Wall Street. As the market value of the stock increased my father sold off portions of it to invest in the farm. He shared his father's vision of a farmer's life so long as it was subsidized by a healthy income that allowed the farmer to see his day as a connection to nature and not one of subsistence living. It was without a doubt, the best of both worlds. When the crash came my father held firm to the belief that things would recover. "Can't really get worse, can it?" he'd mutter under his breath. But get worse, it did. The market would go on to lose more than eighty percent of its value in a few short years. My father's stress level went up in direct proportion to the decline of the market.

Our house as well as our family seemed to have weathered the early days of the depression without much fuss. We were one of the few rural areas blessed with electricity. A direct benefit to my grandfather's connections to local industries allowed the stringing of electric lines to our home, despite the distance from Oakland. In many respects, the house's size, along with the conspicuous electric lines made it look more like a hotel than a farm house. We had a relatively new Philco Model 21 Cathedral radio which had not been bought on time. The farm had a good, albeit older, dark green tractor, also a Fageol, built in 1923. The truck, too, was older but in good working order and most importantly, no installment payments due.

But, by 1932 the Depression had crept into our home. Anne had died ostensibly because we could not afford hospital care for her. My father took that belief and let it gnaw at his insides. Her death became a parasite that sucked any semblance of happiness from him. It wasn't an overnight change, but rather a slow decaying of attitude that Anne's death sent him careening over the edge. The wholesalers in Oakland bought less and less; they paid less and less when they did buy. Prices for crops had dropped some sixty percent in the last two and a half years and the wholesalers tried to drive them even lower. The stocks still left were worth next to nothing. In September of 1929, Pa's General Motors stock traded at seventy-three dollars a share. By 1932, those shares were now worth just eight dollars each. Our needs however, remained constant. Our house became a pressure cooker of sorts with my father stuffed in the pot, ready to boil over.

Pa became furious one summer night shortly after Anne died. A group of veterans from the Great War had camped out in Washington, D.C. demanding a bonus payment be paid early from Congress. The bonus, which was between a dollar and a dollar twenty five per day for each day of service, was due to be paid in 1945. The veterans called themselves the BEF, the Bonus Expeditionary Force. Pa loved the play on words. "A good name for the unit, don'tcha think?" he'd muse. The press referred to the rag tag collection of veterans that had amassed throughout the DC area as the Bonus Army. My father called them, "The Boys." Pa had followed the events in the capital with an eager ear.

"Ain't nobody in this family votin' for no damn Republican this time around!" Pa bellowed as he entered the kitchen.

Jack and I sat at the table together but alone. Without Anne I was always alone now. Neither of us responded to him. We were not trying to be disrespectful or cross. I just didn't have it in me to talk about anything, much less a bunch of people I didn't know. Pa slammed himself down at the table and bayoneted the food on his plate as if it were the enemy. Jack broke the silence.

"Everything okay, Pa?" he asked.

Pa seemed almost relieved that someone asked and his voice rumbled, "They shot two of the boys, Jack!" Pa went on to explain what he had heard and how. "I was over at Shultzy's place and we was workin' on the roof when his girls came running out and yellin' and whoopin' at us. They was listenin' to a radio program and it got interrupted and the reporter fellow said the police shot two of the boys." Sucking in a quick pull of air Pa continued, "The girls said they are gonna clear 'em out."

Jack never had a chance to respond. Pa shoved his plate back and it crackled and spun as it made its way across the table. He left the kitchen with as much fervor as he had arrived with. The radio clicked on in the living room. The static droning paced back and forth as Pa tuned it; and when voices were clear he cranked the volume as high as he could. Jack and I spent the meal listening to reports of what was happening in the nation's capital that evening from the other room. For Pa, the news was grim and infuriating. The newscaster reported the use of tanks and tear gas to clear the ten to fifteen thousand residents who had taken up camp and were attached to the BEF. The camp was in flames and the residents were on the run. Hoover was as good as dead to Pa, a man who was once a staunch Republican would be voting for a man he once referred to as a "pompous overblown rich boy." FDR was now the candidate of choice in the Miller family.

Anne had been gone about six months and the household had returned to a somewhat normal routine, though there were still days her memory came to the forefront instead of lingering in the back of our minds as it almost always did. Every day felt cloudy. The sun was not as warm or as bright as it once was. The farm, life in general, was filled with the dreary doldrums of routine.

It was raining and I was sprawled out on the floor near the foot of the stairs reading. Jack was reenacting the slaughter at the Somme as little British soldiers made of lead were mowed down with his hands. "Aaaahhh! Push on! Push on! The Huns'll fall," he'd yell. But still, the assaulting soldiers were knocked over, sometimes in wide swaths of mock machine gun fire and others by a sniper like flick of his index finger.

Mr. Schultz, our neighbor, who had a pretty thick German accent, had given Jack and me the soldiers almost a year ago when he finally accepted he was not going to have a son of his own. "Three daughters are more than enough for any man to bear," he said. His wife had died in child birth and the burly German was left to figure out how to raise three girls on his own. He was really the only visitor we had ever had; before the UXA started, that is.

The Unemployed Exchange Association was born in Oakland as a result of the rampant unemployment within the city and outlying farming areas. The Bay Area was heavily dependent on manufacturing, and the Depression hit the area especially hard. A collective of unemployed men had created an association that had set aside money for a system of barter exchange. A labor exchange of sorts that despite being labeled as a communist haven, thrived and grew in membership and success if you could call survival success. Word of the exchange, as well as other organizations like it, drew unemployed white men to the area.

So, it was toward the end of 1932 that the stream of visitors began. A man, in his mid-thirties and dressed in a worn suit and tie arrived at our front door. He stood with his head cocked to one side, his dirty tan hat nearly falling off. Both his hands were spread over a worn brown suitcase that he held pressed against his body.

"Pardon me, Lad. Is your mom or dad home?" he said in a timid voice.

The Hobo was short and thin and he reminded me instantly of the people of Pipe City. The old suit looked like it was tailored for a man two sizes larger than him as it hung limply around his shoulders. His eyes looked like targets with a blue bull's eye surrounded by puffy dark circles. He was clearly tired and haggard, another victim of the endless Depression.

I gave him a half smile and set down my book as I rose. Jack's epic battle continued unabated as mock explosions and cries of death echoed through the room unaware of the real life tragedy standing on the porch. Ma was working on dinner in the kitchen and must have heard the strange voice because she ambled into the room wiping her hands on her checkered blue apron. A quick look of shock slipped across her face at the sight of a visitor on her front porch. She recovered quickly though and gave the visitor a smile.

"I'm sorry. We ain't interested in what yer sellin," she muttered politely.

He must have struck Ma as some sort of salesman even though I had never seen one come this far out of Oakland. I supposed that desperation might have driven them further and further from the city. The man smiled widely.

"No, Ma'am. I'm not lookin' to sell ya anything. I was wondering if ya had any work?"

He didn't look like any of the farm hands we ever hired. We did need hands, though. The crops were in and they would need harvesting soon. Even though he didn't look the part, I was hoping Ma would take him on. I don't know why but I did not want to see him disappointed. I didn't know if I could bear any more sadness.

"I'm real sorry," Ma said softly as if the tone of her words might somehow soften the crushing blow she was now delivering to him, "We ain't takin' on any hands right now," she finished the statement with a bit more gusto then she had started it with; but, I could not help but notice the discomfort in her voice. Ma stood wrinkling her apron in her clenched fists trying to maintain her strength. The visitor didn't help her at all.

"I can work for food and a place to sleep. Ya don't need to pay me none," he said barely above the sound of a whisper as if the sentence wounded his pride to the core.

He was the vision Ma had always hoped to avoid at Pipe City. Here on her front porch was the physical embodiment of all she feared might become of our family. "We all gotta have as much Christian charity as we can bear in these times," she would say to us before we headed into Oakland with the donations for Pipe City. Now, she was faced with the need for Christian charity and it hit too close to home. She was paralyzed and she rapidly fidgeted with her apron as she looked to find the right words to cast out this man in need.

"Ma, we do need hands and he won't cost us any," I interjected hoping to save this man the fate of sleeping in a pipe with a burlap door.

Ma looked at me with helpless eyes and then looked back at the gaunt man camped at her front door. She stepped forward and opened the door for him.

"Dinner is at six. John'll be back in about an hour and he can tell ya what you can do to earn your keep. Paul, show him to the spare bedroom upstairs and then take 'im to the well, so he can get cleaned up before supper. I'm Edith, this is Paul, and that's Jack over there," Ma rested her left hand on my head and pushed out her right to shake his hand.

"Mighty grateful Miss, mighty grateful," the visitor gushed. "Name's Frank, Frank Wood."

Instantly I went from pitying him to hating him with venom more intense than any anger I had ever known. I looked defiantly at Ma with eyes as sharp as daggers, "Spare bedroom?" The words carried forth my animosity and there was no mistaking my feelings on the subject. Anne's room, that's what it was. It wasn't spare, an extra to be handed out to some stranger on a whim. Ma glared back at me. This marked the first time in my life I had ever truly challenged her authority and I was doing it in front of a stranger.

"Take him to Anne's room. She don't need it anymore," she hissed at me and then turned and left the room cutting off any hope I had of defying her will.

I watched her leave the room, my fists tightening into solid bricks. I whirled around and shot a look at Jack. He had not even registered the egregious affront to Anne's memory. The presence of this stranger had not impeded the progress of his battle. I doubted he even knew that the man was even in our house. I would get no reinforcements from my brother in this conflict.

"Follow me," I muttered furiously. I began to stomp up the steps trying as I did to shake loose the drywall on the ceilings, hoping it would knock some sense into Ma as it smacked into her head. Mr. Wood followed me up not registering or not caring about the fury in my footsteps. At the top of the stairs I grabbed the doorknob to Anne's bedroom and flung the door open. The sheer curtains covering her window swayed in the breeze I had just sent across the room. Rays of sun danced about, bouncing off the walls as the curtains constantly changed their intensity and direction. The room was alive with light. Mr. Wood brushed me aside and entered her room. He dropped his suitcase to the floor next to her bed and walked to the window pulling the curtains aside. The dance of light ended abruptly and he cast a long ominous shadow across the floor that just touched the edge of her bed. His presence was a hideous stain on an otherwise beautiful landscape. I ordered him out thinking the sooner he was gone, the better, "Come on."

We walked to the well together passing the run down Cadillac he had arrived in. The car was a reflection of its owner. It was a 1926 Cabriolet, dark red and dusty, with numerous dings and overstuffed with personal belongings of all sorts. At a cost of at least five thousand dollars it must have been the envy of its neighborhood. Now, it was a remnant of an all flash and no substance culture that had no place in the hard reality of the day. After all, the car cost as much as ten Ford Roadsters. Someone could have bought a house for what this guy had paid for a car. Mr. Wood, like his car, was unfamiliar with a hard day's work and now his survival depended on just that. Neither had adapted well to their new stations in life.

Mr. Wood tried to make small talk with me.

"Pretty place ya got here," he said despite my attempts to ignore him.

"Where's your pop?" he asked.

"Out," was my curt response.

He was actually over at Mr. Schultz's place helping him pull the engine from his tractor, but I didn't feel the need to explain any of that to the man who was sullying Anne's memory. We reached the well and Mr. Wood pulled some water and began to wash himself. I stood watch over him finding new reasons to dislike him. His hair was unkempt, his shoes were patched with cardboard, his suit had a hole in the back pants pocket, and he was going to sleep in my sister's room. He finished his standing bath, wiping his hands on the back of his dirty pants.

"Where's your sister?" he queried.

"She's dead," I spat and walked away from him feeling I had sufficiently complied with Ma's orders.

I did not see him again until we sat down for supper. Billy was already eating. His little hands filled with baked potato and his face covered in tiny broccoli florets. Pa sat with a stoic expression eying the newcomer to our table with suspicion. Ma broke the silence.

"John. Grace?" she said it like a question.

Pa responded as if it were a choice. "No," he said flatly.

His rejection was, I knew, not of Ma, but of God. She of course took it as a personal affront and was shocked by Pa's apparent bad manners, especially in front of Mr. Wood. Ma said grace with a bowed head and her head did not rise again throughout the meal.

The entire meal may have passed in silence if it were not for Jack. Always the bold one of the family he broke the icy quiet that had enveloped the table after Pa's rebuke.

"Did you serve in the Great War, Mr. Wood?" The question seemed to echo in the stunned silence for a moment.

Mr. Wood smiled politely at him and simply said, "Yes."

His answer did little to satisfy Jack's eager curiosity for war stories. He quickly followed up with, "In the AEF?"

Jack didn't really want to know if he was just in the American Expeditionary Force. He really wanted to know if Mr. Wood had seen combat. Many of the American servicemen of the Great War were vets in name only, having never fired their weapon in battle. Mr. Wood's expression grew more serious as he stuck a forkful of potato in his mouth.

Again his reply was short, "Yes."

Jack countered him with a bit of ham. Ma clearly went all out to impress our new hand since we had not had meat in almost two weeks.

"What branch?" Jack inquired.

Mr. Wood was quick to reply this time, "Marine Corps."

In unison Jack and I turned to Pa. Pa finished what he was chewing and smiled.

"Semper Fi! Who'd you serve with?" Pa said, now welcoming a fellow Marine to his table.

Mr. Wood seemed to hesitate a moment before he responded, "Fourth Marine Brigade."

Jack leapt from his seat, "Pa! That's where you served!"

The meal started to go sour for me then. I had so hoped Pa would dislike the man. I had thought Pa might resent Ma for hiring a hand without his say. I half expected that the man would never even make it through dinner before Pa tossed him. Now, they seemed fast friends, comrades in arms. Mr. Wood could become a permanent fixture. It would be Mr. Wood's room. Anne's memory would be wiped from each of the four walls. His shadow would blot out the sun. I wished he would die.

"Third Battalion, Fifth Marines, C Company under Captain Hersh," my father said merrily, happy to have someone to share the glory days with.

Mr. Wood adjusted on the wooden chair and increased his pace as he ate. He mumbled something inaudible.

"Huh?" Pa said.

A bit clearer now he said, "Hersh is a good man."

Pa chuckled a bit, "was. You mean was. He never made it out of the Wood."

Pa was talking about Belleau Wood, I was sure of it. Jack became even more animated at the thought of meeting a real live Marine, a Devil Dog, that served in the famous battle. The Marines that served at Chateau-Thierry were legends! During the Great War, American Marines had earned the nickname "Devil Dogs" for their valor at the battle.

Mr. Wood back peddled a bit, "Sorry to hear that."

Pa eased back into his chair and set his fork aside. He crossed his arms and the muscles in his arms popped forward. "We spent the first week of June picking off Boche from a distance, remember?" Pa seemed to ask but not really expect a response because he continued without pausing. "They shelled us right into our fighting holes. Trench mortars, even gas, though that wasn't too bad most times. Then we got orders to take the Wood. Told us the Hun only held a small portion of it. Our artillery hit 'em but it only warned that we were on the way. Them machine guns opened up on us before we even got outta our holes." He hesitated a moment before going on. "Crossed that wheat field and got chewed up, we did," he gave off that odd chuckle of his as he said it. "The Germans gave us hell and we gave it right back to them." The sound of his voice trailed off. His eyes were fixed above Mr. Wood's head seemingly looking at nothing. We had seen that stare before. Ma told us not to bother him when it came on.

It was several minutes before Pa came back to us. He looked directly at Mr. Wood.

"Who were you with?" Pa asked.

The question hung in the air and Mr. Wood had risen from his seat taking his plate in his hand. Pa's arms uncrossed in a flash. His hand flew at Mr. Wood and grabbed his forearm. The two men stared at one another. For a moment, I thought they might actually have a fist fight.

"Fourth Battalion, ninth Marines." Mr. Wood said.

Pa released his grip on the man and went back to his food. Mr. Wood left the room with his plate in hand, still half full. Dinner ended as it had begun, in oppressive silence.

In bed that night, Jack was restless, tossing and sloshing in his bed like an animal caught in a trap. Neither of us slept though I desperately wanted to. The room was flooded with moonlight and glowed eerily. Jack decided it was not worth trying for slumber and so started up a conversation. He leaned up and tucked his pillow under his chest.

"Whataya think of Mr. Wood?" he asked.

I rolled over to face him and rubbed my eyes from fatigue. I didn't know if I should answer honestly or not, and so I gave an ambivalent answer, "He's okay, I guess."

A cloud consumed the moon and a dark shroud overtook the room. Jack hesitated before he responded. He seemed apprehensive when he spoke, "Four Nine wasn't at Belleau Wood."

I guessed I was supposed to understand but I didn't; so I waited for him to elaborate. His tone was strained and slow as if he was enunciating each word so there was no way I could miss his meaning.

"Fourth Battalion, Ninth Marines wasn't there. I don't even know if they even exist." Jack took a deep breath of air and released it slowly. "He wasn't there," Jack whispered. "He's lying."

My head sprung from my pillow and my voice was too loud when I blurted, "Do you think Pa knows?"

Jack sat up in his bed slowly. His face was obscured in darkness. "Pa knows. He knew before Mr. Wood even said what unit he was in. Pa ain't no rube. That's why he grabbed his arm, I think . . ." Jack's voice trailed off and whatever he thought remained unsaid.

"What'll you think Pa will do?" I asked realizing this was the longest conversation between the two of us since Anne passed. I waited for a response but got none. "Jack? You still awake?" I said in a tone that was barely a whisper. A voice came from Jack unlike any I had ever heard from him. It was a low tremble, deep and guttural.

"I don't know what he'll do. Paul . . . Pa was mad. Mad as hell, he was." Jack turned in his bed and the conversation ended there.

I smiled broadly. Mr. Wood wouldn't last long.

Chapter 9

An Act of Charity
1932

The morning came hard and fast after a night of late and broken sleep. The restless night had given way to a foggy morning that called for us to stay in bed. Jack was already awake and dressed. He scuttled about the room looking for something. He must have found it in the dresser because he slammed the drawer shut and left the room leaving the door ajar. I rolled out of bed, hurriedly dressed in a pair of old denim jeans and a t-shirt, then headed out. As I passed Anne's room, I glanced in not knowing what to hope for or what I would see. For all intents and purposes it looked as if the room had remained as I remembered. The bed was arranged with a stuffed bear and a doll that stood as sentinels to her memory. Either the room had not been slept in or Mr. Wood had taken great care to ensure that he left it the way he had found it. Regardless, his stock had just gone up a point or two with me and I decided to apologize to him when I saw him. After all, it wasn't his fault that Ma gave away Anne's room so callously. Plus, I now had the added comfort of knowing that he wouldn't last long. Pa could not abide a liar, and according to Jack that was what he was.

Pa and Mr. Wood were not at breakfast and the morning was already rushed. Jack and I needed to get to school, and neither of us had recovered from our late rising. We both moved in measured steps, tentative that we might fall over into our breakfast. The apology would have to wait until this afternoon. I shoveled some toast down and dashed out the door. The thick fog covered the farm like a soggy gray blanket. The air was heavy, moist. I nearly ran head long into Mr. Wood's car. It was just where he had left it when he arrived the day before, but I could barely see it hidden beneath the foggy gray mist. His belongings still protruded from the passenger seat like multi colored flowers from a dull red vase. Little flecks of dew formed around the tips of low hanging shirt sleeves and half opened boxes, containing what was left of an affluent man's life before the Depression. Now, they looked like weeds as they haphazardly poked through the car.

That afternoon, the fog had cleared out and left behind a cool, cheerful day as an apology for the dreary morning. Upon our return from school, I made it a point to search out Mr. Wood. I wanted to thank him for caring for Anne's room the way he did. His lie about the service held little meaning for me, though it seemed to anger Jack greatly.

"What kinda man does that?" Jack muttered as we walked down the path towards the house.

I treated the question rhetorically and did not respond since it was the sixth time he had asked it this afternoon alone. When we came to the house we went our separate ways. Jack tore open the door and went inside while I headed to the barn to see if Mr. Wood was working there.

I poked my head into the door and called, "Mr. Wood." Echoes bounced back in reply but no Mr. Wood. I stuck my head into a few stalls and climbed the ladder to the loft knowing the effort would be futile but trying to be systematic about my search. I finally concluded that the barn was devoid of life and headed out to the fields.

The fields needed tending; there was no doubt of that. We were late hiring hands this year, and other than Mr. Wood, we still had not taken on any others. In some spots we were already too late. Vegetables were rotting before they were even picked. Much of the broccoli was wilting and some of the watermelon had burst and was drying in the sun. I made a mental note to tell Pa when I saw him, not understanding why he had not noticed. Had he forgotten? I doubted that.

After a cursory search of the fields yielded nothing, I headed back to the house. I doubted that Pa would have treated Mr. Wood leniently and there was more than enough work to go around. It was the last and least likely place I thought I would find the man.

Walking towards the house, the outhouse caught my eye. It was a creaky old thing. A wooden shack built before I was born, it always reminded me of the shed Jack and I tried to assemble for Pa when we were young. The outhouse was slapped together from old wood, stained by age and benign neglect. The door was fastened in place by two metal hinges of varying size and shape. The top one was large, black and sturdy, while the lower one was rusted and small, too tiny to hold the weight of the door tightly. The door hung awkwardly as it protruded outward at the bottom and came taut at the top. This gave the effect that the outhouse itself was leaning to one side. The small roof was slanted towards the back of the shack, something Pa always said he intended on fixing so he could have more head room when he was doing his business. Like so many of his well-intentioned plans, he never got to it. I peered through the crack at the bottom of the door thinking I had finally discovered the location of Mr. Wood. When no feet appeared in view I decided to relieve myself before heading into the house. The door squealed softly as I opened it sounding like a newborn piglet desperate to suckle a sow. The outhouse had never offered a pleasant aroma; but, today the smell punched me as I entered, nearly knocking me back out the door. No words could describe the fetid odor that hung like a dark cloud around the outhouse. Sometimes, I thought you could see tiny specks of crap floating in the air around the thing. I grew closer to the wooden hole in the bench. A pungent odor of lime wafted through the air. I forced myself in, holding my breath as best I could and burying my chin into my shirt. Pa had overdone it with the lime this time.

I unbuttoned my trousers and encouraged my bladder to hurry up. Flecks of sunlight poked through the crevices of the wood illuminating small areas inside the outhouse. Looking down I saw a great mound of lime piled high in the dark hole. I aimed at the mound, reducing the mountain under the steady flow of rain I deposited on the lime's snow-capped peak. As the lime eroded, it exposed the bedrock of waste that had grown upwards over time. "Someone must be a bit sick," I wondered aloud to myself because of the odd red hue of the lumps left behind in the pit. Buttoning my trousers, I left the outhouse and took my first deep breath since going in. Little did I know, I had already discovered Mr. Wood, or what was left of him.

Pa was outside the house admiring Mr. Wood's beat up red Caddy. He circled around it rubbing his chin as he did so. His face was thinner now and the first signs of a beard were forming on his face.

"Nifty car," I said, announcing my presence.

Pa shuddered, surprised at my sudden presence. "A beauty," he responded as he turned to me and smiled. He was clearly tired. Heavy black sacks hung below his eyes, and his eyelids drooped low over them.

"Do you need help with anything?" I asked.

Pa returned to surveying the vehicle before he answered, "Nope."

He was running his hands along the door while his chin rested on the metal. The car was six years old but it showed a great deal of road wear. It had been driven great distances, pushed beyond its limits. Though never intended as a makeshift home that is what it had become. The Cabriolet's red top coat of paint had been dinged and pitted from numerous stones kicked up on the road. It reminded me of a kid who lived through a bad case of pox. I waited a few moments more before realizing that he had no intention of elaborating on why he was inspecting the car so intently. "

Pa, what are you doing?" I asked curiously.

He paused a moment and looked at me, then went back to his evaluation of Mr. Wood's car. "Mr. Wood gave us his car to say thank you for taking him in."

I was dumbfounded by the statement. "Really?" was the only response I could muster over my astonishment.

At supper that night there was no Mr. Wood in attendance. I had thought Mr. Wood and his generous gift to us would have been topic number one for conversation. I thought the mood would be jolly, but instead table conversation was dominated by events of a national scale. The Philco radio groaned out a monotonous series of numbers that I didn't understand, and paid even less attention to. Ma and Pa, however, kept hushing everyone as they tried to listen. Pa left the kitchen grumbling under his breath as he did so. "Ain't nobody smart enough to keep quiet when they're told." Billy responded quite poorly to being hushed and apparently decided that negative attention was as good as positive when he started picking up utensils and banging them on the table. Ma hushed him again to no avail. She shook her head and seemed to resign herself to the fact that she was not about to hear one ounce of whatever program she so desperately wanted to hear. Ma slammed a casserole dish into the sink in frustration. A series of stomps began to rhythmically approach from the living room gaining volume and momentum until they sounded like a Kansas tornado.

Pa bellowed as he entered the room, "Quiet! Ya hear me? I said quiet!" Billy nearly jumped out of his seat, a fork plummeted to the floor and he turned on the water works before the utensil even hit the ground.

"There ain't no need for that," Ma chided.

My father's raucous tone put the whole family on edge for the remainder of dinner. Pa sat at the table and Ma started dishing food onto his plate. She then grabbed Billy and rested him on her hip.

"What's got you so riled?" she asked in a tone mixed with condescension and frustration.

Pa's voice started as a rumble and finished in a low moan that was as close to an apology as anyone was ever going to get, "Just wanted to hear the election returns is all."

"Ain't as if it was ever really in question, don't ya think?" Ma asked without ever looking away from her plate.

"Don't know why we ever gave you gals the right to vote. There's more to an election than the President, you know." Pa paused for a moment to catch his breath. He was talking so fast and he was so tired that this fight seemed to take all the energy he could muster. "Most of the seats in Congress going to the Democrats," Pa blurted.

Those results seemed to get the better of his anger over the family noise, but the tension in the room was palpable. To add to it, Billy started to cry again for no apparent reason.

"Shush, child!" Ma scolded.

Pa stormed off from his seat and headed into the living room, a rush of air following close behind. A moment later the radio clicked off and then the storm door clattered shut.

The election returns and subsequent tiff between Ma and Pa had provided a cloud of covering smoke that evening which helped to obscure an obvious fact. Mr. Wood was nowhere to be found, but, according to Pa, he had given us his car; a five thousand dollar gift. The questions of where he went and how he got there were never asked. Nor did anyone bother to wonder why a desperate man would give such a tremendous gift to people he had only just met. Mr. Wood simply disappeared from the farm. Soon after, he slipped from our minds as well, like he had never even existed in the first place.

Chapter 10

Failures
1933

The men of the UXA arrived just before dawn in two trucks that looked like they were assembled from a dozen different puzzles. The men of the Exchange were as eclectic a group as the trucks they had come in. The youngest looked no more than twenty while the oldest might have been sixty with a thick gray beard and nearly no hair under his hat. Most were men around Pa's age or a little younger. There had to be twenty of them, all outfitted in various denim and broad brimmed hats, ready to work.

A cacophony of idle chatter came to an abrupt halt as one of the men greeted Pa with a cheerful, "Morning." Pa shook his hand earnestly and they exchanged a few words before letting the grasp come to an end. The man who spoke with Pa turned and issued a series of commands to the others and they were off to work like bees on honeycomb. The men went at the fields as a child did a perfect climbing tree. There was an excited energy to them. The work was not mundane or arduous, rather a little slice of Heaven to them. They worked nearly straight through until dusk. A few had brought simple lunches wrapped in cloth, but most just nibbled some raw beans or split open a watermelon to sustain them as they worked.

Jack and I spent the day sorting the fruits of their labor. We dug through and pulled out what we could of the stuff that had already turned bad. We moved the crates into the barn and came out to find another set ready for us. The harvest came in because of their labor. Pa had handed over the Cadillac Mr. Wood had left behind to the UXA in exchange for the work on the harvest. There was a great deal of glad handing, slapping and shaking as Pa and the men who had pulled the harvest in thanked one another for the mutually beneficial exchange. Exhausted from the day's work, Jack and I watched from the porch as the men left in the car they had just earned as well as the two trucks they had come in. The small dust storm kicked up by their exit blended with the darkening twilight giving the farm an ominous and disquieting gray hue. The day was long and Jack and I headed to bed knowing tomorrow would come too fast for our tired bodies.

Breakfast the next morning was skipped by Pa as he looked over much of the harvest. Jack and I would go with him to Oakland again. When we were done eating we headed out to where Pa had pulled the truck.

"Morning Pa," Jack said.

"Morning, boys," Pa replied and quickly added, "When ya load the truck make sure there ain't nothing rotten in the baskets."

Our shoulders collapsed like an avalanche, slumping in unison at the order. We had already tried to ensure that yesterday. Our efforts were sincere, but the harvest was late and the collection showed the wear and tear of waiting too long to be picked. Jack and I started to comb through some of the baskets and pick out green beans by hand. Pa tackled the watermelon and we spent most of the next two hours trying to present the best harvest we could.

"Pa, they ain't gonna pay much for this," I said sadly.

"Those mooks livin' in Pipe City won't eat this stuff," Jack added callously.

Pa didn't respond. When it was time, we got in the truck and headed to the city. It was clear even before we left the farm that candy was once again relegated to being nothing more than a distant and fading dream.

Jack and I watched the storefront where the wholesaler was, waiting for the door to open and Pa to emerge. When the door opened it flung with such fury that the door bounced back and hit my father in the shoulder as he stomped out. The truck door got the same treatment. The same smash, followed by a gust of cool rushing air and concluding with a thunderous bang accompanied every exit and entry my father made that day. I bit my lower lip and held it tight within my teeth. We drove past the general store, past the sign, and I tried not to look too longingly at it as we did. We headed to 19th Street and the encampment at Pipe City. When we parked the truck, the burlap curtains swayed and the men came out like ants from a mound.

"Unload it all," Pa said flatly as he got out.

"All of it?" Jack asked astonished.

"It's only gonna rot. Do as I say boy," Pa snapped.

We followed his instructions and started to unload. While Pa spoke with the mayor several men came to the truck to lend a hand. Jack grumbled in protest the entire time. His words were obscured under his breath but I managed to hear, "poor, lazy, good for nothin's." I'm certain the men of Pipe City had gotten an earful. One of the men, a thin frail figure, smiled at me as he took a basket from the truck. I forced a smile back at him.

"Your father is a good Christian. God Bless him and your family," the man said.

"Too late for that," I returned nastier than I had meant it to sound. These people did not need to be insulted by two people now. They didn't need any additional burden. I instantly regretted it and felt horrible for the words. "I'm sorry," I said. "We lost my sister not long ago." The man looked gloomy and distraught.

"You have my deepest condolences," he said sweetly and sincerely as another basket was removed from the truck and a head of broccoli tumbled to the ground.

"Thank you," I whispered picking up the runaway vegetable.

"No, thank you," he said, "and your family."

We exchanged smiles and finished our work in silence. This Depression was destroying good men along with the bad. It was an undiscerning disaster that didn't care who you were, what you had, or who you knew. It ignored age as easily as faith. I looked once more at him and saw Pa's eyes. This would be us soon. I hoped we would bear it with as much quiet humility as this man did.

We now had a harvest worth nothing and had given away a car to get it. Even at our age, Jack and I knew that was not a good sign. We were in trouble even though none of us would speak openly of it. It was what we all knew but could not give it life in words for fear it would become reality.

The family's finances had already taken a pretty severe hit earlier in the year when the East Oakland Trust had failed. President Hoover had led the creation of the National Credit Corporation late in 1931. The NCC was supposed to be the solution to the banking crisis spreading around the nation. The problem was two-fold. First, the NCC was a group of banks that were supposed to loan money to other banks. The problem with that was obvious. Banks didn't like to give out low costs loans, especially during a depression. Therefore, they did so very reluctantly. Second, it had done nothing to settle the growing panic cutting across the nation. The lucky ones got their money out before everything collapsed. We were not one of the lucky ones.

By the time Hoover had been convinced of the need for a federally funded initiative to aid the struggling banks it was too late. The Reconstruction Finance Corporation did not open its doors until February of 1932. For California, it was a month too late. The panic that had cut across the state had wiped out many of the small banks that serviced the suburbs and rural communities. As the banks became buried in debt and died, the savings of local residents were sucked into the coffins with them. We did not know it until many months later but we had lost our entire savings to the failure of the East Oakland Trust. I lost $12.62 and Jack lost over 17 dollars. Both of us cried when Ma told us. We never knew how much our parents lost but it was substantially more than our childhood accounts. As kids, we never considered what had been taken from them. We were too busy wallowing in self-pity to care. We needed someone to blame and so we blamed Herbert Hoover. So, too, did the rest of the nation.

After the bank failed, Pa had still supported Hoover, but it was a tenuous support at best. When the Bonus Army was broken up, Pa's support withered on the vine. So, too, did our crops. A seed of support grew in him for Franklin Roosevelt that grew with every passing day. The months crept by and nothing got better. Ma and Pa fought now. Pa was always apologizing, Ma always yelling at him for any perceived slight. Pa now waited for the day when FDR would be president. "Someone's gotta help. They just gotta. We can't last much longer," he would mutter in frustration to Ma or to himself. Pa had gotten his wish. Hoover had been trounced in the election and FDR was inaugurated in March of 1933. We listened to his inaugural speech on the radio. He began:

"President Hoover, Mr. Chief Justice, my friends: This is a day of national consecration. And I am certain that on this day my fellow Americans expect that on my induction into the Presidency, I will address them with a candor and a decision which the present situation of our people impels."

I sat and listened because that was what I was supposed to do. I had no idea what he had said, no idea what it meant, either. Ma and Pa were resolute in their efforts to take in every word of it.

"This is preeminently the time to speak the truth, the whole truth, frankly and boldly. Nor need we shrink from honestly facing conditions in our country today. This great Nation will endure, as it has endured, will revive and will prosper."

Jack yawned. It wasn't from fatigue. Though older than me, he lacked my mind and any ability to sit and listen to anything that did not involve humor or a detective.

"So, first of all, let me assert my firm belief that the only thing we have to fear is fear itself -- nameless, unreasoning, unjustified terror which paralyzes needed efforts to convert retreat into advance. In every dark hour of our national life, a leadership of frankness and of vigor has met with that understanding and support of the people themselves which is essential to victory. And I am convinced that you will again give that support to leadership in these critical days."

The President went on to talk about moneychangers and temples, swarms of locusts, executive power, and so much more that I did not have any inkling of then. It was difficult to follow, but he did talk about getting people back to work. That I understood. Pa seemed happy with his choice. Ma seemed pessimistic.

"What can he do that Hoover didn't?" she wondered. "How's any man supposed to fix this," she said desperately, waving her hands in the air, pointing to everything and nothing all at once, as she asked the question. She stared at Pa with a gaze so intent that it made me uncomfortable.

Pa countered, "Hoover failed us. He failed the country, Edith. It wasn't me that did this. He failed us." He returned the uncomfortable stare Ma had leveled at him.

She clicked off the radio and left the room without further commentary. Pa's remarks had struck me as very strange, even then. "Your choices, your consequences," he would always tell us. He was an exemplar of rugged individualism. This was the first time in my life I had heard him blame someone else for anything.

Chapter 11

The Legend Spreads
1934

FDR had said we had nothing to fear. But we did have something to fear. We were running out of money. The stocks were either sold or nearly worthless. The crops were rotten and even if they were fresh they wouldn't fetch more than a few cents. The car Mr. Wood had left us was now gone. I started to wonder if a place like Pipe City was in our future. It was the first time since the crash of '29 that I started to feel the Depression. It was the first time I felt afraid.

By 1934, I was thirteen and nearly as tall and as strong as Jack, despite the fact that he was fifteen. I had grown in leaps and bounds and though Jack had grown as well, my own spurt far outpaced his. Regardless, he spent most of his time asserting his continued dominance over me. Playful but firm, he would grab me and toss me around, punch me as hard as he could or trip me while we ran. Jack wanted to make sure I knew my place. Ma would intervene on my behalf when she was in earshot, but for the most part, I was on my own. For my part, I didn't want her help. I wanted her to remember Anne. Ma had not visited her grave. She never spoke of her. She had taken up giving her room to total strangers. Ma seemed busy erasing Anne from existence while I did my best to remember her.

It was in that year, that the fear of the Depression became very real for us. We had come in from the fields and washed quickly at the well, barely stopping as we splashed ourselves. We were ravenous with hunger. With Pa a few steps behind, Jack and I had dashed into the kitchen looking for Ma. We did not find her there. Instead, Ma was sitting on the rocking chair in the living room listening to the radio. The music was old and had a Latin flair to it.

"What's for supper ma?" Jack asked quizzically.

"We're famished!" I added with a sense of urgency.

Ma did not look up at us. She didn't even move a muscle. "There ain't nothin' for supper."

Our stomach's rolled with need.

"Whattaya mean there ain't no supper?" Pa demanded an answer as he entered the room.

Ma stood up defiantly and looked at him for a moment before she said, "There ain't nothing to eat. We don't have anything, and we don't have no money to get anything." She walked out of the room before the tears welling in her eyes had a chance to overwhelm the dam.

We went to bed hungry that night surrounded by food not ready for harvest or too rotten to eat. We were starving on a farm! Sleep was difficult to come by. Jack and I tossed and turned trying to force rest upon our famished and tired bodies. When I finally slipped into a restless sleep the nightmares came. The darkness was so thick that I could not see my hand in front of my face. The air was hot, and stale. When I tried to sit up my head smashed against hard stone and I reeled back in pain. I tried to roll out of bed but met resistance on both sides. I seemed encased in some stone tomb. There was a small glimmer of light, and I started to crawl forward trying to reach it. My arm desperately grasped for the light. My arm pushed aside the barrier, and my eyes blurred as the light blinded me. I continued to crawl out of the pipe and suddenly, I dropped. I kept falling and falling, waiting for the earth to meet me and shatter my body. When I finally came out of the nightmare, I had been yelling and Jack had apparently hit me with his pillow.

"Stuff it," he said as he rolled over. "Gimme back my pillow," he added.

I tossed it back. It hit him in the head; a soft thud told me I had found my mark. It was payback for his first strike against me. My heart beat aggressively trying to escape my chest. Perspiration dripped from my forehead and shoulders, trickling down the small of my back. I lay back down in the damp sheets thinking about what my life would be like in Pipe City. I pulled my blanket tight to my chin. I didn't sleep the rest of the night.

Ma kept taking in stragglers that showed up on our doorstep looking for work despite the fact that she couldn't even feed her own family. Anne's room had ceased to be her's anymore, and I resented every man that took up residence there. I resented Ma so much more for taking these men in. None of them ever stayed long. "There's never anything much to eat most days," I thought to myself. "Why would they stay?" There was a factory worker from Oakland who came and lasted two days before he was gone. He was a gruff man who answered every question with grumbles and grunts. He showed up one day on foot. His shoes were taped together and he smelled of body odor. After him there was a fellow who came south from Washington State looking for work. He spoke of riding the rails and the ruthless men who beat those who hid on the trains. He lasted four days before he was gone without a word. It was usually after these men left that a modicum of food would appear in the house. "Maybe Ma is holding out and makin' sure she saved food for us," I thought. The reality was there for me to see, but I was too naive, too innocent to think it possible.

In late June of that year Ma took in another stray. This man was different than the others, though. The car rolled up and the brakes squeaked as it came to a slow stop. The man who exited the car was a burly young man in a brown t-shirt and jeans. His arms were thick and strong and they seemed to be just a bit too big for the rest of his body.

"Excuse me, son, is your mama home?" he asked. His voice was a tad high for his look.

"Ma, there's a man here to see ya!" I yelled into the house. I had become resigned to the situation though my abhorrence for it had not dissipated. The new arrival had waited at his car, leaning against the dull black frame.

"Howdy, Ma'am," he said as my mother arrived at the door. He approached slowly and shook her hand. "Would you have a bed and a warm meal for me?" he asked politely and added quickly, "I can pay for them." He thrust his hand into his front pocket and pulled out several dollars to prove his point. Ma's eyes nearly popped from their sockets.

"Come in, come in."

"That was a mighty fine meal, Mrs. Miller," the stranger said as he patted his stomach and pushed his chair back.

"Please, call me Edith," she said and smiled at him. "Do you have any pie? I sure would love some pie," he said as he looked left and right searching the room for dessert.

"Sure thing, Mr. King, sure thing," Ma said as she scurried from the room taking his plate with her as she did. It was the first time I had heard his name, and so I put it to good use.

"Mr. King, what brings you out to California?" Just as I asked the question Pa came ambling into the room. His hands were clean but his overalls were a mess. Mr. King rose from his seat, introduced himself, and explained his presence.

"Nice to meet you," Pa said as he sat down at the table. Ma had returned with a piece of apple pie for Mr. King that was made not from apples, but from Ritz crackers and an assortment of other cheap ingredients. Pa gave her a look that was as clear as if he had spoken the words themselves, "What are you doing giving this man food?" Mr. King returned to my question.

"Have you heard about this strike at the docks?" he asked.

"Yup," I replied not understanding the purpose behind his question.

"I work for West Coast Shipping. Ever hear of them?" he said.

I shook my head thinking I might have.

"The company is bringing me out to help end the threat from these subversives and communists who are trying to Sovietize the dock workers. You ain't a communist, are you?" he smiled as he said it.

Pa slammed his glass down on the table.

"See, your daddy doesn't like communists either," he said not taking his eyes off me. He shoveled another piece of pie into his mouth and continued to talk. "I help end strikes and get good people back to work. I'm headed into San Francisco tomorrow. Your Ma and Pa are kind enough to let me rest here for the night." Another overloaded spoonful went in and his hand went to his pocket. He took out three dollars and left it on the table. As he rose he flicked a coin my direction. "Remember, keep away from those reds, ok?"

I caught it and looked into my hands. A quarter!

"Thanks!" I said shocked.

He messed my hair and said, "I have to visit the outhouse. Which way?"

I jumped from my seat and walked to the door with him, pointing to the right where the outhouse was.

I went back to the table with my shiny new quarter in my hand. I sat at the table staring at it. Pa was quietly seething. Had I looked up to ask my question I would have realized that.

"Pa, are communists really behind the strike? I mean, are they really tryin' to . . ." Pa cut me off before I could finish.

"No," he said as anger turned him red. "People are desperate. Desperate people do desperate things." He paused a moment before he finished. "My father told me once. Never mess with a man's job cause that means you're messing with his family."

I didn't understand. "Pa?"

Before I could frame the words he made himself plain, "Mess with a man's family and there ain't no limit to what he might do."

When Mr. King returned from the outhouse he was shaking his head. "Who-eeh! You boys can be proud o' that stank, I tell ya," he announced. "What does your mama feed you?" he asked rhetorically as he walked past us.

He was right. The outhouse had a very distinct odor and no matter how much lime Pa dumped in it the smell never quite went away. Jack and I had suggested digging a new one but Pa flatly refused.

"Can you show me where I'm sleepin', son?" Mr. King asked me.

The quarter he had given me had temporarily allowed me to like him. I had forgotten, if only for a moment, where he would sleep.

"Upstairs. First door on the right," I said curtly. I fingered the quarter in my pocket thinking I might give it back. I didn't.

As Mr. King headed to the stairs Pa stopped him.

"Mr. King!"

He paused a moment and turned.

"I wondered if you could give me a hand in the barn for a few minutes before you retire for the evening?" Pa asked with an air of sweetness and formality I had never seen from him.

"Be happy to," Mr. King replied.

"Go to bed, boys." Pa said as he walked out the door without Mr. King. "I'll meet you in the barn," he called over his shoulder as he left.

Mr. King and his car were gone by morning.

Chapter 12

Return to Normalcy
1934

The San Francisco General Strike got bloody not long after Mr. King disappeared. The Industrial Association of San Francisco, an organization of businesses and employers, tried to break the maritime unions. Deciding to move goods from the docks to warehouses around the city, they would be forced to use strikebreakers and to make their way through the striking union members. The Joint Strike Committee had barricaded the imported goods on the wharf and were not about to let it pass without a fight. The city was on the verge of something bad.

On Tuesday, July 3rd, a warehouse two blocks from the marina became the sight of ferocious riots between strikers and police. When the radio reported the location as King Street I popped from the floor where I had been listening.

"Do you think Mr. King is there?" I asked Pa, "on King Street," I added thinking he had not seen the irony in it. Pa did not answer me, instead turning the radio louder. "Guess Mr. King isn't very good at his job," I muttered mocking his efforts to stop strikes and communists. He wasn't the only one trying to stop them, though. Police employed clubs, tear gas, and even bullets as the strikers attacked the trucks in and around King Street. The striking workers were joined by other unemployed union brothers. They attacked the passing trucks with rocks and bricks; often times hitting trucks not associated with their employers. Drivers were pulled from the vehicles and threatened or even beaten. Men would gather in force and overturn the trucks. Police tried to place guards around pallets of bricks left outside construction sites, but even they could not stop the swarm of men from using them as weapons in the growing conflict. Both sides blamed the other for the violence. They had a day of rest on the nation's birthday, and then the government and the people fought another round.

The day came to be known as Bloody Thursday. Emboldened by the support of the government, the Industrial Association decided to open the port further on July 5th. The unions and police clashed again, but this time two striking workers were killed. Police used vomit gas and even fired on wounded workers being carried into the union hall. Once National Guard troops arrived, the strikers backed off and the trucks moved unimpeded through the city. It looked as if the government and the businesses had won.

Four days later, on July 9th, a funeral procession crawled down Market Street in San Francisco. Some fifty thousand people lined the streets in silence to honor the two striking workers killed during the melee with police. Two trucks, draped in black and each carrying a coffin, proceeded down the street followed closely by over a thousand working class men. They walked, many with their hands held behind their backs but all with hats in hand. As one reporter put it, "Not a hat could be found on a man's head today." In the days that followed, union after union voted to support a general strike. San Francisco was shutting down.

The shut-down was beginning to spread to other areas as well. The teamsters in Oakland voted to strike. Up and down the coast, union after union was joining the cause. The Longshoremen even opened their membership to African Americans. Once used almost exclusively as strikebreakers, African Americans had supported the strike and many refused to be used as scabs. As far away as Portland and Seattle, rumors of general strikes began to spread in support of the workers in San Francisco. Non-union workers began to join in. Barber shops closed, theaters shuttered their doors, and only food deliveries moved in the city. Things were changing. Things were spreading.

The International Longshoremen's Association and their union allies along with many working class people sympathetic to their cause literally shut down an entire city for nearly four days. Their employers tried to break the union. The mayor and the police force stood against them. The Governor of the State of California called out the National Guard to disperse them. Newspapers, fearful of their own employees trying to unionize, wrote articles against them. None of that mattered anymore. The city ground to a halt in support of them. When it ended both sides claimed victory, but it was the workers who won. They had obtained near the wages they wanted and many of the rights they demanded. It was a tipping point for the nation, for the city, and for our family.

While it seemed not a soul was at work in San Francisco, our farm buzzed with movement. Pa had taken on three sturdy men as hands. The first was a tall, thick fellow with dark black hair named Tim. He was usually quiet and always seemed a somber man. Well-kept and tidy, despite his stature as a farm hand, Tim seemed more concerned about his appearance as any man I had ever known. He washed incessantly, always smelling of lye soap and could easily have donned a suit and run for political office. He oiled his hair and manicured his nails. He was both vacuous and vain. He was also cruel and heartless. He butchered animals with an unabashed joy, kicked any living thing that got in his way and never said a kind word to me, or Billy, or even Jack.

Just as tall as Tim, though far less concerned with his appearance was Stephen, a most prodigious worker who didn't shy away from any job. Thin and gangly, he was a talkative man but never really spoke to anyone in particular. He seemed to have conversations with the air, answering himself as often as other people did. He was the oddest one of the group, and Jack and I always tried to avoid him as best we could. Billy, however, loved him. Stephen and Billy took an instant liking to one another. The man owned a large straw hat with two peacock feathers poking from the sides of the thing. A truly hideous sight to anyone but a six year old, Stephen would put in on Billy's head and the two of them would giggle together for half an hour.

Lastly, there was Connor. Connor was a freckle faced, red-headed Irishman who had left New York in search of work. If Tim and Stephen were tall then, Connor was a giant. The man stood a full head taller than the others. His arms were near as wide as my entire head and his shoulders seemed to stretch on into infinity. Yet, despite his great mass and enormous strength, he was amiable and always avoided conflict, preferring to walk away instead of fight. In lieu of discourse, Connor told stories. His tales were fascinating and he had an anecdote for every occasion. In a thick Irish brogue he would lighten any situation with one of his silly stories. Connor was the one I spent most of my time with. Once, I slipped and went face first into a load of manure. Jack nearly burst at the seams from laughter but not Connor. He meandered over to me, thumbs tucked at his side and pulling at the edges of his trousers. When he stood over me, his massive frame blotted out the sun and cast a dark shadow over me. Connor reached a massive paw into his pocket and drew out a hankie. He gently dabbed the edges of it at my face and gave me a crooked smile as he did. Just as he was about to speak, I raised my hand and cut him off. "I know, I know . . ." I muttered with horse-crap dripping off my chin. In my best imitation Irish accent I muttered, "Ya know, back in Ireland . . ." and Connor gave a hearty laugh and pulled me up. He was a great guy and worth whatever Pa was paying him.

At the time, I never bothered to ask where we got the money to pay them. I chalked it up to FDR and the New Deal. Maybe the Agricultural Adjustment Act was really working. Maybe Pa was selling stock I didn't know about. Heck, maybe the price of crops had finally come back to life. Whatever it was, however he was doing it, life felt somewhat normal again. The nightmares about Pipe City went away and for the first time since Anne had died, I slept peacefully.

Chapter 13

Escape
1936

The next two years were relatively happy ones for us. Thankfully, we did not have any repeats of the infamous no dinner nights. It wasn't as if we were rich, not by a long shot. The world had not turned so much that we had no cares, but the ones we did have paled in comparison to many in the nation. We seemed safe from the dire portends of Pipe City. We would not find ourselves slithering slowing along a line waiting for a bowl of soup and some bread from some overzealous missionaries. We were insulated from bill collectors and repossessions. It was as if we had just caught a slight case of the economic disease ravaging the nation. Our family had a high fever, coughed a bit, and then recovered. For whatever reason, we had survived it. It seemed as if we had developed an immunity to the depression surrounding us.

The slow train of migrants ebbed and flow like an undulating tide. Sometimes, we would get two in a day, mostly traveling on thumb or who had jumped the blinds and came west by rail. Other weeks came and went without so much as the churning of dirt and stone under the weight of tires. A few came and went within a day while others lasted a week or two, but none ever stayed long. They mingled with our three steady hands but never really blended with them. Tim would organize the new arrivals and set them to simple menial tasks at first until he could sort out the brains from the rubes. Those that lasted more than a day learned to take a wide birth around Stephen and his clumsy insanity. Their reaction to Tim always made me chuckle. They saw him and thought by his immaculate appearance that he must be someone important. Tim was always able to employ his image to convince them to do his work for him.

"That man is useful by default," Connor would remark, fascinated by how Tim would manipulate each of the newcomers.

I always just thought it was mean. "Why do you let him do it?" I queried as we sat on the porch together enjoying a respite from the sun.

He seemed to ponder my question as he whittled a small piece of pine with a knife nearly twice its size. He paused and leaned back, parted his lips and then thought better of whatever he was going to say. His massive arms and broad chest were barely contained within his shirt, and I never understood why he let Tim run everything when he could do it.

"Why don't you do something about that man?" I demanded.

Connor shrugged his shoulders. "Dunno. Why should I? He don' bother me none."

"Yes, he does!" I snapped. "He pushes you around just like he does everyone else." I was furious at him now.

"Does he? Recon' I don't notice, so there ain't no need to bother the man any 'bout it." Connor's demeanor was a constant. A rudder that never turned, a wind that never shifted directions, Connor was steadfastly passive. It was the only part of the man I didn't like.

Once, Connor had left the tractor out in the rain. I had discovered it the next morning and had quickly taken steps to hide the mistake from my father. I toweled it off as best I could and then used it to pull some burlap sacks of seed out to the northern field. My father would have thought it lazy to use the tractor to take a few bags of seed so short a distance. I felt his consternation and disapproval was more than worth the cost so that Connor could avoid trouble. The last thing in the world I wanted was for him to be fired. I pulled the tractor into the barn and left to find Connor. He was alone, doing the heavy lifting, unloading bags and boxes from the truck.

"Connor," I said flatly, greeting him.

"Kiddo," he said, wiping his brow with the back of his forearm.

"You left the tractor out in the rain," I said, barely above a whisper.

"Dang it!" Connor yelled. "I meant to go back in the evening but never made it. Guess I should go talk to your pa."

Connor seemed quickly resigned to the fact that he may lose his job. Work was not easy to come by and a man could easily starve in this new America.

"I pulled it into the barn and wiped it down with towels. He doesn't need to know anything."

Connor looked at me quizzically.

"Thanks," he muttered. Then, he shocked me with his intentions. "Still, I gotta let him know I fouled up."

Dumbfounded by the man's apparent stupidity I said, "What? Why would you do something so dumb?"

He placed the big mitt of a hand on my shoulder and smiled coyly at me. "Kiddo, no matter how far you bury your mistakes, someone always comes along and digs them up. No matter how deep you think you hide a thing, it ain't really hidden. Look at them Egyptian folks, right? What was that guy's name who they unburied?"

I answered almost automatically, "Tut. Tutankhamen."

Connor smiled in appreciation of my quick intellect. We had read an article on it in school. They had been looking for the tomb for almost fifteen years, and then late in 1921, they tore down a worker's hut and stumbled on the stairs to the tomb.

"That's right. Tut. See what I mean? Nothing stays hidden forever. Tim sure ain't gonna keep it a secret for us, now would he?"

I shook my head, knowing that Tim would find a way to report it to my father at the first opportunity. Resigned to the truth of

Connor's words I prayed my father would not send him out onto the road again.

Luckily, Pa never fired Connor, and I had not been denied his friendship. However, Billy was not so lucky. His fascination with Stephen had lasted the better part of a year before it came to an abrupt end. There was no one particular event that severed the relationship. Maybe it was just the fact that by the time Billy had hit the age of seven he was more mature than Stephen was at forty. The peacock feathers had wilted, the straw hat had frayed and Billy had totally lost interest in the man and his weird quirks. For my part, I had learned to tolerate Stephen more than like him. He became a part of the landscape of the farm and blended in with the eclectic mix of it all.

I had been happy that Billy had realized how strange Stephen was. I had hoped he would adopt Connor as his new surrogate, but alas, that was not the case. "Paul, you wanna race?" he would ask when he was three steps ahead of me. Even before I offered an excuse or just a flat no, he would be churning his legs and turning his head to check if I was in pursuit. "Paul, you wanna swim in the pond? Paul you wanna climb trees and pretend we are monkeys? Paul you wanna . . ." Over and over again all day, every day, Billy chomped at my heels like a lost puppy. Truth be told, he was a lost puppy. He had never really been happy since Anne died. I was too busy being sad and angry to even notice how lost he was. I felt selfish and unkind, and so I capitulated to his demands as often as I could. He had not done anything to deserve what had happened. None of us did, especially Anne.

Pa had the newfound influx of men build a second barn on the property. It was about half the size of the old one, but it went up quickly, especially with the extra hands Pa now had working on the farm. He said it was going to be for new tools and seed storage, but Ma quickly adopted it as her own. She turned half of it into a sort of barracks for the hoboes that came through. Pa wasn't too happy about it, but it brought a great smile to my face. The unintended consequence of Ma seizing the new barn from Pa was that I didn't have to endure any more migrants taking up residence in Anne's room.

Ma had made a big deal of Jack's birthday. Ma made a big deal of everyone's birthday, but her first born son turning sixteen seemed to give her license to make a capital issue over this one. The morning was spent consuming a hearty breakfast of eggs, bacon, and biscuits. While the family ate voraciously, Ma snuck out of the room and returned with a large box wrapped in bright red paper. She plopped it on the table and kissed Jack affectionately on the head.

"Happy birthday."

Jack plunked his fork down and tore open the box. He pulled out a pair of fine work boots.

"Thanks!"

Jack dropped the boots to the floor and started to knead his feet into them. Pa gave a knowing smile as he did so. Jack's face turned sour.

"Ouch. Something's sharp, Ma." He pulled his foot out of one of the boots and turned it upside down. Shaking it vigorously, he poured out the contents onto the floor. A pair of keys gave a loud clink as they dropped to the floor.

"Enjoy it, son. It's yours," Pa said proudly.

Jack had just become the proud owner of a car.

We all funneled out the front door, a stream of excitement that followed close behind Jack. Jack moved with meteoric excitement. By the time I had nudged my way in front of Ma and elbowed past Billy, Jack had made impact with his car. It was a 1931 Desoto Coupe in a horrible sandy brown color. Whoever the previous owner had been, he hadn't added many options. The car had no bumpers nor did it sport any spare tires. I realized quickly how jealous I was and tried to stop looking for negatives. Jack walked along the length of the car caressing it like a champion horse. While we all gawked at him, he hopped in the driver's seat and started her up. A low purr emanated from the engine, and it was clear that what she lacked in aesthetics, the car more than made up for in mechanics. The remainder of the day was spent taking turns in the Desoto; Jack a permanent chauffer, never relinquishing his hold on the steering wheel.

That evening, after supper, Ma had invited the Schultz's over for cake. Mr. Schultz arrived in his classic boisterous fashion, clapping Pa on the back and taking Jack into his arms and lifting him from his feet.

"Herzlichen Glückwunsch zum Geburtstag, my boy!" the burly German spun Jack in his arms like a toddler, not the sixteen year old he was.

I knew Jack was unhappy about the scene, but there was not much to be done about the man. He was affectionate, loud and generous to a fault. It was those qualities I always saw in the man, and I was certain that it was what my father saw in him as well. When Mr. Schultz returned Jack to the floor and to a modicum of dignity, each of the Schultz girls formed a line in front of him to wish him a happy birthday. Jane, the eldest of the three, led the parade.

She planted a polite kiss on his cheek and said, "Congratulations! Happy birthday!"

Jack blushed visibly and managed to stammer out a polite, "Thank you."

Next in line was my favorite of the three, Sarah. I liked all the girls, but Sarah was a bold girl with little fear. When we played together as children there was no tree, no swing, nothing that intimidated the girl. Sarah mirrored her elder sister's actions, and I felt a pang of jealousy as she did. I suddenly wished it were my birthday. Finally, the youngest of the girls, Elizabeth, acted as the caboose of the train and did the same as her sisters. She needed some extra encouragement from her father to complete the task as she was the shyest of the group. She scampered over to her father as soon as the deed was done and stayed close to him until Ma coxed her into the kitchen.

"You look so pretty!" Ma took the crinoline fabric at the edge of Elizabeth's dress and rubbed it between her fingers in appreciation. "Would you help me in the kitchen? I could use some help," Ma held out her hand to the little girl and offered a big smile as well. When that was not enough she enticed her further, "I bet we could even frost the cake together and have a few licks before everyone else. Whattaya say?" Elizabeth took her hand tentatively and was led away into the kitchen. Jane and Sarah dutifully followed suit.

We sat and listened to Pa and Mr. Schultz banter about politics and the dismal economy. For two men whose personalities were totally different and that had served on opposite sides of a war, they could not have agreed more on the finer points of life. There was one point, however, that they disagreed vehemently on.

"We gonna listen to the fight?" Mr. Schultz queried.

"Of course!" Pa blasted back at him with feigned anger. "Your ruddy German is gonna go face down!"

"Doubtful."

"Come on Schultzy, ya really think Schmeling can knock out Joe Louis?" Mr. Schultz seemed to ponder the question for a moment, letting it hang in the air.

"Ten rounds and he's a goner!" he replied slapping his hands down on the table and rising from his seat.

As we headed into the living room to turn on the radio, Pa mumbled under his breath, "Doubt your German lasts five." It was as if the Great War was about to be fought again, this time by single combat.

Mr. Schultz was wrong on one point. It took twelve. Joe Louis lost to Max Schmeling in twelve rounds. It was his first defeat. For

Mr. Schultz it was sweet atonement for the Great War. Pa took it hard, as it allowed Mr. Schultz seemingly endless bragging rights and it appeared to have painted a smile as broad and mountainous on his face as the frown was wide and cavernous on my own. I took it harder because I really liked the man, not just as a boxer, but as a person. Yes, he was a Negro, but I never quite understood the big deal about race and color. To me, he was a strong, hard-working guy and gutsy as all Hell! He was someone to aspire to.

When it came time for dessert, the girls put out plates while Ma and Elizabeth spread cream cheese frosting over the yellow cake. We sang to Jack while Mr. Schultz sang in German and was louder by far than all the rest of us combined, still in the happy throngs of celebratory victory. The girls clapped frenetically as the singing ended, and Mr. Schultz banged his fist on the table several times in merriment. Once cake was served, the room fell silent except for the clanking of silverware on plates as we all devoured our slices of cake.

"Sarah dear, would you mind bringing some cake to the men in the barn?" Ma asked sweetly.

"I'd be happy to," Sarah smiled. "Wanna help me out?" She looked at Billy, not me, and I felt deflated.

"Sure!" Billy sprang from his chair and began orbiting Ma, waiting to have anything handed to him.

Ma poured some milk into some glasses for the farm-hands and with that there was too much to carry for the two of them. Before I could offer my assistance, Sarah gave me my orders.

"Let's go Paul. No dilly dallying over there."

I sprang from the chair happy to oblige. My frown had reversed itself.

Connor, Tim, and Stephen were all in the barn engaged in some activity or other when we arrived. The arrival of cake seemed to have a similar effect on them as it had on Billy. They dropped what they were doing and trotted over to us.

"Well, ain't you a welcome sight?" Connor said cheerily.

"Much obliged," Tim offered up in his most pleasant voice which still left a great deal to be desired.

Stephen came at the cake fluttering his hands like a bird trying to take flight. He started clapping them together as he got closer and cooed audibly as he took his slice from Sarah.

"You're welcome," she uttered, a bit put off by his strange behavior. Stephen had already stuffed a massive chunk in his mouth and simply shook his head as a thank you. While Stephen ate as if it was the first and last slice of cake he would ever have, Tim went off on his own. Connor leaned against the heavy metal plow.

"Good cake, this is."

"I love cake!" Billy agreed with gusto.

"Ya ever have Christmas cake?"

"Yeah! I love cake on Christmas!" Billy seemed to find the conversation he was born for.

Connor shook his head, "Not cake on Christmas, Irish Christmas cake. It's got raisins, nuts, fruits and best of all, brandy!" He hesitated a moment. "My ma used to make it," he muttered, suddenly looked sad, then added, "When we could afford it."

Connor regaled us with stories from his childhood in Ireland. He told us of his brothers and sisters, and of family traditions great and small. Sometimes, his cheeks nearly cracked as huge smiles broke across his face. Other times, it looked as if he might collapse into violent sobs. We sat happily listening to it all until Tim ruined it.

"Don't you have work to do?"

Connor stopped his story short and handed his empty plate to Sarah. "Thank you kindly."

I never understood why he allowed people to treat him like that. We gathered the dishes and headed back to the house.

"Can we play Lemonade What Was Your Trade?" Billy asked unaffected by Tim's gruff treatment of Connor.

The Outhouse

"Sure!" Sarah replied smiling, not at Billy, but at me.

We hurriedly placed the dishes on the porch steps and ran off to start our game. I was too old for this now but I liked her. I wanted to be near her. Plus, the game always gave me fond memories of Anne. Sarah, Billy, and me played for hours together. She unabashedly acted out some of the strangest things, a monkey in a zoo, an elephant on parade, a jockey and more. Her hair was tied with a large green bow, and I felt the urge to pull it and let her hair rain down freely. I restrained myself but kept becoming distracted by the vision. I performed poorly in the game. I was focused instead on her beauty. The sun set and we still played by the light of the stars. The soft glow of moonlight only made her prettier. When Mr. Schultz finally came to collect her, we were all exhausted and my cheeks hurt from smiling. Soon after, I collapsed into my bed and fell fast asleep.

I stumbled from bed and bumped into the walls as I traversed them, half asleep. My bladder was full to capacity and my bowels ached for relief. I deserved this. I had eaten and drank too much and ignored my body's needs. It was all because I didn't want to leave her. Sarah was pretty, so pretty that I found myself dreaming of her. That was added pressure that the areas below my waste did not need. I hobbled down the steps taking two or three at a time and nearly stumbling twice. Once I hit the front door, I quickened my pace and made a dash to the outhouse. I was awake now and hoping that I could reach the finish line before the pressure became too much to bear.

I reached the door and flung it open. The hinges creaked and then threw the creaky wooden door back at me almost hitting me in the behind as it walloped back into place. I had not taken a deep breath before coming in and paid the price for my forgetfulness. The stench made my nose curl and my eyes furrow. I didn't have time now to go back out for a gasp of air. I tore down my breeches and let everything flow. Relief! I lingered in the darkness for a while, allowing everything that I had stored to make its way out before wrapping things up. I nudged the outhouse door open and with a spring in my step headed back to bed. That's when I saw Pa.

Chapter 14

Discovery
1936

I watched my father walk along the outside of the house. At first, I assumed he had a similar purpose as I had. That assumption was quickly washed away as Pa approached not the outhouse, but the old barn. I went to call out to him but thought the better of it. He would scold me for waking up the family or some such nonsense. I walked back towards the house trying not to let curiosity take root. Something told me not to look. Whatever it was, whatever was going on in there was none of my business. Still, I wondered what would have Pa out of bed at such an hour. Why would he need to be in the barn in the middle of the night? Was this the answer to how Pa could afford a car for Jack? I stopped and peered over my shoulder. A faint light undulated through the cracks in the barn. The flickering light danced, twisting in and out of view, teasing me, enticing me to look. So I did.

I moved slowly towards the barn trying not to make any undo noise. Stealthily, I crept along the outskirts of the barn. The dirt along the edges of the barn took to the air as I scratched along the walls. I tried to peer through the cracks in the walls but it was no use. I could see nothing but the occasional glare of the small light. The tiny dust storm I generated combined with the darkness to further obscure my view. I continued to skirt along the edge of the barn trying not to lift my feet. The dust tickled my nose and I held my breath, holding back a sneeze.

Suddenly, something or someone had grabbed hold of me. A vice grip tightened at the top of my night shirt while I wrestled to gain freedom. My hands swung into the air, desperately seeking to free me. I could not reach whomever or whatever held me. After a few frantic moments I realized that I was caught. I was done for and there was no other recourse but surrender. My hands fell to my side and I stopped struggling against the hold. My heart pounded and I started to try and fabricate some excuse for my skulking about the barn at this hour. My mind did not work as fast as my heart, and I had no reasoning for my actions real or imaginary.

Oddly, as the tension eased in my muscles so too, did the grip held on me. Slowly, I rose to my feet and felt the grip release completely. A quiet thud quickly followed, and I abruptly came to the realization that I was safe. I had not been caught by my father. I had been snagged instead by a hook, hung low on the outer wall of the barn where we kept a small hatchet with a flat hammer end on the back that we used almost daily. My pulse slowed and my heart grew calmer. I had to suppress a nervous giggle at my foolishness. I swished my hands across the ground until they felt the cool metal tip of the hatchet. I held it tightly in my hands and listened carefully for any indication that my struggle had been overheard. After a few moments I decided I was safe. Replacing the hatchet on the hook, I continued my quest for discovery.

Soon, I had reached the door to the barn. It was closed but I knew it was unlocked. The only way to secure the door was on the outside. The concern was always keeping things in, not keeping people out. While on my knees and using my right hand to hold myself steady, I slide my left hand into the crevice of the door and began to slowly peel it open. Carefully, I craned my neck trying to see within. The door was open a mere six inches, just enough for me to see a wide swath of the interior of the barn if it was light. In the darkness, the crack revealed nothing more than a black abyss. An alternating series of thuds and eerie scraping noises came from the corner of the barn where the light emanated from. I would need to go inside if I wanted to satisfy my curiosity. Inhaling quickly, I gently encouraged the door to move ever so slowly until it offered space enough for me to squeeze inside.

I slid myself between the door and the frame, small pieces of wood splintered under my weight and poked into my skin through my shirt. I ignored the little barbed teeth and pushed my way through their defenses. Once inside, I took position behind a large metal plow. Resting my back against it, I allowed myself a moment of respite before continuing on. The metal was cool, like ice sliding down my back. I enjoyed the sensation for a second or two and then decided it was time to take a peak. The on again, off again thudding and scrapping continued louder now, no longer muffled by the walls of the barn. I allowed the sound to dictate the side I would initially peer out from.

Slowly, I stuck my head out from the side of the large metal fortification I had established for myself. Pa's legs were visible on the far end of the barn. Occasionally, they would be obscured by the thin wooden legs of the table he was working at. I could not see the cause of the noises nor could I see what he was doing. I watched for a moment. The thumps and scratching noises continued and I became aware of a new sound. It was a sort of slurping, like a wet mop slapping against a floor.

Something hit the floor with a slap. I thrust my body backwards behind my defensive structure. Slowly, I extended my head back to its initial position trying to see what had fallen. A small pile of stringy material lay on the floor. It looked moist. A hand shot down to pick it up. When it did it, became clear what had hit the floor. Pa's hand had grasped an end of the long tubular pile and drew it upwards. The bloody entrails of some poor creature seemed to slither upwards to the heavens. I rested my back against the plow again and considered what I had seen. Why was Pa slaughtering a pig at this hour? Should I reveal my presence and simply ask him? I hesitated a moment before deciding to peak out the other side of the plow gaining another vantage point. This time it became very clear what Pa was up to.

The red wheelbarrow Jack used to push me around in when we were kids had a new passenger. The hobo who had arrived yesterday and been taken on as a hand, sat awkwardly upright in the wheel barrow. Something was off, though. He was too large a man to fit in the small conveyance; yet, there he was in it. I rubbed my eyes, still somewhat dry from dust, trying to comprehend what I was seeing. Pa stood at the table, a large knife in hand and a bloody apron covering his trunk. He scrapped at a large bone, cleaving the meat quickly from one side and then spinning and doing the same to the other. He dropped the meat into a bucket and tossed the bone into the wheelbarrow. It landed with a thud that shifted the weight in the wheelbarrow slightly. It was just enough to knock the man's head from its macabre perch. It teetered to one side and then went rolling from his shoulders. The head hit the dry dirt floor of the barn and rolled a few feet towards me. I nearly screamed as it settled in the muck, the hair matted in a stew of coagulated blood and mud. Pa walked nonchalantly over to it and picked it up by the hair. The head dangled a moment before he deposited it ungracefully amidst the assorted bones and flesh it had once topped in life. Pa raised the large knife and brought it down near what was left of the man's torso. A dull noise was followed by a slight sucking sound as he yanked the knife from the flesh. Again, the knife rose and fell. A third time and the man's arm separated from his shoulder like ripened fruit from a tree. I watched in stunned horror as Pa repeated the sequence of severing, rending and cleaving. His face was placid, serene. He showed no signs of trouble at what he was doing.

I watched Pa leave the barn covered in the blood and gore of his victim, pushing a wheelbarrow full of some grisly stew. Severed limbs poked out of a thick sludge of innards. The head of the man stared at me as it left the barn. The lips open as if to call out but no sound would come. I held both hands over my own mouth, clasped tightly to muffle any sound. Tears streamed from my eyes and mixed with the mucus flowing from my nose as if they were working in tandem to lubricate and loosen my hands, exposing my cries. I pushed my hands ever tighter against my lips. My teeth began to throb under the pressure. My legs shook uncontrollably. I was consumed by confusion and terror. Darkness crept at me from all sides. Finally, I succumbed to the dark wave, for how long I do not know, though the sun peaked over the horizon when my eyes opened again.

Chapter 15

Apathy and Ignorance
1936

"Jack! Jack! Please, you have to help me. You have to help me stop it. We have to stop him." It was difficult to breath. I was hyperventilating. Panic and fear filled me. I was driven by shock and a lack of understanding. My voice cracked and wavered as I spoke. I thought at the time that this was a one-time event. Pa had been provoked or had grown angry and lost his temper. Maybe the man deserved to die. The thought didn't last long. Pa was carving him. Butchering him like next week's dinner. Did he intend on feeding the man to us? The thought made me shutter and my eyes narrowed, blackness closing in all around, and then a loud thump.

I awoke, spread on the bedroom floor, with a heavy pressure on my belly. The weight was Jack's. He sat atop me like a bird nesting and his arm held high in the air like he was ready to take flight. He smacked me in the face. How many times I did not know. I only understood that my cheeks were throbbing and tingling with pain.

He raised his arm again to deliver another blow and I yelled, "Stop!" and raised my arm as a shield. When I had deflected the blow I lurched to the side and used my arms to jettison Jack from his perch. Jack tumbled to the floor and we both glared at each other and said in unison, "What gives?" It was coming back to me now. The bloodied apron. The fleshy mess that hung from the bones. The severed head. The smell of blood and death. I felt myself swoon again and tried valiantly to fight against the blackness. I let loose a deep sigh and steadied myself. I realized that I must have fainted before and a wave of embarrassment broke over me.

"Hey!" Jack blurted, glowering at me. "I said what gives?"

My eyes locked with his, and I put up a trembling hand to tell him I needed a moment. Once I started I didn't stop. The words tumbled from my mouth, an avalanche from Hell. "Pa killed him! He cut up that man that arrived yesterday. I saw him! I saw him! He killed the man and he was covered in blood. I saw all the blood on the apron. He did it Jack. He killed that man. I saw it!"

Jack didn't say anything at all. He sat there with that dumb look of his, and his lips pursed ready to speak but he didn't. I was scared, but Jack's response to my revelation made me more angry than scared. Finally, Jack spoke and when he did I was seething with rage.

"You saw him kill that man? You actually saw him kill him?"

I hadn't. Now, I had to admit that I hadn't actually seen him kill him, but I saw the result sure enough.

"No. I saw the . . ." I struggled to say what I needed to, the memory still etched indelibly in my mind. "I saw the body." I nearly choked on the words as bile tried to push its way up my throat. "It was all cut up. The blood . . . so much blood."

Jack shook his head in disgust, his hair bouncing as he did. "Didn't happen," he said flatly.

"But I saw it," I protested. "You saw a pig, you had a dream, I don't know what you saw. Even if you did see what you think you saw, what's it to us? Pa would have had good reason."

Jack started to walk from the room, but I grabbed him by the arm.

"Jack, he killed someone, don't you care?"

Jack looked down at my hand and tore his arm from my grasp. "No." His eyes filled with pressure and tiny veins spread throughout the whites of his eyes like blood dripping on a white apron. "No. I don't care."

Connor was tilling the fields. The afternoon was crisp and perfectly clear. A light breeze carried the scent of jumbled fruits and vegetables, giving the air the taste of a sweet juice. He saw me approaching and stopped the tractor. His burly frame dropped from the machine and the tires rose in relief.

"Hey kid," he greeted.

I didn't say hello.

"You alright, Paul?" He asked.

I started to cry. I was too old to cry but I cried. I sobbed and heaved and bawled. Connor took me into his great burly limbs and scooped me up. I don't know how long he held me, but he didn't let go until the river had run dry.

When my eyes had become a desert he asked, "So, what's goin' on?" The words were soft, a gentle inquiry to elicit a vicious tale.

I told him. I told him everything I saw. I described the grisly contents of the wheel barrow, the blood, the hacking and slashing, the blood, the cold veneer of my father's face, and the blood. I had seen blood before. I had seen lots of blood before but never from a dead man, never from a man my father had killed. Connor listened intently to all I said. He never interrupted; he never even seemed to bat an eye. He stood; a massive, stoic, and silent witness to a living horror story. I told him about Jack. How could my brother not believe? How could he not care? When I was done my lip quivered and my hands shook, but I stood firm, knowing that Connor would believe me. He knew I was no liar.

He knelt down on one knee, but his head was still nearly as tall as my own. Leaning in close to me Connor put his hands on my shoulders.

"I doubt you saw what you think you did, Paul." Connor ruffled my hair trying to mollify me. "Go find somethin' to do and I'll speak to him when I'm done. I'm sure it was nothin' to be worried 'bout."

I tried to argue my case but Connor wouldn't have it.

"Your Pa is the most generous and kind man I know. He's a good fellow, the best. Whatever you saw wasn't what you thought." Connor bounded up to the tractor and before I knew it he was fifty feet away and working as if we had never even spoken. That was it. He didn't believe me.

That night we lingered on the porch as we often did. Connor whittled while I read. I was angry at him for not believing me. I thought he was afraid of Pa, afraid of what my father might do to him. I muttered "coward," under my breath each time I passed him throughout the day. I had not spoken a word to him since the fields. I ignored every advance he made; every playful jest he tried met with cold derision. Occasionally, I offered a scowl in his direction that he either ignored or missed altogether. Only the slow steady grind of metal on wood could be heard to break the silence. At least until the car pulled up.

The sheriff's car arrived at the house and parked just before the porch. When the passenger exited I nearly dropped my book in surprise. Pa walked slowly from the car, the sheriff walking two paces behind him. I couldn't see if the sheriff had his gun drawn on him. There was no other way he could have controlled Pa. I had always thought the man was too slight of frame and just a tad bit too old to be a sheriff. More a grandfather than an officer of the law, he was always pleasant enough to me and never harassed the kids in town. Yet, I was stunned that Pa had walked from the car with the sheriff. My mind raced with an uneven mix of joy and terror. Had Connor really believed me? Had the coward actually done something about what I had told him? If Pa was taken away what would happen to us? It was Pa's first words that cleared my mind and made me realize what was happening.

Pa pointed at Connor and coolly said, "That's the man. He's the one that stole from me."

"Damn liar!" Connor roared with a strength and ferocity I had never seen from him before.

It was as if he had expected this attack and had girded himself to respond in kind. He reared up from his seat on the porch and the steps added to his already enormous height. The sheriff moved his boney hand subtlety down his side and placed his hand on his revolver. Connor never even noticed it. Pa, stunned at Connor's sudden courage took a step back.

"I ain't no thief and this man knows it!" Connor spat, moving forward towards Pa like predator stalking its prey. "He's the liar and I won't stand for it!"

Pa nearly stumbled head over heels trying to avoid the sudden swipes of Connor's massive paws.

"You're under arrest, son," the diminutive sheriff declared placing himself between Connor and his intended target. Ma and Billy had dashed out the front door just as Connor stopped in his tracks.

"I ain't going to your jail, sir. You need to take this man here. He's a right cold killer."

Understanding flushed over me. Connor did speak to Pa and this was his way of getting rid of him! Connor waited a moment and then turned to leave. He walked away while the sheriff ordered him to stop. Everyone was yelling. I was screaming, "Connor!" The sheriff was demanding him to halt and then it happened. The sheriff lurched forward and grabbed Connor's wrist. His hand barely wrapped halfway around it. Connor quickly shoved the rickety old sheriff backwards and the man seemed to skid across the ground and bounce as he careened towards us. Connor pointed at him, glaring a silent ominous warning as he did. Then he turned his back on everyone and walked away. He didn't get far.

The air exploded in a thunderous crack! Connor seemed to take another step before stumbling and dropping to the ground. His heavy frame thudded as it impacted with the earth. His body lay twisted, one of his arms pinned underneath him and his legs crossed like trees felled in a tornado. The sheriff sat on his behind, his gangly arms outstretched and his revolver aimed at Connor's lifeless body. The smell of powder poisoned the air. Ma screamed, Billy broke into tears, and Jack stood silent staring at the dead man who was once my friend. Pa looked briefly at Connor and then to me. He did not know how I had discovered his secret, but he knew I had done so. His eyes were cold, stern, unyielding. At once I understood him. His gaze was a silent portent of things to come if I spoke of what I knew again. Connor had died because of me. I had told him what I knew and he paid the price for it. I watched as the dirt turned to a dark mud, blood pulsing, spilling out the last remnants of a good man's life. I wished I had never known. I wished I could forget but I couldn't.

Chapter 16

Condemned
1936

The smells of bacon grease and warm bread filled the house as I entered the front door. Strange to think that those very smells used to make my stomach ache with joy. Now, I associated them only with death. A guest meant a big meal. A last meal for the condemned. I didn't need a crystal ball or a set of cards to know the man's future. I wondered if every man's palm who came to this house looked the same. Did they have a short lifeline? I had not met this one yet. I didn't know his name or what he looked like. I had no idea who he was or what he had done in life. I only knew it was over. In a matter of hours he was going to be dead. My father was going to butcher him like a pig. I wondered if he would squeal when it happened. I wondered a great many things and none of the answers brought me any comfort.

I heard voices in the kitchen. The stranger chatted with Jack while Ma chimed in with a few of her usual quips that she used on company. I tried to go straight up the stairs. I tried to avoid what connection to the man I could for as long as I could, but my feet would not listen. My head leaned towards the stairs; my feet remained cemented to the floor. The stranger gave a polite chuckle at Ma's observation about the similarities between behaviors of children and pigs. It was something about depending on the mother and then sucking her dry. It had ceased to be funny years ago. Jack asked a question about where the man was headed. From the spot I was glued to, I could not make out the man's answer in its entirety. I heard words like "work" and "nothing" and the phrase "gotta do something, ya know" came through clearly.

The Outhouse

I decided to look to see what Pa's loot would be after he murdered and robbed the poor man. If my feet would not let me upstairs maybe they would let me go outside. Slowly, painfully they slid across the floor and the voices from the kitchen faded to the background and then to oblivion. I opened the door as quietly as I could, knowing just where the hinges would start to creak. Slipping outside, I stood on the porch and looked left and right for the vehicle that would be used to fund the Miller household for a few weeks, a month or even a year.

I walked off the porch and began orbiting the car in an ellipse, bringing myself closer at times and further away at other moments. It was a beat up Ford Model A roadster. It was the Tudor version in green, not even the Town Car variation. It was cheap and nearly worn out already. I was certain the engine would cough and gag, like a teenager dying from tuberculosis. Though it was not more than a few years of age, the car showed signs of heavy use. The tires were dusty and bald; the front grill was broken in two places and tied on with a mix of twine and rope. One headlight was missing altogether and the front bumper was bent on the left side. The passenger door looked like it might fall off if it was opened. Yet, the rear of the thing looked pretty good; if you saw it only from behind, it might be worth something. Otherwise, there was nothing special about it at all. This man was going to die for next to nothing.

I had laid the groundwork for a fake stomach bug earlier in the day when Ma offered me a piece of leftover pie.

"No thanks, Ma. I think I might be coming down with something cause my stomach is a bit achy," I whimpered.

She felt my head and sent me on my way with a quick hug and orders to drink more. So, by the time dinner rolled around I felt I could execute the plan with relative ease. I splashed my face with some water and tucked my arms tightly under themselves. Rubbing them quickly together I brought my hands to my head and tried to create some measure of artificial warmth. I had seen Jack do it twice before and it worked both times. I was confident that my artificial pallor and warmth would relieve me of meeting the man who was about to die. I was wrong.

Ma heard the shuffle of my feet before she saw me.

"Pick up your feet when you walk boy," she scolded.

I tried to let loose a muffled groan, but it was completely disingenuous and came out more like a squealing balloon. Before I knew it, Ma was almost on top of me. One hand poked at my stomach while the other acted the part of thermometer and read the temperature across my head. She slid downward and took my chin in hand and lifted my eyes to hers.

"Get something in your stomach and then it's straight to bed with you," she ordered.

She pirouetted and shuffled away without me having so much as uttered a single word. It wasn't as if you argued with Ma and won anyhow. It was official, I had been foiled!

His name was Wilson. He was in his forties, had a family in Kansas or Arkansas, someplace like that. He was looking for work and trying to send money home to keep his boys in school. His story was like all the others. Sure, the details changed here or there. Sometimes they had daughters instead of sons, sometimes they were trying to save their house or keep up payments on a radio or vacuum. None of it mattered once they came here. None of the payments were ever going to get made. There was no job waiting for them. Only Pa, only death. I tried not to look at him, not to see his face. God, I tried so hard not to hear him, not to see him. I didn't want him to be real.

I moved a green bean around my plate. Wilson chatted amiably with Pa on the merits and pitfalls of the New Deal. They seemed to get on just swimmingly. The two of them thought the most recent addition, the Social Security Act, was taking the nation too close to socialism. My father was a reformed republican at best and his support for FDR often waivered especially as the memory of Hoover and the Bonus Army faded. Wilson was smart enough to find consensus with his host on any number of issues and avoid topics they tended to disagree on. Our house had seen enough guests over the years where even little Billy probably understood the dynamic and how it should play out.

"May I be excused?" I said as soon as a gap in conversation appeared.

Ma looked at my plate and shut down any hope I had of getting out of there. "You need to eat. Keep your strength up if you're coming down with something."

I continued the long and lonely travels of the solitary green bean. It passed through mashed potatoes and congealed butter only to find itself back amongst friends. It looked as if we were in for a long night.

Ma had made the ultimate in extravagant desserts. She had produced a peach cobbler full of butter and syrup and sugar during the height of the depression. The smell of it nearly sent Wilson into a tizzy. He swooned and lavished compliment after compliment on her as she carried it to the table. His dark eyes widened like a kid at Christmas. I wondered how she could be so blind to everything. Did she ever wonder how Pa was able to keep the household in the black? She knew what had happened to the bank accounts. She could see what was going on around her, so why couldn't she put it together? How could she not know what he was doing? Yet, she never showed any signs that she suspected anything was wrong at all with our lives. She just kept making apple pie and peach cobbler and never once stopped to ask why other people were homeless.

Ma dished out a hardy portion to Wilson and he dug in without waiting for the others to get theirs. It was the first gap in otherwise perfect manners I had seen from the man. As I watched him eat he became real to me. I had made it through nearly the entire meal without accepting him as a person and now there he was, a man. For all intents and purposes, a nice man. But he was a dead man, too.

Wilson must have felt my gaze upon him. He looked at me and smiled. As he did the flesh seemed to melt off the side of his face. He was half flesh and half bone, skull and jawbone staring at me, chewing like the cobbler was a piece of cud, the teeth shifting from side to side. I blinked, trying to clear the image from my mind. He brought the spoon to his bowl and I saw his arm drop to the table. His fingers twitched and the spoon seemed to freeze within his grasp. Dangling pieces of flesh protruded from his forearm and blood spurted rhythmically from where his elbow had once been.

"May I be excused, please?" I asked urgently.

I was already half out of my seat when Pa ordered, "Sit down and finish your dinner."

Why was he making me get to know the man? I didn't want to watch his little foreplay. Pa toyed with the man like a cat batting around a hapless mouse before the kill. At least the mouse knew the end was coming. I didn't know which condition was worse, man or mouse.

I tried to fix my eyes on my plate. I could see entrails running through my mashed potatoes. Green beans became hacked off fingers with gnarled knuckles. The pork chop, partially cut up, started to ooze blood. My eyes darted away and landed on my father. He stared at me, menacingly. He looked like a hungry vulture waiting for its victim to take one final breath and then he would be on me, tugging at my flesh. He held a spoon in his hand. The spoon became a knife. The knife became a massive blade, covering in gore and dripping bits of flesh as he raised it towards his mouth. I blinked hard, slamming my eyes closed. They opened again and suddenly it was a spoon again. The utensil ran over with a cacophony of ingredients. Syrup dripped like flayed flesh, ice cream melted and slithered like exposed sinew and bits of peach dropped from it like little splatters of brain matter. Pa was eating it, smiling now. I felt myself retch. I looked away but it was too late. What little of my dinner I had forced down had returned with a vengeance. I leaped from my seat as vomit exploded from my mouth and spewed across the floor.

Ma had seen to my care after that. She doted on me like she used to when I was little and it felt nice. She helped clean me up and then tucked me into bed as if I was six again. I was too old for this sort of treatment, but it felt good anyway. She brought me a glass of warm milk with a touch of honey. She sat with me and read a bit from *The Wonderful Wizard of Oz*. I missed Anne. I started to cry a bit and Ma joined me. She put the book down on my bed and sobbed as if Anne had only died yesterday. She looked old and tattered now. Part of me was still angry at her for letting strangers stay in her room, but part of me was starting to understand. It was too painful for her to remember Anne and so she tried not to. While I desperately tried to hold on to her memory, Ma was busy erasing it. I hated her once for that but now I pitied her. Her grief was greater than my own, invisible and silent, harder to bear. I sat up in bed and hugged her. I held my mother tight and we both found solace in each other's arms. Anne had left a hole in our lives that was never going to be filled.

After a time, Ma extricated herself from the embrace and wiped her eyes, erasing any evidence of her grief. The unyielding matron had returned. She forced a smile at me:

"You need your rest," she croaked, her voice sore with crying. That, at least, she could not hide.

"Good night," she said.

"G'night Ma," I whispered. I watched her leave the room and then began the slow decent into fitful sleep.

A faint light snuck into my bedroom. I rose from bed to investigate. The light seemed to flicker as it entered my bedroom window. I traveled across the room. Jack was fast asleep in his bed, one arm hanging languidly over the edge. I rubbed the sleep from my eyes and looked out the window. The light emanated from the outhouse. The door was ajar and there was movement inside. A shadowy figure seemed to be coming up from within. He was small and thin. His clothing was ragged, torn and filthy. He moved towards the house slowly, dragging one leg. As he moved, the lame limb suddenly fell from his frame and filled the ground with a patch of dark crimson. The figure screamed a high pitched blast, sat down, and tried to reattach the leg he lost. As he reached for it, his arm became dismembered, blood spurting from the gap in his tattered clothes as it did so. The figure looked up at the window and stared at me, perched on the sill. I could not see his face, and I craned my neck outward trying to see who he was; what he was. The moonlight spread across the ground and crept toward him. In a moment he would be revealed.

The clouds stifled the light for a moment, and I felt like I would fall from the window as I leaned to see. Suddenly, the clouds broke and the moon was as bright as day. It wasn't a man I was looking at. It wasn't one of Pa's victims. Anne's face could be recognized despite the flesh that had been flayed and torn from her. The worms that had eaten at her had not done so much that my sister's visage was not plain to me. She waved a gentle boney wave at me and I slipped and fell from the window. Jack's pillow was already in midair when I awoke. When I tossed it back to him I couldn't help but notice that there was a faint light coming from the window. I was too terrified to look, but it could only be from one thing. I shivered and pulled my blanket over my head.

I rose late the next morning. My mouth still held a hint of bile and the taste of it irritated my empty stomach. The room was devoid of life. Jack was already out in the fields with Pa and the others. Well, most of the others. It didn't take long to realize that Mr. Wilson was already gone and I knew just were to find what was left of him.

Chapter 17

Honor Thy Father
1938

My sixteenth birthday arrived and passed with little fanfare. Jack's eighteenth birthday, however, had been greeted with pomp and circumstance befitting royalty. Then, the house was adorned with homemade decorations and the kitchen had already filled with the smells of assorted pies and other baked goods. They had acted like a lure, enticing each member of the family in the hopes of getting a nibble without getting caught on Ma's hook. Pa would enter the kitchen with his nose high and his eyes half closed as if his sight would interfere with the appreciation of the aroma.

It had been nearly two years since I had discovered my father's secret, and a sort of morbid understanding had been reached between us. We never spoke of it. We never really spoke about anything at all in the last two years but nevertheless an arrangement had grown between us. Pa continued to fund the family in the manner he had grown accustomed to and I was excused from any meal that found guests present. This morning's breakfast was devoid of any future victims, and so I found myself across from the murderer who had sired me some sixteen years ago. On that day, our conversation had consisted of a hardhearted happy birthday and a vacant thank you.

"We gonna have cake tonight, Ma?" Billy asked in his shrill, excited tone.

"Of course, dear." Ma replied, showing just a hint of irritation. It had been the sixth or seventh time the question had been asked by my little brother.

"Are the girls coming? Are they?" Billy seemed to ricochet around the room. Ma slammed the pot down that she had been scraping clean.

"Are you gonna ask me the same two questions all day?" Billy shook his head vigorously and receded from the kitchen in a quick back-peddle.

"Are the Schultz's coming, Ma?" I asked. She may have answered the question a half a dozen times for the runt of the litter, but I genuinely did not know. I hoped they were. That would mean Sarah was coming.

"Yes." Her tone was still curt but at least she answered. I rose happily, planted a kiss on Ma's cheek and headed out at a cantor.

"Well, thanks," I said merrily.

Ma stood, mouth agape, in shock at my affectionate gratitude. Sarah made me feel strange. A good strange, but still strange. Clearly, the thought of her had been enough for me to set aside the animosity I carried for my mother for ignoring my own birthday.

There was no thought, however, that could get me to set aside my ever growing disgust for my father. In the two years since I had discovered his secret I went from shock and disbelief to being terrified of him. Now, it seemed, I simply hated him. Every word I spoke dripped with loathing and disdain. It was impossible for me to even feign respect for him. As the days passed my behavior towards him became ever more mocking and derisive. As I aged, I had less and less motivation to reign in my true feelings for him. I began to wear my contempt for my father like a badge of honor. No one who spent any time with us could avoid seeing it.

"Do it yourself, old man. Why should I help? I'll do it when I'm good and ready. Don't tell me how to do my work."

There were countless examples of the scorn that billowed forth from my mouth. Mr. Schultz once gave me a slap in the back of the head that almost sent me head over heels after one such comment.

"Don't go talking to your pa like that, son," he chided.

I respected the man and so reigned in my behavior only when he was present.

I surely wished that Mr. Schultz had been around when I entered the barn that morning. Pa was tinkering with the tractor, preparing the plow for seeding the western edge of the farm. He never looked up when he heard me come in. Maybe he thought it was Jack because when he spoke it was matter of fact, not curt and cold.

"Get me that wrench, would you?"

"Get it yourself," I belched back at him in disgust.

"What?" He was taken aback, probably expecting Jack's cordial assistance, not my cool derision. I ignored his question and began to gather some nails. I searched for the hammer. Whoever had used it last had not replaced it on its hook.

"Who in the Hell do you think you're speaking to?" Pa rose up from his position near the tractor, his lower half obscured by muddy rubber wheels.

I turned and proffered up a scowl, nothing more.

"Answer me!" he yelled.

I could see his hands curling tightly, fingers disappearing within fingers, like a snake curling before a strike. He repeated himself, overemphasizing each word for effect.

"Who in the Hell do you think you're speaking to?"

This time I offered him a response, but it was one born of hate rather than any sort of admiration. "A murderer," I muttered under my breath.

"What?" he demanded and I too willingly obliged.

"A murderer!" I said without turning to face him.

"Don't you judge me!" He flung his hand towards me. "You don't have the right ta judge me, boy! Ya don't understand anything at all."

His condescending tone bit at me and I bit back just as forcefully, yelling loudly as I did.

"What don't I understand? Enlighten me! Explain to me just what part of all this that you are doing I don't get!" Pa looked stunned. "You take people in; you kill them, and steal from them. What part of this is confusing?" Now, I amped up the condescension. Pa's eyes drooped and his brow furrowed. He didn't yell but his tone was fervent.

"You can't understand." His eyes fell and he looked longingly at the ground for help that would not come.

My tone softened but only by inches.

"Make me understand then."

He started slowly, still looking at the ground. "When Anne . . ." The name seemed hard for him to utter. "When your sister passed . . . I promised it wouldn't happen again. I wouldn't let it happen again. It was my fault . . ."

I cut him off, furious at what he was doing. "Damn you! Damn you, Pa! You ain't got the right to do this! Don't you go blaming this on her! She don't deserve this! She's clean and innocent! Don't you go putting your crap on her like you're doing this for her. Anne never asked you to kill no one and neither did we! This is you. This has always been you. We don't need this stuff. You think Jack needed a car? It ain't about need and it sure ain't about Anne, so don't go putting all this on her. She deserves better than that."

My diatribe had been equal parts anger and shame; all directed at a man I once aspired to be. He was once the Lone Ranger to me and I happily played Tonto by his side. He was my hero. Now, I barely recognized him as kin.

"Paul, please . . ." Pa pleaded. His contrition lacked any sort of sincerity. "I did these things to keep our family safe. You don't know what the world is really like. I kept us from the pipes."

The Outhouse

A shiver walked a snail's pace up my spine at the mention of Pipe City. I remembered the man who once brought food and old clothes to the men there. I remembered the good man, the charitable man. He was a younger man then, with fewer wrinkles and not a fleck of gray hair. His face was sun-kissed and not as careworn as it was today. I remembered the gaunt Mayor and his family. I recalled the vision of his daughter clinging to his leg looking up at him proudly. She loved him for who he was even when they were homeless. I swore I would have loved my father if we were homeless. I just couldn't love him as he was now. I would have preferred living in squalor and crawling into a pipe to sleep.

"Better innocent men die then for us to sleep in a pipe, huh?"

"It's not that simple," he said, frustrated.

"Liar," The words were out of my mouth before he even finished his sentence.

Pa's hands slapped against his sides. "I have had enough of you and your ungrateful ways." Pa began to march towards me. "You need to learn some respect." He hadn't taught me respect. I had learned one thing from him though; revulsion. So, I told him to go where I thought he belonged.

"Go to Hell."

His fist crashed into my face. The shock of it sent me reeling backwards. The second and third punches missed by inches, but by the fourth I had no place left to retreat. His hands slammed into my chin and forehead. Within seconds, I crumpled to the ground. One second later he was on top of me, his fists tapping a lively tune across my whole body. A medley of black and blue, or rather, a lament of all I once held true.

I writhed like a worm on hot pavement but to no avail. My father had me pinned. My face ached and I could feel my eye swelling. Blood dripped from my lip and sank down the back of my throat in a salty tang. My left arm was pinioned between my body and the ground underneath us. My right arm worked tirelessly in an effort to spring my father off of me or to block his blows. I was growing tired and could offer less and less resistance as the minutes passed.

"Respect me!" my father continued to shout, his face close enough to my own that I wondered if he intended on biting me next. His breath was hot and it mixed with cool flecks of spit as he yelled. I was so angry. Angrier than I had ever known I could be. I railed against him. I railed against the bonds he had me in, against all that he had become.

"Murderer!" I spewed at him turning my head to face him as best I could. "Murderer!" The word became a chant. Some sort of symbolic mantra that I threw at him hoping that it might give me strength over him. It was futile, though. Worse, it fueled the man's rage all the more.

I felt the weight on me lessen for a moment. Pa had risen to his knees though he still held me down firmly with his hands clasped on my shirt. I felt my body heave upwards as if I had suddenly taken flight. Like a rocket in the funny pages, I flew across the room. My trajectory landed me against the barn wall. Tools of metal and wood clanged and fell as my impact tremor radiated outward. Then my father landed. His hands scurried around my shoulders. His fingers dug at my skin, looking for placement. When they found my neck, he brought them together with force. I had taken a quick breath but it wasn't enough. His hands slowing began to squeeze, tightening around my neck while he lifted me off the ground.

"I'll kill you! I'll kill you!" he intoned, spit flying from his lips. As I gasped for air the realization was beginning to form in my ever clouding brain. He meant it.

This was the end for me. I wondered how it would feel. Would it hurt more than this? Were God and Heaven real? I doubted it, but furtively hoped for their existence. I couldn't breathe. I couldn't call out for help. I felt my fingers tingle and my head began to feel heavy, dull. I kept my eyes on Pa's face. He was incensed, the rage and animosity in his eyes boiled over and seemed to fuel his arms. His hands spread over my throat like an iron scarf. They acted like a vice clamp, slowly applying more pressure, and I was unable to do anything about it. I didn't want to die. I didn't want to get chopped up like a pig and have my mutilated corpse shat on. I was terrified. The tears rolled and I prayed earnestly to God, for forgiveness, absolution, and most of all, for intervention. Then, I thought of Anne. I thought of her frolicking, of us playing near the pond together. Pa had claimed he was killing these men to protect the family, to keep us safe and free from the depression that shrouded so many families. He said he would never let it kill another one of his children. He was a liar. It was all lies. Pa lied; Ma lied; God lied most of all. There was no help coming to save me from the clutches of death. I took one final look at those unyielding eyes and then closed my own. There was no light at the end of a tunnel, only a dark abyss and the feeling of eternal falling.

"Oh, didn't mean to interrupt." I heard Stephen's penetrating voice come through the blackness that had been pressing against me.

I felt my father's hands slacken and air rushed blissfully but painfully into my lungs. Life! Stephen had saved me. I thanked God and made dozens of promises about how I would spend the rest of my days now that I had at least one more to live. The clamp loosened and my back began to slide down the wall. My feet felt faint glimmers of the ground as the tips of my boots edged closer to it, though, Pa's grip on my neck remained.

"If you intend on killing the kid, that's surely one way of going about it."

I could see clearer now. Stephen walked leisurely towards us. Pa still held me by the neck, but I now had firm footing and could breathe though it hurt to do so. Stephen tapped Pa's hands with his index finger and circled nonchalantly around him.

"Though he'd probably stink the joint up worse than the smell of that outhouse if you did kill him," he said, a sly smile cutting across his face.

Did he know? Pa let go of me and left me gasping for air. He walked from the barn uttering not a single word. My body crumpled down the wall of the barn as if it was carelessly tossed sack. I coughed and gagged. My hands felt gingerly around my neck checking for what, I did not know.

"Thanks," I croaked through the pain. I wanted to hug him or shake his hand, but I couldn't seem to get my feet under me.

"Get yourself together and meet us in the field." Stephen disappeared as quickly as he had arrived.

We spent the day working in the western fields. I was last to arrive as it took me some time to regain my feet.

"What in tarnation happened to you?" Jack blurted when he saw me.

I realized he had the benefit of seeing what I looked like after the pounding Pa handed me before I had. Instinctively, my hand rose to my face and touched the puffy area around my eye. I recoiled at my own touch, the pain searing through me. I limped past Jack not knowing what to say.

"Well, it's an improvement!" he called out and chuckled at his own joke.

Stephen whistled a lively but repetitive tune as we worked. I could hear him occasionally stop and comment, making idle small talk with Pa.

"Would you shut up?" Pa blurted not long after we had started; why, I could not say.

Stephen's shrill whistling returned mere seconds later. Tim tried and failed to shut him up. I tried to stay as far away as possible from all of them. Yet, my curiosity was insatiable as the day was continually punctuated by unheard comments from Stephen and loud bursts of frustration from my father. As the day wound down, I found myself gravitating towards them, trying to hear what was going on. Stephen eyed my approach.

"Jack. Jack. Jack." Stephen said, repeating my brother's name over and over again in tune to that infernal song he had been whistling. "So, that is a lovely car you have." Stephen observed as if it was the first time in two years he had noticed Jack's car.

Jack responded cautiously. "Thanks."

Pa's back stiffened visibly at the interchange between them.

"Must have cost your Pa a pretty penny," Stephen said in a sing song voice, again in tune with that annoying song.

"Don't you have work to do?" Pa countered through gritted teeth.

Tim had decided to stay out of the whole affair by now, and quietly buried his head in his chest, avoiding any eye contact. "Now Paul, you didn't get a car for your birthday, did you?"

I smiled awkwardly at him, my lip split as I did and I could taste blood again. I shook my head silently and stole a glance at Pa. Long thin lines of muscle raced down his forearm. His hands were slightly swollen and covered with blood and dirt. Stephen ignored the tension.

"Do you think another hobo might pay your father with a car for a few days of food and shelter? Though I doubt you'd get the automobile before Billy. It's pretty clear how your Pa feels about you, isn't it?"

My jaw was agape. He knew! He had to know! But what was he doing? Before I could find out, Pa ended it there.

"We're done."

We returned to the barn and began putting away tools. Stephen grabbed the pitchfork and started mucking out a stall. He whistled the same tune that had so irritated my father throughout the day; this time it was louder and more piercing, seemingly echoing off the walls. Pa stopped and stared at him. Stephen paused a moment under his glowering eyes and then raised his hand and plunged it towards his own heart. Stephen fell unabashedly into the hay and disappeared within it. His arms and legs were splayed out and only the tips of his fingers and a lone boot sole were visible. A mock death at his own hands or was it Pa's hand he simulated? I was beginning to think he was smarter than we had given him credit for.

"Sometimes, I really think you just ain't right in the head," Pa blurted, frustrated with the antics of the man. Stephen's steady stream of off-color jokes and antagonizing statements throughout the day had chipped away at Pa, especially after his dealings with me. "Are you an idiot or something?"

He rose and dusted the hay from his body. Stephen pulled the old straw hat that had stuck firmly in place from his head, wiping his brow with the back of his hand. He leaned on the pitchfork and blew a final piece of hay from his shoulder. His response, when it came, was measured and calculated. The words seemed hand selected from the thousands of possibilities he had to select from. There was no discernible smile or scowl, rather a flat, emotionless expression.

"So, Mr. Miller, what exactly do you do to keep hands on so long? After all, most only survive a day or two here."

Again, Stephen seemed to deliberately antagonize my father. The word "survive" seemed to be dragged slowly across his lips. The topic and the sarcasm of his comment were not lost on Pa, or on me. I shivered with fear, or excitement, I did not know. My father held his pose for only a moment and then lowered the hammer both literally and figuratively.

"I expect them to show some respect and appreciation for what I done for them, is all."

The words were ominous, full of venom and spite. Pa tramped past Stephen, his feet slamming into the ground. The two men nearly collided. Their shoulders brushed together. Stephen gave ground but not enough to let him past without bumping into him. Both men bounced to the side as they drove their shoulders into one another. They stared menacingly at each other and I thought for sure it was going to come to blows. Surprisingly, it was Pa who walked away first. He was three steps past him when he ended it.

"You're fired. Get your things and get off my property."

I skipped dinner as well as the birthday party that night and breakfast the next morning. My stomach ached, but those pains paled in comparison to the tenderness of my face and neck. I was desperate to avoid Ma and the inevitable questions about my bruises. That evening the men of the family had gathered in the living room to listen to the rematch between Joe Louis and Max Schmeling. I had avoided contact with everyone, especially my father, but I couldn't bear to miss this. The fight had come along with all the hype of the charged political climate that was growing ever tenser by the day. Schmeling was the example of Nazi Germany and all its racist ideology; while Joe Louis embodied the "everyman" of America. It was genetic superiority versus grit and moxy. Schmeling had taken the first fight in twelve rounds and had given Mr. Schultz and every German a sense of pride. This time, we listened to the fight without him, hoping that the results might be different.

For all the hype, it took just one round. Joe Louis had knocked Schmeling down several times and the referee had stopped the fight. God, I wanted to be in New York for that fight. I wanted to be able to see it happen. I wanted so much to see the giant brought low. Despite my bruises and puffy eyes, I yearned for my own rematch, one that with hard work and honesty would come to a different conclusion than my first battle. I dreamed of a second fight with my father, a fight that would end quickly with me standing over his shattered, defeated frame.

Chapter 18

An Awkward Breakfast
1938

Stephen was gone; any hope of reconciliation between my father and me had vanished while my bruises were turning from shades of purple and blue to black. My sense of isolation continued to grow. Anne was a distant memory. Connor, though more recent, but still gone. Now, Stephen had left and all that remained was Tim. Cold, steel-hearted Tim, who didn't care when Connor was shot nor did he feel Stephen's absence. All that was left to me was my family. I had a father who murdered innocent migrants, a brother who could care less as long as it didn't harm him, and a mother who seemed oblivious to it all. My only solace was in Billy's wide-eyed innocence and Sarah. She was an oasis of happiness in a desert of despair.

"What happened to you?" Sarah said frantically the moment she saw me.

"Jack," I blurted. I blamed him, not wanting to answer the questions that would come if I told the truth. A lump clustered in my throat. It was harder to lie to her than I thought it would be. The taste was unpalatable and sour.

"Why?" she spat, her eyes furrowed in confusion and anger.

"Family stuff," I couldn't bear to lie to her again. At least there was truth in this.

"What's wrong?" Sarah asked. I hadn't heard her, and so she laid her hand on my shoulder and asked again. "Paul, what's wrong?"

"Nothing," I scraped my feet along the ground, digging into the grass with a vengeance, head hung low.

She hesitated a few moments before moving herself directly into my path. "Is it me?"

"No. No, it's not you. You're perfect. I . . . they love you." I stumbled on the words. Yes, I meant them, but I wasn't really prepared to say them, nor for her to hear them. I felt my face flush with the warmth of embarrassment. Thankfully, she was merciful and didn't take advantage.

"Then, what's eating you?"

"I hate my family." I gushed. "Well . . . most of them, at least."

We stopped and sat at the tree. Anne's tombstone lingered in the background. I picked grass and let the wind blow it from my hands. I stared at Anne's stone longingly. I missed her dearly.

"It's hard, isn't it?" she asked.

"What?"

"Life. Losing people you love. Missing them. Loving the ones you still have even when they make you mad." Her eyes glistened and she looked like she was going to cry. "Life's just hard."

I didn't quite know what to say. Words were never my strongest ally. I sat silent and waited, hoping she was going to continue.

"It's easy to love people when they are gone, isn't it? You can love all the happy memories of them, all the moments you shared, and you can forget any of the bad stuff. They're not here to renew it. The bad stuff, I mean. We get to make them perfect in our minds, but they probably weren't, you know. They probably made us mad, but we just can't remember or we don't want to recall." She took a deep, sad breath and the next words seemed to deflate from her like air escaping a balloon. "Life's just hard."

A tear fell from her eye. Just one lonely tear, and suddenly, I remembered that Sarah had lost her mother. I took her into my arms and held her close to me. She returned the embrace, cautiously at first. I rubbed her back ignoring the pain in my arm that had been inflicted by my father. My hand slid up and down. I felt the muscles in her back, the slow steady curve of her spine, dozens of soft locks of golden hair. Her chin rested on my sore shoulder. Sarah inhaled and exhaled at a slow cadence and each time she did, I drank in her sweet breath. Her breasts were nuzzled against my chest and they pressed firmly against me each time she took a breath. Her lips were inches from mine. I wanted desperately to kiss her but I lacked the courage.

"I'm sorry."

"I'm sorry. You were sad, and now, so am I," Sarah said as she pulled away from me. She was right, now I was sad.

By the time I had gotten home that evening I had determined to try and recover some measure of my relationship with my mother. Sarah had lost hers by accident, and I was beginning to feel I had lost my own mother through a mix of tragedy and neglect. Anne's death had driven a wedge between us, but it was a wedge of our own creation. We didn't need to be distant or cold to one another. There was the briefest of moments where we had connected again. It was the night after I had discovered my father's activities. That night she had cared for me, nurtured me, and let herself feel again if only for the barest of moments. I went to bed hoping that our relationship could be salvaged.

I woke up the next morning and lingered in bed. I wanted to ensure that everyone was out of the house before I went down to the kitchen. I hoped to catch Ma by herself so we could talk. Pa would be angry that I was late on my chores, but what could he do, beat me? He had already done that. It hurt, I had to admit that. I still ached in several spots, most of all, my neck. There were deep purple imprints in the shape of my father's fingers all around it. I had seen Ma for a moment after it happened, but this would be her first glimpse at Pa's handiwork. I wondered how she would react to the assault on her son.

"Morning," I said as cheerily as I could muster.

No response. I tried again. "Good Morning."

Ma spoke without turning. "Sit and eat. You have chores to do."

Her tone was callous. So much for the little talk I had planned. I did as I was instructed. I sat and immediately began to eat a piece of toast with molasses, though I had to bite and chew on one side of my mouth. My face looked like a newborn pig, rosy and oozing. Unable to keep my lips together, bits of toast fell from my mouth. I gazed at my mother's back, waiting for her to turn and see what her husband had done.

When she finally did turn, she took a deep breath and whirled around quickly as if she was yanking off a band aid. Although she immediately tried to hide it, I saw in her face a sense of horror at what I looked like. The shock of seeing it all at once had the same effect on me. I knew I had been beaten but didn't realize how bad until I saw myself in a mirror. I knew that this morning was worse than when things first started to swell. Now, there was swelling on top of swelling make the fleshy valleys deeper, and the purple and black tipped mountains all the higher. I waited for her shock. I waited for her dish-panned hands to caress my face. I waited and I waited but it never came. She just stood at the counter and stared blankly at me.

"Good toast," I said desperately trying to break the silence. I felt stupid the moment I said it. I doubted my face could handle changing any more colors. She hesitated a minute and then a serious expression took over her round face.

"Are you quite finished?"

I didn't understand. "Wha?"

"Are you quite finished being obstinate with your father or do I need to speak to you?"

The corners of my toast crashed onto my plate and bits of bread sprayed forth. My hand remained at my mouth, though now devoid of food. It wasn't possible. It couldn't be possible that she would take his side.

"Look at me," I said imploringly. "You think this is my fault?" My eyes grew wide and the working side of my lip curled as I said it.

"You've been disrespectful," she muttered, seemingly forced. "Your father told me everything."

I doubted that very much.

I just came right out with it. I was sick of secrets and sick of being the bad guy. "So he told you he kills those men and steals their stuff? He chops them up and sticks them in the outhouse. He told you that? That's why we have to keep burying the hole and digging new ones, ya know? Cause their full of dead men who did nothing wrong but show up here. I suppose he told you that?" I was yelling by the end of it, all that pent up emotion just flooded out of me.

Ma stepped towards me and locked her eyes on mine. "No," she whispered, "No. He didn't tell me all of that."

A sense of satisfaction began to refill the reservoir of emotion that I had just emptied at her. Finally, I would have someone who I could talk to. Maybe, just maybe, she might be able to stop him. Satisfaction was replaced by hope. My heart quickened in anticipation. What would she think of it all? Would she scream? Leave? Yet, she seemed so calm. There was no argument, no disbelief at all. Why?

"I've known a long time what your father has been up to." She bowed her head in shame.

"Why didn't you do anything? Why didn't you stop him, then?"

She looked at me again though her head had not risen fully. Ma looked sullen and pale.

"What would you have me do?"

Was this a plea for forgiveness? I didn't know.

"Stop him. Call the sheriff. I don't know. Something at least!" I shouted angrily at her.

"Those men . . ." she seemed to choke on the words. "Those men were dead anyway. They were going to starve out there. You don't know what it's like. They were dead anyway." Her words were hollow and devoid of passion. They came from her lips like a series of lines from a horrible actor. She believed nothing that she said. "Dying might as well have done somebody some good at least." They were my father's words though they crawled unnervingly from her lips. "He kept us out of those horrible camps. He kept us from the pipes. He kept us from the pipes." She whispered trying to make herself believe in it.

"He's a killer!" I shouted. I wanted to take hold of her and shake her. "I don't want to do this Ma. You don't want this. There has to be another way . . ."

Ma's hand came sharply across my face. The sting of it on an already bruised face exacerbated the pain.

"What other way? Don't be foolish boy! There is nothing for us. People like us, they're starving, homeless. Most of these migrants that come through are just boys. Pa sends them away. He don't hurt them none. He takes in the ones who are older. The ones who've lived a bit. Don't you act like you got all the answers! You don't! You think you're better than us! You act like what the man has had to do has been easy on him. On us. He deserves better from you."

Ma stormed out of the kitchen tears streaming down her cheeks, her feet punishing the floor for my perceived sins. She offered up the same tired arguments in defense of his actions. I realized then that I could no longer see them as just the actions of one person. I sat at the table in stunned silence. She was a silent accomplice to it all. She fattened them with a ghoulish last meal and then fed them to the monster. I had thought all along that she was oblivious to it. Now, that illusion was shattered. She was as sinister as he, as evil as the murderer himself. I tried to hold it. I fought so hard against the torrent, but when it came the tears flowed like a tsunami washing away every loving memory of my mother and any hope of reconciliation.

Chapter 19

Malaise
1938

I had come to the awful realization that my father was not unique. No, it wasn't his murderous ways that I saw as an epidemic, rather that he had become self-centered. Once, when he was in a comfortable economic position living off inherited property and money, he cared about others. Yet, when the world seemed to threaten him he regarded others as expendable. Where once there was we, now he saw only himself and his needs. Jack, too, was as egotistical as a young man could be. He was all the bravado and bluster of a man who had decided how he would handle every situation life threw at him while having little to no actual experience. Ma was passively concerned with her own little world. The world around her was too terrifying to view in a real sense, and so she had buried her head in the sand and pretended that nothing bad was happening. I was simply the fly in everyone's ointment. I refused to ignore the reality of what Pa was doing, what it meant for our family, and what was happening in America and around the world. While they enjoyed their fantasy world in which murderers and their accomplices thrived and were just and defensible, I remained firmly rooted in a reality in which many went hungry, more were unemployed, and if the radio was right, a great deal more would soon be dead on the field of battle.

"Ever wonder what might happen?" Sarah asked as we walked along the edges of the pond together.

"With what?" I wondered if she meant us. More and more, I had been thinking of us as a couple, although I didn't know where she stood on the subject, and I lacked the courage to find out.

"Europe. Hitler. The Soviets. The whole mess." Her arms flung out to her sides trying to encompass the everything she was referencing.

"Do you mean if I think there'll be war?"

"I think it's coming sooner rather than later, don't you?" she asked, a sort of sadness in her words.

"I doubt he's done with Austria. Probably Czechoslovakia next, maybe Poland. I doubt he'll try his hand against the French. Pa says we'll sit this one out, though. Me, I'm not so sure of that." I listened to the radio intently each evening, I read what newspapers I could get my hands on and I asked a great deal of questions.

"If it happens, if we get into it, will you go?" Sarah's voice was shaky. I shouldn't have liked that her voice quivered at the thought of me going off to war, but I did. It meant she cared. I shrugged my shoulders.

"I suppose I might have to." Pa had been drafted. He hadn't volunteered in a fit of patriotism like so many others had done when Wilson had called for war against Germany. If Roosevelt called for war would I volunteer? I hadn't really thought about it.

"I don't agree with what they're doing, you know?" She murmured.

It was easy to forget her German heritage. She lacked any of the outward signs that her father illustrated. There was no thick accent, nothing that said I am from half-way around the world. I realized then that she was a child of two worlds. Loyal to a homeland she could not remember. Her father extolled the virtues of a land that existed only in her imagination. He loved Germany; she loved him and so loved Germany, too. Yet, here she was telling me that she did not agree with what they were doing. As if she wanted to ensure that I did not see her as a potential enemy. As if I could ever see her that way.

"I know," I assured her. "How is your dad handling all this?"

"He wants to join the army," Sarah half giggled and half grimaced when she said it.

"He wants to go back?" I asked a bit shocked.

Sarah laughed now. "No. No. Not like you think. He wants to join the American army so he can go kill Hitler. He calls him the hand dancer. He says he wants to go nail his hands to the door of the Reichstag. You have to see him, Paul! He gets so animated; I think he's going to start breaking dishes." A warm smile slowly receded from her face and was replaced by a look of concern. "I wish the whole thing was a farce. I wish Welles made the whole damn Nazi Party up, and we were going to read about how silly we all were for panicking over nothing. I wish it were so." Her hope that the Nazi's were no more real than the radio program, *The War of the Worlds* by Orson Welles was a happy fiction, but a hopeless one.

I smiled at her, not knowing what to say or do. After a prolonged and awkward silence, I reached out and took her hand in mine.

"Pretty funny what the papers are saying about it, isn't it?" I said.

She nodded grimly.

"An alien invasion in New Jersey. Really, just too funny. I wonder if people really did start to evacuate." I smiled at the thought of all these city folk in their fancy clothes running for cover. I rubbed my thumb gently back and forth over the tops of her small fingers.

"Can you imagine how many people would die?" she whispered.

I giggled a bit at the thought. "Well, I'm sure the heat rays would cause a great deal of damage. I bet there would be looting and all sorts of chaos." She yanked her hand from mine and scowled at me. "Paul!"

"What?"

"How can you joke about this?" she demanded.

"It's funny." I said defensively. "Don't ya think?" It was a stupid question. Clearly, she did not.

She turned from me and pulled her arms around her shoulders. It looked as if she was hugging herself and I wanted to be the one to do it, but clearly it wasn't the time. "I'm not talking about the stupid radio show. I still have family in Dresden, you know."

Dresden was a far cry from Grover's Mill, New Jersey, I knew. I wondered if the family she mentioned was Jewish. I didn't have the heart to ask. I stepped forward and put my hand on her shoulder.

"It's going to be okay. Everything will turn out all right, you'll see." I hated lying to her. She rested her back against my chest and nuzzled her head in the nape of my neck.

"Paul," she said, her voice wavering slightly, "You're an awful liar."

I held her in my arms, and we watched the sun slip behind the growing clouds and settle in for the night. The starlight was obscured by the cloudy night. A deep darkness enveloped us as we headed for home. It weighed heavily on Sarah; she remained silent for much of the trip back. Occasionally, she would reach out and take my hand to steady herself or have me guide the way. My heart would skip a beat at her touch. Just as quickly as she took my hand she would let it fall limply from her grasp and my heart tumbled over a cliff. I walked her safely to her doorstep.

She left me with a simple, "G'night."

I watched the door close behind her. "Goodnight," I whispered into the night air. "I love you."

Chapter 20

Distractions
1939

I had never experienced this before. My stomach alternated between a low guttural rumble and a steady churn. My hands were shaky. I pulled on the hand-me-down jacket that I had inherited from Jack when it no longer fit him. I tried to get a glimpse of my semi-transparent reflection in the window to find that something was tragically wrong. I looked like a hobo. I buttoned my shirt wrong with one hole at the top and two buttons remaining. The dark brown jacket didn't quite match the lighter variation of brown in the trousers. I looked down at the walking disaster I had become, and the white shirt I had chosen puffed steadily up and down in time with my elevated heart rate. It made no sense. I had known the girl for years. Why, suddenly, did I feel like I was going to simultaneously melt and freeze all at once? I knew the answer but I didn't want to accept it. It was the kiss. Soft but firm, sweet but salty, it was everything and nothing at once. Mostly, I was hoping it would happen again and this time I wouldn't mess it up.

Two days before, Sarah and I had been skipping rocks across the pond. Our friendly competition led to some flirty shoving and bumping as we tried to derail the other's toss. Then, it was grabbing of arms and hands and suddenly it wasn't about the rocks skidding across the pond anymore. I held her arms, stopping her from throwing.

"I'm not letting go. I won't let you beat me," I said playfully.

"I bet you I can get you to let me go." she dared.

"Doubtful."

Then she kissed me. She came in fast and then the world went into slow motion. I relinquished my grasp and slid my arms around her back. I wanted to hold her and keep her always but not by force. I wanted her to be mine because she had decided to be mine. I felt her lips draw away and she turned quickly from me. My face pressed against her golden hair.

"You know you have to court me properly now," she said and then sent her rock careening across the pond as she walked away.

So, tonight would mark our first official date.

That evening, we decided on the earlier show, holding dinner off until after the picture. Sarah suggested it and I agreed blindly despite that rattling in my gut. She wore a white, sleeveless dress with light blue strands passing through it in a somewhat haphazard fashion. Her hair was pulled back a bit with a blue band, and her curls were banded together with simple white ribbons. A hint of rose blush adorned her cheeks, her eyes were outlined with a dark line like the ocean on a moonlit night and her lips were ruby red. I wanted to kiss her. I wanted to run away. I wanted to marry her. She was beautiful. People stared at us on the bus. They ogled her in both subtle and obvious ways, and I felt a strange sense of pride that she was with me. Yet, as soon as we arrived at the theater I felt overwhelmingly shamed. Standing next to her, I felt out of place as if someone else deserved to be here and not me. She should have someone better than the destitute son of a murderer. She should be arriving here in style, in a new Cadillac, not by bus. I was starting something I could not hope to finish.

We sat three rows from the back of the theater in velvet red seats. I was sixty cents poorer now, after two twenty-cent tickets, some buttered popcorn, and soda pop to share. But the company was the best I had ever known. Our elbows rubbed together and we jokingly nudged each other from the armrest. Sarah was sweet. She was beautiful. She was funny. I was enthralled.

The news reels were dominated by news from Europe. The gray celluloid illustrated the rise of Nazi Germany and its leader, Adolf Hitler. A frail little English chap with an umbrella smiled and shook hands with the Nazi in his tidy uniform. Neville Chamberlain had just purchased of few more months of peace at the cost of their ally, Czechoslovakia. Years later, I remember reading a quote from Winston Churchill on the subject of the Munich Conference. He said that England had been given a choice between shame and war. She had chosen shame and would get war. Within those colorless film frames a perceptive person could read the tea leaves and see the future. Sarah sat with her hands clasped together, fidgeting nervously in her seat. I watched her furiously quick motions and shuddered to think what obstacles our future might place before us. My stomach rolled and growled angrily, a mix of nerves and hunger. The world was hanging over a precipice and death was pulling hard at its feet.

The mood of the theater reflected mine, remaining somber and gray throughout the news reels, but it was noticeably cheered with the appearance of a certain sailor and his lanky girlfriend. The first Fleischer offering, one where Popeye tried to become a Hollywood stunt man was hysterical. The theater chortled at the sailor's ability to fly a plane. Bluto wound up getting tossed from one wing to another and then from the front of the aircraft to the back. The propeller nipped at his cubby behind as Popeye aimed the plane downward. Then, the big man went careening toward the tail of the aircraft to have his genitals crushed. The whole sequence was repeated several times to applause and laughter. Yet, all of Popeye's efforts were wasted when little baby Sweet Pea arrived with his own motion picture to show the director. Sweet Pea's daring rescue of Olive Oyl, infused of course, by a can of spinach, won the baby the stunt position. The second cartoon had Popeye heading into the jungle in search of Bluto. A sign said, "Jungle! Keep alive, keep out!" Popeye ignored it. He battled an assortment of African animals; a lion, a rhino, and even pulled the trunk of an elephant through its tail and tied it off in a ribbon. He went through all this effort only to pick a fight with his arch enemy.

"Neville Chamberlain could use a few lessons from Popeye," I whispered.

When the feature began, Sarah settled into her seat and nestled her head on my shoulder. She was brash and affectionate, almost to the point of inappropriateness. I was shy and reserved, unwilling to make any advance towards her. As the MGM lion roared on screen, I thought how perfect we were together.

Judy Garland's song, "Somewhere Over the Rainbow," touched Sarah. I could hear her humming along to it towards the end, her vocal cords vibrating on my arm as she did. Instinctively, I knew I had found a kindred spirit, one that wanted to escape nearly as much as I did. The tornado that brought Dorothy to Oz was an amazing piece of special effects for the day, and the theater "oohhed" and "aahhed" as the house spun. Yet, it was the landing that was really amazing. The transition to the color of Oz was shocking and wonderful. Sarah's hand tightened on my arm with childlike excitement when little munchkins started to pop up from their hiding places. Her hands broke into a full blown slap; tapping in time to "Ding Dong the Wicked Witch is Dead"! Anne Hamilton's arrival as the Wicked Witch sent her jumping a tad-bit in fright. There was nothing to love about the witch, but I appreciated her at that moment. By the time the Wicked Witch set the Scarecrow on fire, Sarah's arm was wrapped tightly around mine and her fingers rested neatly between my own. I decided I had a new favorite character.

When the film ended we left the theater with a throng of people pouring out the wide double-doors. The street was lit in an array of colored lights emanating from the various neon advertising signs that encouraged passersby to grab a pack of Camels or purchase the newest RCA offering. The smell of stale popcorn piggy backed along with the patrons. There was a great chatter that seemed to follow the crowd like thunder trails lightning.

"It was amazing!" a middle-aged woman in red exclaimed. Her counterpart nodded his agreement bobbing through the crowd as he did so. That seemed to be the general consensus of the crowd. Words like thrilling, majestic, incredible, nothing like it before, etc. seemed to dominate the clamor within the group.

"So, what did you think?" Sarah inquired.

I hadn't given it much thought until she asked. It really was incredible. Yet, I didn't know if I liked it. There were no dainty china dolls, no quadlings, and I hated what had been done to the flying monkeys. They never got a chance to help Dorothy. They were relegated to serving the witch alone. I don't know why that bothered me so much, except that, they were always my favorite aspect of the book. I supposed I couldn't abide the change. Gone, too, was the Queen of the mice, but I cannot say I missed her all that much. Although, I loved the colors of Oz itself. It was exactly as I had imagined it as a boy. Bright and beautiful, populated by all manner of interesting creatures, Oz lived up to my demanding expectations. The songs were great and the Wicked Witch stole the show. I suppose the greatest change in the film that I was wrestling with was turning Oz into a dream for Dorothy. As I child, I needed to believe it was real, tangible in a way. Now, as a young man, I accepted it as nothing more than a child's imaginative concoction. Yet, I was wholly jealous of Dorothy. She had everything I did not. She was surrounded by men who protected and loved her. She had family that cared deeply for her. Her home was a refuge for her; a place to feel safe and warm. Finally, the thing I wished most for myself was that, like Dorothy, my parents would be gone, too. Apparently, the pondering in my head had taken too much time, and Sarah asked her question again.

"Paul, what did you think?"

I wasn't about to share everything that rambled through my head. "Pretty good, I thought. You?"

Sarah beamed with excitement, "I loved it. The songs were spectacular and the color was amazing. I don't know how they did those trees. Did you see how scary they were? They reminded me of Snow White. Did you see Snow White?"

I shook my head no trying not to interrupt her. She continued an unabated and unabashed celebratory review of the film. Whether she realized it or not she had taken my hand in hers. I know she said some things, comments on the motion picture, but I didn't hear one word of it. Her hand was nestled in mine. Our fingers blended together, a mix of calluses and silk. We walked together, arm and arm. Suddenly, all my thoughts calmed. *The Wizard of Oz* became the best film I ever saw because I saw it with her.

We meandered the city streets together.

"I think it was better than *The Adventures of Robin Hood*," Sarah declared with a glint in her eye.

One hand brushed a lock of stray hair that had slipped in front of her perfectly blue eyes. I repressed a smile at the thought of how much she intoxicated me. She knew it was a personal favorite of mine, so her comment was meant as bait; a playful challenge to me. She had me hook, line, and sinker.

"Come now, Sarah," I chided her sarcastically, "a film without sword fights is no film at all."

I was an adventure addict. Most of all, I was an Errol Flynn addict. He was everything I was not. Brash and confident, words and women came easy to him. I was never so lucky. I loved *Captain Blood* and *The Charge of the Light Brigade,* but *The Adventures of Robin Hood* was the best of the bunch.

"There were fights!" she bit back playfully and gently slammed her hip into my own. "The scarecrow's insides wear torn out!"

I tried to interject, but she had barely taken a breath before pushing her position further.

"What about the ugly green guards in those big hats? They fought them," she jutted her finger out like a sword, her nail a sharp point, then poked me in the side as if she was running me through with a rapier. I lurched back, playfully drew my own finger as a sword and nearly tumbled over an unsuspecting pedestrian. I apologized profusely, dusting the man off, while Sarah giggled with her hand held demurely over her mouth. I sent the man off and turned to her.

"Well, I guess you won that fight," I said with an embarrassed smile.

"Take that, you Saxon outlaw." she said, jabbing at me again.

"Norman or Saxon, what does that matter, my lady?" I returned, my hands held high in mock submission, playing along with the Robin Hood theme.

"You know you are very impudent?"

I took a chance and said what I felt in my heart but used Flynn's words, "But you do love me, don't you, don't you?"

"You're a strange man," she countered using Olivia De Havilland's line from the scene in Sherwood Forest.

Her head dropped and her eyes found some blemish in the sidewalk that required her undivided attention. My first attempt at boldness had failed miserably. Then, Sarah's head rose slowly and she looked me straight in the eyes.

"Tell me, when you are in love, is it hard to think of anyone but one person? Do you want to be with them all the time?"

She smiled coyly and I returned the grin, wide and happy. She stepped into me, her shoes brushing past the tips of my faded brown soles. Instinctively, I moved to step back but she took my hand in hers and I was unwilling to withdraw. She smelled of flowers, of buttered popcorn and soda pop, and of sunshine. I lifted my free hand

and let the back of it stream down her alluring cheek like a warm waterfall. She pressed her face to mine.

"I do love you . . . I do," she whispered in my ear. Her lips slid open slightly and we fell inexorably together in a passionate kiss, forgetting everyone and everything around us. Nothing mattered but her. I don't know who kissed who, but I do know it was the greatest moment of my life to that point. I let myself nearly drown in it before I had to come up for air. I hated to, but I had to end it.

"Sarah, we shouldn't." Little old ladies passed by and scowled at us with disapproving eyes. Men smiled knowingly and the world pressed in like a great weight on us. Our moment had come so quickly and passed in mere heartbeats. But what beats they were!

"We should go," Sarah demurred, her face blushed slightly and her hand fell limply from mine.

I feared I would never again find a moment like that.

Chapter 21

An Interesting Character
1939

Hitler had invaded Poland on September 1st. Europe was at war and America was officially neutral. None of the politicians wanted to make the same mistakes that had slowly pulled the nation into the Great War, and so we buried our heads in the sand and pretended that it wasn't happening. It was a collective, national attempt to blatantly ignore reality. Outwardly, Americans would proclaim, "It's not our fight," or "Europe needs to sort out its own problems," and "Hitler's no threat to us." Inwardly, we all seemed to understand the lie we were telling ourselves. Maybe lie was too strong a word. Maybe it was a vain hope that Europe could sort out its problems without us. We hoped that the Brits and the French would be able to stem the tide of aggression. It was a futile hope. Hitler was done in Poland within a month, the British and French were doing nothing but waiting, and the Russians seemed to be aiding the Nazis. The world was growing darker and we pretended the sun was still shining.

Our house was a mirror of the world around us. A great evil grew among us. He acted with impunity and no one bothered to notice. Those that did were eliminated. Anyone willing to turn a blind eye to the slaughter were left alone or benefited from the wickedness. Then, there was me. I knew what he was doing but felt powerless to stop it, and so I clung to hope. I hoped that he would stop. I hoped that the man he had just carved up was the last one he needed, and there would be no more. I hoped that maybe the slew of visitors would somehow end and Pa would be left without fodder for his habit. I hoped and I hoped and I hoped, but it didn't change reality.

Hitler had taken Austria and the world had done nothing. Of course, he claimed that it was a unification but it did not change the facts. Hitler had demanded the Sudetenland of Czechoslovakia. European leaders met at Munich and gave it to him on the promise that it was the last thing he would demand.

"Never give a bully your lunch," Jack had said, "He'll be back tomorrow if you do."

It was the only astute thing I remember coming out of his mouth. Of course, six months later the whole of Czechoslovakia was gobbled up by a hungry German nation. Even Mr. Schultz decried what was happening, "This is not Germany. They will rise up against him. They know this is not the way."

Even he was living a dream. By 1939, we all understood who he was even if we refused to face it. We clung to false hope that something would change. It was only getting worse.

Both the world, and our family, were at a moral crossroads of sorts. We needed a good man to enter our lives. For the world, that man seemed to be Winston Churchill. For our family, the man was named Mr. Simmonds.

"Excuse me, son," a fluid, almost languid voice said.

"Can I help you?" I asked, pulling my head from my book. I stood up and dusted my legs with one hand, a puff of light brown air glittered around me.

"I was wondering if you had any work?" he smiled cheerfully at me. The gleam of his white teeth struck me like a light bulb being flicked on in a dark room.

My countenance must have darkened because he immediately apologized for his question.

"My apologies, I didn't mean to put you on the spot like that. It's just that . . . well . . ." He had a hard time finishing it. They all did. It's just that I'm starving or poor or desperate or some other unspeakable condition that no one could ever have imagined themselves being in. I couldn't look at him.

"We don't got any work." I sat back down and stuck my head back into my book.

I could see his feet from the tops of my downward facing eyes. He wore black dress shoes that had grown faded and scuffed like they had been shined by sandpaper. I grew angry that those shoes had not turned and left. I went to repeat myself, but he beat me to it and spoke again.

"Ever read it before?" he queried.

"What?" I said astonished.

The Wonderful Wizard of Oz. Ever read it before?" he repeated

I looked down at the book in my hand and then to him. I was flabbergasted. I had read it dozens of times. If the truth were told, I really didn't even need the novel in hand to recount the story. Reading it had become a habit of sorts, a way to honor and remember Anne.

"I'm a bit of a bibliophile myself. You know, there are a number of sequels, too." He took a seat next to me. He smelt of dust and perspiration. He reeked of the depression.

"Bibliophile?" I asked dumbfounded.

Mr. Simmonds patted me gently on the shoulder. "Sorry. It means lover of books. Biblio, books. Phile, lover of. It's Greek. Used to be an English and history teacher. When there were kids in school and not riding these bloody trains trying to find work." He rubbed his face aggressively with both hands as if to try and wake up from a bad dream.

I pitied him. He reminded me of my own school teachers who had encouraged me to read and get a good education though I had only ever had two men as teachers.

"I read *The Emerald City of Oz* once. My teacher let me borrow her copy when I was young. I liked that one. Dorothy got to bring her family to Oz in it. Life got too hard in Kansas so they escaped to Oz just in time to save the city from the Nome King." I glanced back at the house and pondered the course of my family. Dorothy and her aunt and uncle had chosen to escape their troubles. My family had chosen a different route, a malicious but otherwise successful path in protecting their farm. Oz was a playful child's fiction; my life was a horror story.

"That's the one with the magic belt and the wish, right?" Mr. Simmonds queried. I suspected he knew the answer to his question and was merely engaging in conversation.

"Yes, sir, it is." I replied, trying to end things quickly.

"Ever read *Dorothy and the Wizard of Oz*?" He asked with a coy smile.

"No."

"There is an earthquake that sends Dorothy, her kitten, a horse and her cousin to a world populated with vegetable people in a land of glass." He began the plot summary ignoring my strong desire for him to leave. I thumbed through my copy of *The Wonderful World of Oz* trying my best to be rude. "They travel with the Wizard of Oz through all the strange lands that the Oz books are so famous for. They face invisible bears, wooden gargoyles, and dragons, all while trying to find a way to the surface."

He smiled broadly in the telling of it, reliving the fond memories of reading it. My curiosity got the best of me and I asked, "How did it end?"

"Well, I wouldn't want to ruin it for you."

"Not like there's a steady stream of books coming my way anytime soon," I said, waving my hands around and pointing out various parts of the farm.

"Are you certain you want me to tell you it?" he asked proudly. He was like a fisherman reeling in his catch.

"Please."

He leaned forward and rested his elbows on his knees. A small puff of dust arose from his legs as he recounted the ending.

"The Wizard had some piglets with him and when they all returned to Oz, one of them went missing. Dorothy's kitten was a tad rude and was blamed for the missing piglet. The kitten faced murder charges and the Scarecrow actually becomes the kitten's defense attorney! It's the Tin Woodsman who really defends her, though. He uses one of the other piglets to convince the jury that they were wrong to condemn the kitten. Then the surly kitten ruins it and demands to see all nine piglets together. The kitten knew where the missing piglet was all along and thought the trial was merely entertaining."

I laughed out loud at this. It was so typical of Baum and the silliness of Oz, yet, still unpredictable. Without really knowing it, I had given up my efforts at sending the man away. We chatted amiably about any number of topics, from Oz to FDR and beyond. He was a brilliant man who seemed to intuitively see the subtleties in a book or situation. I was fascinated by his opinions and his seemingly endless knowledge on all topics great and small. As the day dragged on I remembered my manners and offered him coffee and food. He politely declined, but I forced a large cup into his hand and a hardy piece of pie onto his lap. He was gracious and restrained; eating slowly though I was certain he was starving. I liked the man tremendously, so what I had to do next did not come easily.

"You really are a very nice fellow. I wish we could do something for you but there's no work here."

The lie came easily and I prayed it was convincing. He remained stoic but his eyes were sad. I tried to remind myself that I was not rejecting him, rather saving him.

"Besides, work on this farm has been known to kill a man." That, at least, wasn't a lie. I thrust out my hand and offered it to Mr. Simmonds trying to say goodbye. He pumped my hand and went to say goodbye, but we were suddenly interrupted a deep voice that sent shudders through me.

"I really don't know what you're talkin' bout Paul."

My head snapped around to see Pa standing in the doorway, his face looking pale and ashen behind the dusty screen door.

"We have plenty of work to go around." He smiled menacingly as the screen door creaked open. "Always room for one more."

Chapter 22

Reprieve
1939

Mr. Simmonds had accepted my father's offer of a job along with room and board as any man in his situation might, with gusto. For Mr. Simmonds, hope seemed alight again, little did he know the depths of darkness Pa had in store for him. The man had come to the farm penniless and with nothing of value. These were the types of people Pa turned away flat, not even considering their value as farm hands. If he could not steal anything from them; he was not about to waste time on them. Murder had to be profitable, after all. There was just one reason Pa had taken the man on as a hand, to torment me. Pa would bat the man around a bit, toy with him like a cat would a mouse, and then pounce and destroy him for his amusement and my pain. In his own twisted way I knew that in Pa's mind, he was trying to teach me a life lesson. People die all the time, sometimes for a purpose, sometimes for nothing at all. Deal with it, move on, and above all, take care of yourself and your family. I understood the theory, but the practice was more than I could bear. And so, I too, stalked Mr. Simmonds, waiting for my chance to pounce.

I spent most of my time skulking in the shadows, trying to ensure Mr. Simmonds safety from a short distance. Any time Pa came within range of the man I leapt from cover and appeared as nonchalantly as possible. Pa would eye me warily and go about his business. Mr. Simmonds always seemed to welcome my arrival; though, I doubt he understood why my appearances were so important to him. We talked while we worked, passing the time together in friendly banter. A somewhat symbiotic relationship developed between us. He would share his knowledge of books with me. He retold stories from memory that I might never get a chance to read myself. He was a wonderfully animated storyteller, and I often found myself dreamily pulled away from my work and into his tales. I would be jerked back to reality at points only by what I contributed to the relationship.

"Paul, what do I do here?" he would ask or, "Is there another way to do this that's easier?"

I would show him how to use a tool or where to stand when moving hay that made life a bit easier on the back. Then, I would wait patiently to be whisked away to a far off world in one of his stories. In this way, we both eased the burden of farm life for the other. A faster friendship had never been made.

As the days passed, it became increasingly obvious to me that this system was bound to fail. Pa needed to be in the right place at the right time only once; while I needed to be right there one hundred percent of the time. I knew that Pa would not act in front of me. If he was going to kill the man in front of me; he had had numerous opportunities to do so. Still, I was exhausting myself trying to keep vigil over Mr. Simmonds. I had to do something to get rid of him before my father did.

I had thought that the manner in which Tim interacted with Mr. Simmonds would have driven him off. Tim had bossed him around, treated him like a child, and had him perform all of the most mundane or tedious tasks the farm had to offer. Yet, Mr. Simmonds took to each task patiently and without complaint. Even Tim had begrudgingly learned to like the man in the few days he had been with us. I could not rely on his crass personality to do my work for me. As hard as it was going to be, I knew I had to shun him. I knew if I was cruel to Mr. Simmonds, the betrayal would hurt him and if he was lucky, it would be enough to drive him away. Unfortunately, I never got the chance.

I was idly tossing rocks at a can that sat precariously on the edge of a stack of graying lumber when Pa stormed past me. He was red faced, full of rage. His shadow passed me, blotting out the sun and covering me in an instant blast of cool air. A great ruckus arose from the barn in the moments after Pa had passed. Tools clanged and then thudded to the ground. It sounded as if he were tearing the place apart. With my head turned, trying to see what he was doing I never saw Tim coming until he had passed me and entered the barn. In truth, he didn't really enter the barn. It was more of an invasion.

"He's a nice man," Tim said, seemingly entreating with my father.

The riotous search came to an abrupt conclusion and silence reigned supreme for a moment. I slid into the barn and took up a position near the exterior wall. I would have gone unnoticed if not for the loud crash of an eclectic mix of unused hardware spilling from the bucket I bumped into. Oddly, neither man bothered to look towards the sound.

"He's a nice man, Mr. Miller," Tim repeated.

Pa had clearly found what he was looking for. Ending his search, he took whatever it was up in his hand. He did not respond to Tim. In fact, he didn't even really bother to acknowledge Tim at all. Silently, he stepped from the shadows. Understanding flushed over me. I had run out of time.

Pa flicked his wrist, dismissing Tim, the glint of a butcher's knife shimmering at his side. He made no attempt to hide it.

"Go find somethin' to do." Pa ordered.

Tim's face hardened to stone and went as white as marble. He looked scared but he didn't move a muscle. That alone was more defiance than he had ever shown my father in all the time I had known him.

"Leave," Pa spat.

Tim's sun-burnt face darkened and his muscles tensed. "Mr. Miller, ya ain't gonna do this one like ya done the others." Tim turned and faced me, his eyes wide. "Why don't you see Mr. Simmonds off, Paul?" He may have asked it like a question, but Tim's voice said it was an order. I couldn't believe what he was doing. "Your father and I need to talk," he added.

Wordlessly, I left the barn and headed to the house at a sprint.

Mr. Simmonds had gathered his bag and was headed towards the road.

"Mr. Simmonds! Mr. Simmonds!" I called. He slackened his pace and allowed me to catch up with him though he never actually stopped walking.

"I'm leaving, son," he said. There was confusion in his voice as if he knew he had to leave but not exactly why he had to. Something had clearly happened between him and my father.

"I know," I muttered trying to catch my breath a bit. "Where will you go?" I asked.

"Haven't really considered it," he admitted. "Maybe one of the camps or to the docks. I heard they need men in the bay area."

He wasn't cut out for dock work. Even if they were hiring they wouldn't take a man like him. The nation wanted a strong back and thick skinned hands, not a keen mind and thin arms. I didn't know what would happen to him. I thought of the mayor in Pipe City and my heart broke for him. "Good luck," was all I could say.

"Thank you." We walked a few feet further together in silence. "Paul . . . Paul, your father . . ." Mr. Simmonds struggled to put his thoughts into words. If he knew something was wrong, maybe even horribly wrong, I never knew. "Paul, you be careful, okay?"

"I will. You too."

We shook hands amiably and parted company. He was alive. Though I didn't know what his future held, I knew he had one. That was enough to make me smile. I would never know what had driven him away. It was strange to feel such happiness at the parting of a friendship, but I did. Missing the living was easier than mourning the dead.

I watched like a sentinel as Mr. Simmonds disappeared over the horizon before returning to the house. I was already midway up the stairs when I realized that I had left Tim with my father. Frantically, I shot off the stairs, leaping to the floor. There was no loud thud because my feet barely had hit the floor before they were off again towards the door. As I threw open the door I reasoned with myself. Tim was safe. Tim was safe. I kept repeating the words in my head. As I dashed to the barn the farm was eerily quiet. Mr. Simmonds was gone, and there were no other hands around. Pa had not replaced Stephen or Connor, preferring to use the transient labor to his advantage. Permanent help just complicated his ability to steal and murder. I quickened my pace at the thought.

There was no hesitation in me anymore. I threw the barn door to the side and stood at the entrance, waiting for my eyes to adjust from the bright sun. My sight soon went from dark splotches to translucent haziness. I rubbed at them trying to speed the process.

"Tim!" I called brazenly. "Tim! Are you still in here?" I lowered my hands, wiping them on my trousers.

I could see Tim's frame, obscured in shadow, sitting against the exterior wall on the far side. I called to him again but he did not answer. The palm of his hand rested on the ground by his side and his arm was straight out like a kick stand. The other hand was held up at his face as if he were about to sneeze. I was relieved to see him safe. I hadn't really liked the man at all. Frankly, I thought he was a selfish jerk. Yet, he had helped me save a life and I appreciated that. Moreover, I didn't want anyone to be a victim of my father whether they were selfish or not.

"Tim, I just wanna say thank you for your help," I said as I meandered over to him. "What you did today was a good thing."

Tim started to move a bit at that. His arm slackened and his elbow bent. His torso slid slowly towards the side as the support was removed. He did nothing to slow his descent and his head thumped against the ground. I noticed his other hand was not at his mouth, rather holding his neck.

"Tim?" He tried to answer but a horrific gurgle filled the air and my stomach sank.

I raced to the man's side and took his head into my lap. He was covered in blood and dirt. I saw the wound at his neck and screamed aloud. I gently tugged at his hand, trying to get a better look at it. At first, he resisted but then slowly he assented. I peeled his hand away. Blood spurted from the wound in a slow steady fountain. Quickly, I forced my hands onto his neck and tried to put pressure. I felt the blood push against my hands in undulating waves. There was no hope.

I watched, aghast, as Tim's life slipped away. Hands covered in blood, I wiped at his face, caressing his cheeks.

"I'm so sorry. I'm so sorry. Please, forgive me." Tears fell from my eyes and mixed with the streaks of blood on the dying man's face. "We saved him," I choked out trying to give meaning to the horror in front of me. "You did it, Tim. He's safe." Tim's eyes stared into my own. Gurgling noises emanated from the wound in his neck as blood spurted in ever shorter eruptions. The heart he had just found was slowing and growing silent. I rested my head on his chest listening to the softening thump-thump of his heart. Slowly, the sound ebbed into oblivion like the drone of a bagpiper walking off into the horizon. "Thank you," I whispered to him as his body convulsed and grew suddenly quiet.

Chapter 23

Beatings
1939

I had ensured a burial for Tim that was as respectful as possible, not wanting Pa to add him to the growing pile of remains in the cesspit under the outhouse. It took the better part of a day, but I was able to dig a deep grave not far from the tree for him and drag his body to it. I was exhausted, utterly depleted of hope.

The tension continued to build, unabated, within the house. Pa knew I had no respect or love for him, Ma was an accessory to his crimes, Jack was simply apathetic to it all, while Billy was too young and too naïve to understand. For a group of people I once loved there was little tolerance left in me. To allow Pa even the opportunity to attack Mr. Simmonds was the last straw for me. Mr. Simmonds had escaped with his life, blissfully ignorant to how close he came to death and dismemberment. For that at least, I was happy. Had he become aware of what this house of horrors held, Pa would never have let him leave alive. Mr. Simmonds was my first victory, costly as it was. His marked the first life I had acted to save. His rescue emboldened my behavior once more. I was a man now, and I was determined to stand up against what was happening here.

Tim was gone, too. He had helped me to save Mr. Simmonds and it had cost him his life. I never loved the man, never even liked him really, but in the end, he was good. Pa was never gonna let him leave here knowing the secret. Tim knew that before he had acted; and yet, he acted all the same. Tim had knowingly sacrificed himself to save an innocent man. For a man who had been nothing but selfish and vain, it was the greatest act of compassion I had ever seen. Tim was a hero and no one but me would ever know it. In the scores of things that were unfair, that fact seemed to rise to the top of my list of life's little cruelties. I had decided that if Tim could do it, so could I.

The first test of my newfound courage would come against my elder brother Jack. We had fought repeatedly throughout our lifetime, and I was often on the losing end of those conflicts. When we were younger they were simply skirmishes where little damage was done, and the two sides spent most of the time testing the other's resolve. Back then, Jack had two years and twenty pounds on me. He would use his size and strength to torment me as older brothers do. A punch here, a shove there, but never anything too drastic. It was only after I had told him about my discovery in the barn and watching Pa deposit the mangled corpse into the outhouse did the contest between us become a full blown war.

Jack had beaten me more consistently and more severely than Pa had ever done in those early days. But, I was near eighteen now and Jack might still have two years on me but I had a clear advantage in size and in strength. The balance of power in our conflict had slowly been shifting away from him. He found it more and more difficult to beat me or restrain me. Despite this change in dynamic, Jack found ways to continue to gain advantage over me. When I was sixteen, Jack had punched me in the chest as soon as I entered the barn. I grabbed at my torso and gasped for air as the wind left my body. Before I could take a breath Jack was on top of me, pounding at my ribs. By the third jab he brought his head to my ear and said, "You need to show Pa some respect, Paul." His words were whispered venom pouring into my ears. I tried to give some sort of snarky reply, but I had yet to be able to fill my lungs. Several more shots to the ribs followed and I felt like I was going to suffocate to death. Jack finally got off me and walked out. I lay there, recovering from the ambush and spent the next couple of days feeling as if every breath caused an invisible stab wound into my gut.

In a fair, straight up fight, Jack probably couldn't win any longer. I didn't realize it then. I had no consciousness of the shift in tactics; only the shift in intensity was impressed upon me. As each fight broke out, my desire to inflict pain on Jack grew. I became determined to give as good as I got. There were times when I knew I had hurt him, though, he gritted his teeth and showed no pain. The hostilities between us became not just a contest of physical force but also of psychological warfare, as well. Each one determined that the other would not have the satisfaction of seeing the other admit pain or defeat.

Jack was driving the tractor and tilling the fields while I worked on sorting the seed and prepping for the afternoon. He had come back from the south field in a foul mood. I suppose my mere presence was enough to turn his demeanor sour.

"You ain't done yet?" the words dripped from his mouth like acid.

I did not respond. He was trying to engage me and I was determined to avoid it.

"Lazy, that's what you are. Useless and lazy!" he bellowed as he kicked up dirt from the ground.

Again, I offered no retort but my blood had begun to boil. I continued the work I had set out to do trying not to make eye contact with him. Jack had taken to leaning on the fence. His hands held the rail as the small of his back rested there and his one leg crooked to the side. He started to swing his foot back and forth lazily at first and then with force and speed. Rocks sputtered towards me in time to his swaying leg. The force and intensity increased and soon a thick cloud of dust enveloped us.

"You wanna stop that?" I grumbled like rolling thunder before a storm.

This time it was Jack's turn to feign deafness. His prodding continued unabated and the cloud of dirt became a dust storm. I coughed on the particles as they invaded my nose and throat.

"Cut the crap, Jack!" I shouted.

With stunning speed Jack was through the cloud and his hands were grasping my shirt.

"You don't tell me what to do!" he barked.

I reacted in an instant. Knocking his hands down and away from my shirt; I shoved him backwards. He fell to the floor as both of us were stunned by the ferocity of my response. I had finally given him the reaction he was looking for, and he seemed unprepared for it.

Jack pushed himself up from the ground and briskly dusted himself off.

"You shouldn'ta done that," he forced himself to say.

Jack leaped at me as soon as he finished the sentence. I was ready for him, though. Jack lowered his head as he came at me. I raised both my arms and clenched my hands together. I lowered the boom onto his upper back just as he began to wrap his arms around me. I heard the distinctive huffing sound of the air rushing from his lungs and what little grasp he had on me quickly faded. Jack had fallen face first into the dirt and I took a step back letting him decide his next move. He had hit the ground twice today. That was more than his ego could bear.

Jack did a modified push-up and thrust himself to his feet. He was red faced and his mouth was covered in dirt on one side. A small gash had opened up on one side of his lip and the blood combined to make a stream of auburn mud trickling down his chin. His eyes were full of fury as he raised his fists into the air and came at me swinging. This time, I decided that retreat was the better part of valor. I took several steps back and Jack quickened his pace as I did. When I figured he had hit full throttle I let him catch up to me. Sidestepping his lunge, I let my foot do all the work for me. Jack went over splaying out as he did. He went head first into the ground and tumbled over himself landing on his backside before coming to a stop. It had to have hurt, bad. It was his third trip to the dirt in a matter of seconds. Jack struggled to get up. He rubbed his back and his head. I heard him whining about some ache or pain. It didn't matter much to me at that point. I left Jack there to wallow in his misery. A new dynamic had been established that day, and I was cognizant of the fact that Jack was a worry for me no longer. It was great. I felt like a true man that day.

I had things to do. Wrapping up the last of my chores, I headed off to take a bath and get dressed. Sarah and I had planned on spending the evening together. We never did much more than talk together as we walked, and yet I looked forward to my time with her. She was a little bit of parole in my prison of a life and it was a jail I intended on breaking out of.

Chapter 24

An Inconvenient Discovery
1940

Sarah smiled playfully at me as the moonlight caressed her demure skin. The soft light given off by the star-speckled, half-mooned sky made her flesh look like milk and her blue eyes sparkled like a shimmering horizon. She was stunningly pretty and I wanted nothing more than her at that moment. Sarah rose from the steps of the porch and walked several feet in front of me. Stopping suddenly, she whirled around sending her dress spinning as she did. As her olive colored hem flew in circles it rose into the air revealing more of her alluring legs. When the spin came to a halt my eyes remained glued to her legs.

"Look at me," she ordered.

I thought I had been, very intently at that! My eyes walked slowly up to hers. They took in as much of the landscape as they could; the narrow valley between her legs, the flat plains of her stomach, the rolling hills of her breasts; and then finally, the deep ocean of her eyes.

"I was," I said, then corrected myself, "I am."

Sarah replied, "Really?"

Apparently, while my gaze was locked on her eyes, her hands had been busy. She ran her hand down her side, her fingernails moving slowly as they took my eyes with them. Sarah had let loose the top off her dress and her breast was exposed to the cool night air. Her nipple grew and pointed at me as if to draw ever closer. I stared, mouth agape at her. She looked like the Greek statues I had seen in our history books at school, still and perfect. So I stared at her, painting the image onto my brain like a Renaissance artist so that I could always see her now, at this moment. I adjusted my seat on the porch letting my legs fall to the sides as more space between them became needed. I watched her hand move upwards to the other side. She tugged at the lace near the sleeve of her dress. A second breast appeared and the pair now stood firm as her fingers spread wide and slipped back across the mounds. I found myself watching her fingers more than her breasts. They stroked across her breasts and gently tugged at her nipples.

Apparently, a wide smile broke across my face because Sarah giggled quietly and said, "You like what you see?"

I did, though I couldn't believe it! The thought of getting caught had crossed my mind, but I was well past caring.

She raised her hand and pointed her index finger at me. Turning her hand, she now beckoned me towards her with a wiggle of that same finger. I was a fish on a hook and she reeled me into her. She placed her hand on my chest and stopped me about a foot from her. I intended on embracing her and kissing her, but my will was not in command here. She took my hand and fiddled with my fingers a moment before bringing it up and placing it on her breast. Not knowing what to do with it; I simply held her and waited for further instructions. She leaned in and kissed me sliding her tongue into my mouth as she did so. Breaking off, she moved back a few steps before enticing me further, "Come with me."

I followed her staying a few steps behind as I did. She turned occasionally, ensuring my continued pursuit. It was unnecessary to check on me, the vision of her nude body ensured that I would follow her to Hell and back if I had to. I was happy that she checked up on my progress, though. Each time she did offered me another glimpse of her bosom. I thoroughly enjoyed watching her breasts bounce gently as she walked.

We reached the barn and Sarah turned and stood against the door. Pulling me tightly to her, she kissed me again, longer and more passionate this time. My body pressed against her and I dared to raise my hands to her breasts again, this time as an uninvited guest. The arrival of my hands seemed welcome and was reciprocated by a soft grasp between my legs. Sara used her other hand to search for the latch on the barn door. I heard a light thump as the latch gave way and the two of us stumbled into the barn.

Sarah untangled herself from me and quickly went to work on the rest of her dress. She let the light green dress fall to the ground around her feet. She stood before me, sand colored hay darting through her toes, the sky in her eyes and her blonde hair like the warm sun above. She was the world to me. Her smile beckoned me. I drew closer, and as I did, I watched her smile turn to shock, then confusion, and finally terror.

"Sarah! What's wrong?" I blurted. I didn't understand what had changed so drastically in just a few seconds. I looked down at myself wondering if there was something wrong. Seeing nothing out of the ordinary I asked again, "What is it?"

Sarah was standing naked in the middle of the barn frozen, paralyzed with fear. I followed her eyes and turned to see what had her locked in this state of terror. There, in the corner of the barn was the cause of her paralytic shock. A flickering lantern stood on a table in the corner of the barn. Pa was working at the table and he had seen Sarah standing there totally naked. At first, I thought it was simply embarrassment at being caught in the act that had so confounded her. Then I realized what Pa was doing. A large apron, covered in blood and gore was wrapped around him and he held a large butcher's knife in his right hand. The table was covered in blood and innards. It looked as if he was in the midst of slaughtering a large pig. A wheeled cart rested next to the table. Protruding outwards from the top of the cart were the severed remains of Pa's ghastly work. A hand stuck from the top of the wooden cart covered in a crimson sauce. The fingers curled in some childlike wave.

"Sarah! Go!" I yelled at her.

She did not move. Instantly, Pa was across the barn and in between Sarah and me. He was seething with anger and muttering curses at her. Taking hold of her with both arms he lifted her off the ground as he shook her.

"You don't belong here you little whore!" he spat at her.

It took seconds for me to react but they felt like hours.

"Pa! Pa!" I yelled. It was not a begging tone, more a demanding one. "Get your hands off her!" I ordered.

He ignored me and continued to shake Sarah vehemently.

"Damn you. You don't belong here," Pa kept repeating.

He was in almost as much shock as poor Sarah. Sarah's head rocked back and forth in a rhythm, and my father's grip dug into her arms. My arm shot out and grabbed Pa at the wrist. My grip almost slipped off the moist target, but luckily it held firm. I pulled one of his hands from her and spun him as I did so. I had grown tall and Pa was forced to look up at me now. We locked our gaze upon one another, an inexorable rage fueling both of us. Pa seemed to gain his composure. He pulled away from my grasp and turned his back from us. I looked at Sarah and she still stared at the cart. Her chest heaved heavily and her breathing was rapid and short.

"Sarah, please . . . go now."

My fear for her safety was palpable. I did not know how far Pa would go to protect the family secret. What I did know was how far he had gone in protecting the family as he saw it. That was farther than I had ever thought possible in my worst nightmares, and now, I did not know if Sarah would be able to leave alive.

Pa walked back to the bench where he was working. His head pointing downward at the table, he said clearly and firmly, "She can't speak of this to anyone." He hesitated a moment and then said, "It's our secret."

I watched him intently and that's when I saw it. Slowly, his hand cut across the table and picked something up. I could not see what it was, but my stomach turned at the thought of what it might be. His hand slipped in front of him and when he turned around the same hand had rotated around his back without ever revealing itself. With a measured pace, he walked back towards Sarah.

I had mere seconds to think. My eyes shot around the barn looking for anything. Nothing but hay. Rope hung on the wall closest to me. Seed bags at the foot of the wall. Nothing I could use to save her. I was going to watch her die. Would he carve her up in front of me? Would she find a shallow grave in the bottom of our outhouse? Would Pa shit on top of her remains satisfying his need for the twisted little joke of it all? Not her. She was too good. She was too pretty. I loved her. I'd kill for her.

Sarah still did not move, but she had found the ability to speak, if only a little.

"I can't . . . I can't . . ." she kept repeating.

Pa approached her and whispered, "Ssshhh." He looked at me and promised, "Everything is going to be alright."

I didn't believe him. I started to scramble, a feverish search for anything that might help, fueled by a deep and pressing panic. Something. I need something. There was nothing. I dashed in front of Sarah and stood in front of her. A sentinel standing guard for her, though, I lacked the bravery one would expect from such a man.

I tried not to shake as I insisted, "Stay away from her."

Pa kept coming and repeated his promise.

"I don't believe you!" I shouted, realizing that I had started to cry.

Sarah's strange chant continued behind me, "I can't . . . I can't . . . I can't . . ."

Pa was like a juggernaut. He was not going to stop.

"What's in your hand, Pa?" I demanded to know.

He did not answer. He was three steps away from her. I swore he would not reach her.

Without any plan at all, I acted. Leaping forward at him I wrapped my arms around his midsection. Included in my grasp was the arm he had wrapped around his back with his hidden surprise. We plowed through boxes and tables, tools and anything else that stood in our path as we punched, elbowed and wrestled for our lives. I held onto his arm and promised myself not to let go. Pa rained blow after blow onto me but still I held. I held for my life. I held for Sarah's life.

I was losing. I had to end this but I couldn't compete with his strength. Working my foot between his, I managed to trip him while he pummeled me with punch after punch. Pa dropped to the ground and the force of my weight fell on top of him as I held firm to his arm. I heard the air forced from his lungs as I tried to maintain my weakening hold on him. That's when he returned the favor. His free arm came crashing down onto my back and I uttered a loud guttural moan as the air slipped from my lungs. I lost my grasp on him and found myself turned over. Pa was now on top of me and he sat on me like he was riding a horse. He was enraged. His eyes had that horrible stare Jack and I had learned to avoid. He did not look at me but through me. My hands were splayed across the ground and they searched frenetically for anything I could use to defend myself. As Pa raised the knife above his head my hand grabbed hold of a small wooden handle. Closing my eyes I swung it as hard as I could at his head. A warm liquid sprayed across my face and I anticipated the next cut hoping it would be over soon. Hoping that it would not hurt much. Hoping that Sarah didn't suffer much. So many hopes, but I knew they were futile. I was dead and Sarah would be next. There would be no union in Heaven for us. We would find ourselves united at the bottom of an outhouse.

The Outhouse

A heavy weight dropped on top of me with a dull thud. The warm sprinkle of blood continued and it was difficult to open my eyes under the deluge of rain falling on my face. I used both hands to wipe the blood from my eyes. Shaking and blurry I looked up to see a hammer sticking out of the side of my father's head. Blood squirted in a rhythmic pattern that reminded me of water from a well being pumped. I pushed him off me and stood up. Covered in blood and bits of brain and skull, I kicked him in the side. His body shivered a bit. It was the death rattle of my father.

Chapter 25

Mourning

I held Sarah for a long time afterwards. Her breathing slowed over time and her grip on me became tighter, as if, she were slowly waking from her nightmare and realizing that it had been a reality. We were both now drenched in blood, the blood of my father.

"What am I going to do?" I whispered.

Sarah adjusted herself and nuzzled into my shoulder.

I uttered an audible, "Ouch!" and flinched away from her.

My tumble with Pa had left me tender and bruised but otherwise alright. The idea that we were alive warmed me tremendously for a moment. Sarah was safe now, but I had to deal with the aftermath of it all. How was I to explain all this?

Sarah moved off of me and said, "I'm hurting you?"

I held her to me and responded with a lie, "No."

She looked across the barn and saw the shattered remains of my father and I felt her shake as she turned away. For my part, I stared trying to process all that had happened and all that would have to happen in the next few days. I considered calling the sheriff. I could tell him the truth, laying out all that I knew. But, I had known for some time. Would I be arrested for my complicity or inaction? Sarah's body warmed me and I did not want to risk losing her. I could tell the sheriff that Pa had attacked her. That he had intended her harm and I had to act. Pa was a popular man; known around the community for his generosity, kindness, and willingness to lend a hand. No one would believe me. It had to be an accident.

"Sarah," I said, "We need to talk about . . . about this." I did not know what to say or how to say it. She buried her head deeper into my chest and the pain came over me in a torrent. I bit my lip, holding back the groan pushing up from my gut. "Sarah . . ." I waited for a response but she would not or could not answer. "Sarah, let's get you cleaned up and dressed," I said in a kind but firm tone. She looked down at herself and seemed to register her own nudity. She attempted to cover herself, but the effort was in vain. I gently moved her off of me and rose to my feet. My body cracked and I was starting to get a better assessment of just how badly Pa had beaten me.

I walked over to her dress and bent to pick it up. This time the moan could not be contained. "Yow!" I yelled, louder than I should have. I hobbled back to Sarah and tenderly handed her the pretty olive green dress that she had let slip from her shoulders a mere ten minutes ago. "Was it just ten minutes," I thought. It felt like it had been hours, at least. "Let me get you a washcloth and some soap and water," I said, "Before you get dressed, you can clean yourself off."

She stared at me for a moment without answering. I took the silence as agreement and headed for the door. Sarah screamed in sheer terror after I had taken just two steps.

"NO! Please, no!" Her panic filled the gloomy barn, echoing from the loft and bouncing around the beams.

I returned to her and she again dove into my arms. "Come with me then," I whispered.

She rose slowly and we both seemed to lean a little on one another as we left Pa's body behind.

After we had cleaned up at the well and Sarah dressed I brought her home. The parting was not easy, but eventually, a light appeared inside and even Sarah knew she had to go. I promised her that I would come over early in the morning. We agreed that we would not tell anyone what had happened. Pa's body would be discovered in the morning. He would have tripped and the hammer would be imbedded in his head. We hoped that was the story Ma and Jack would believe. Even if they didn't believe it, they couldn't report it as a murder. They knew I would then tell everything I knew. I kissed Sarah's dry, chapped lips goodbye and headed home through the darkness of the night.

Arriving home, I slipped silently into our bedroom. The rhythm of Jack's breathing mixed with the squeaking floorboards as I made my way to my bed. I shed my wet, bloody clothes, though with some difficulty, as my body disagreed with many of the motions I had asked it to perform. Lying in bed, my body and my mind warred with one another. The exhausted body demanded sleep, but the mind would not allow it. I saw Pa coming at Sarah. Relentlessly, he moved at her. He wouldn't stop. My feet seemed glued to the ground. I was too late. I saw Sarah lying on that awful table with Pa standing over her. Her eyes stared at me, but they were dead lifeless things now. Pa worked silently as he hacked and slashed at her once beautiful, innocent frame. Then, it was me on that table. Pa looked down on me, covered with his bloody apron. "You betrayed me. You betrayed the family," he whispered. His arm rose high in the air and the knife plunged into my chest. I awoke from the nightmare. My body felt worse than before I had gone to bed. Jack was still asleep but dawn was slowly breaking over the horizon. I had wished for an endless night. One that would renew my body, refresh my spirit and clear my mind of what had been done. The morning light slithered through the trees and would soon reveal last night's horror.

I knew Ma had to be awake by now. I knew she would have noticed that Pa never came to bed last night. She would be looking for him. It would not be long now before she would find him. I let my legs fall from the bedside and tried to pull my body upright. I was sore and the first signs of large bruises were beginning to appear on my left shoulder and down my ribs. I took a deep breath but that only added to the pain. I dressed slowly, allowing my joints and muscles extra time to creak and pull, consumed with dull aches.

I went downstairs. Ma was nowhere to be found, and so I took some coffee and headed out to the porch. I sat on the stairs and waited for it to happen. I wished the discovery would come soon because the anticipation was becoming worse than the reality. I just wanted to deal with it now. How would they respond? How would I? Would it be accusations and sheriff deputies? Would it be a pretend accident with recriminating looks and barely veiled hatred? I heard Jack moving around inside. He would be out soon. "Well, let's get the show on the road," I thought.

Jack took a seat a few feet from me on the porch. "Morning," was all I got from him these days. I returned the greeting and we sat in silence. I had thought all night about how it would happen, but nothing I imagined could prepare me for the reaction. Ma walked from the barn and made her way to the house. Her head was cast downward and her feet shuffled along the ground, barely rising or falling in movement. Her whole body seemed still, yet it moved towards us. She seemed to float along like a ghost. Jack noticed immediately the strange mannerism Ma was exhibiting and rose to greet her.

Ma arrived in front of us and stood so we could not see her eyes. There was a deafening silence for a time. Her hands clenched tightly and her body began to shutter. Her eyes rose slowly and they were strawberry red and full of tears.

"He's dead," she hissed.

Jack grabbed Ma's arm, pulling her close to him.

"What are you talkin' 'bout Ma," he said. "Pa's dead?"

Ma spit back at him. She wrestled herself free from his grip and spun back to look at me.

Jack was in shock. "Where?" he asked.

Ma never took her eyes off me as she responded, "In the barn."

Jack was three steps off the porch before she finished the sentence.

Ma's eyes flared with rage and sadness. There were no words I could offer her now that could undo what had happened. I was consumed by guilt over what I had done. Killing your own father, no matter the reason, didn't feel right. I thought about hugging her. I thought about slapping her. Unable to bring myself to do either I simply apologized.

"I'm sorry," I whispered.

Ma didn't respond. She didn't move. She stood in front of me, fists clenched and body rocking back and forth, a boundless container of fury. I never felt hate like that before. I was genuinely scared and sad. My own mother could not stand the sight of me standing alive in front of her.

Jack had returned to the porch a few minutes later. He looked back and forth at us, taking in all that the scene foretold. Turning, he looked at me confused and shocked.

"Leave," he ordered.

I walked down the porch steps. I turned to Ma again and repeated, "I'm sorry."

Jack slapped the coffee cup from my hand sending the contents careening into the air.

"LEAVE!" he bellowed as he began to quake with rage. I walked past him and left the house, not knowing if I would ever come back.

I walked to Sarah's house. I had promised her I would come early. Mr. Schultz was outside when I arrived.

"Mornin' Paul," he said cheerfully as he moved from towards the fence line.

"Morning," I responded as nicely as I could.

Mr. Schultz put down the tools he had been carrying and looked at me quizzically, "Somethin' wrong?"

I knew I would have to tell him. It was going to hurt him and I didn't want to hurt him. He was such a good man and I had grown very fond of him.

"Pa died last night," I blurted. "He fell in the barn and landed on a hammer," I added.

It was the first time I had ever lied to the man and it did not feel good. Little in the last twelve hours of my life had felt good. It took only a minute before he took me in his arms and held me tightly as a father should. He held his grief at bay, so he could offer comfort to me. In his eyes, his needs were secondary to mine. I was exhausted and sad; angry and scared. I let all of it out for the first time at that moment, wrapped in the warmth and comfort of his arms.

Jane had made breakfast and called out to her father to come in. When she saw me she greeted me cheerfully.

"Good morning, Paul," the warmth of her words became infected with confusion as she saw the grief in my eyes. "What's wrong?" she asked, quickly slamming down the frying pan she held in her hand.

Mr. Schultz walked to her and placed his hands on her shoulders.

"Mr. Miller passed away last night," he said.

"Oh . . . Oh, no . . ." Jane muttered and then broke into tears. "He was such a kind, generous man," she sobbed.

As Mr. Schultz took her into his arms Sarah's voice came barreling down the stairs.

"No, he wasn't," Sarah said through gritted teeth, announcing her presence.

Her little sister, Emily, was walking down the stairs holding her hand.

Mr. Schultz turned to her in shock and said, "Hush, child. That was uncalled for."

Sarah had a haggard look but her eyes were full of anger. She heeded her father's words and brought Emily to the table. We all sat and ate together. I did my best to answer their questions as to what happened to my father while avoiding Sarah's eyes. I hated lying to her family, and I hated that lying was becoming a bit easier every time I did it. I was on my own, though, because Sarah never uttered another word. After all, she wasn't there and had no idea what happened. That was the story we needed to adhere to. The truth was too terrifying to consider.

When all of the questions had been answered and the usual condolences given, I collapsed back into the hard wicker chair and took a deep breath of air as if I had just come up out of the water. Mr. Schultz stared at me with a look of profound pity.

"I'll come back with you," Mr. Schultz offered.

It wasn't really a suggestion, more a decision he had already made and I was expected to comply with it. He was not a man prone to losing an argument, but on this occasion he would receive none from me. Little did he know how welcome his company would be for me. We left the job of tidying up breakfast to the girls and headed out. Sarah averted her eyes as we left. I wanted to speak to her, to find out how she was. I wanted to hold her in my arms.

"I know there was something between you two," Mr. Schultz said as we walked side by side.

My body tensed. Had Sarah told him about us? Did he know we were in love?

"For what it's worth . . . I know he loved you."

My shoulders slackened. Now, I knew Mr. Schultz was both lying and uninformed about both, Sarah and my father. In an effort to provide solace to me, he had shown me how little he had known his friend. I remembered when I was that naive and the memory of it was like a wave of shame that crashed into me. What Mr. Schultz d¹ ˙ know was what everyone knew. It had been obvious to anyo⌐ had known either of us, that Pa and I did not get along. Schultz's attempt at comforting me was hollow, as emʃ of love as my father had become.

We walked on and he tried to change the subject.

"You and Sarah seem to get along real well," he ˹ it.

"Damn," I thought. He had beaten me to the conversation. "I've been meaning to speak to you about that," I said, slowing our pace as I spoke. I turned and looked him in the eye and spoke as firmly and as bravely as I could muster. "May I have permission to court your daughter, sir?"

Mr. Schultz laughed out loud as soon as I had finished. It was the burly, jolly variety he was so well known for; the type of laugh that filled a room and infected others with happiness. It seemed so out of place, considering what had just happened.

Slapping me on the shoulder and resuming our walk he responded, "You need hers more than you need mine!" A low chuckle continued to emanate from him as we walked. "You know, she is a willful and stubborn woman. Every bit of her just like her mom." He grew somber at the last remark.

I had no memory of Mrs. Schultz nor really did Sarah. She died when she was very young. Her memory must have been at the forefront of his mind as he absorbed the loss of my father, his friend.

"I miss her. Sarah reminds me of her in many ways. Maybe, that's why I let her get away with a bit too much," Mr. Schultz mused.

I smiled at him and said, "She really is stubborn, isn't she?"

We both laughed a bit and finished our walk together sharing stories of the ladies we loved. In doing so, we both helped each other set aside a difficult day.

Mr. Schultz had spoken with Jack for a few minutes before he headed inside to speak with Ma. We all kept up pretenses that it was an accident that killed Pa. In order for that illusion to remain intact, Ma and Jack had to concede that my continued presence in the house was necessary, though they detested it. Mr. Schultz had offered his ndolences and his aid to the family before returning home. Before ng me alone with them.

aul, if there is anything I can do, just ask," he said as he left. I 'o scream out to him.

"Take me away from here," I thought. Instead, I merely said, "Thank you."

As I watched him walk off into the distance, a small dust cloud forming around him as he did, a terrifying thought struck me. The body! What had happened to the body? I dashed to the barn, heedless of everything around me. Twice, I stumbled and almost fell, but momentum carried me forward and I slammed into the barn with force enough to shake the old wooden walls. I looked around frantically, spinning, and darting my head from side to side. It was gone. The body wasn't here. The outhouse! A controlled jog brought me to the outhouse. I grabbed the iron handle and the door swung open. The hinges creaked under the forceful tug and I hesitated before entering. I knew what I would find. I understood what it would mean. My feet simply didn't want to carry me forward to confirm it. I willed myself to take the single step required to confirm my suspicions. I dropped my head and slowly opened my eyes. Amidst the lime and waste was the unmistakable sign of a fresh human corpse. What looked to be a thigh sat tucked in the corner of the hole. Someone had deposited the body to cover Pa's tracks. I didn't care if it was Ma or Jack. They were both co-conspirators in my eyes.

Funeral preparation began the next day. Jack had built a simple pine coffin for Pa. I proffered no assistance, nor would it have been accepted if offered. Ma had decided to bury Pa in the church cemetery. The decision was a selfish one in a way. When she died, she wanted to be in the church yard "to hear the bells for all eternity." She also wanted to be next to Pa. This left little debate in her mind as to how final arrangements for Pa would be handled. Again, I extended no helping hand, and had little interest in pretending to care where his remains were to be interred. Sometimes, I envisioned him burning in Hell for his crimes; the visage of his face screwed up with pain brought me a measure of joy. Other moments would come and I would see Pa kneeling before Jesus, his head bowed low and Christ's hand resting on his head. Christ would look at me with consternation in his eyes and condemn me for my inability to forgive.

Pa's funeral became a happy day for me in an odd way. Sarah had taken hold of my hand during the service and held it throughout. We walked from the church together, hands clasped, in full view of everyone. My mother, Mr. Schultz, and anyone who cared to notice would now see that Sarah was my girl. I had feared that the night I had killed him had also killed our burgeoning relationship. Her fingers entwined with my hand put those fears to rest. Pa was dead. Sarah and I were alive. What's more, we were together. Nothing else could matter to me at that moment so long as I was a part of her life.

I was no longer welcome in my own home. Oddly, I understood why. There was more than a small part of me that felt I deserved their treatment. That I was a pariah and the ostracizing was natural, inevitable, and warranted. I had committed patricide. The details mattered little to them. No mitigating circumstances would undo the harm I had done to the family. I remained. I endured. To the people that were once my family, my existence was their bane. I had killed the man they felt had kept them from sleeping in the Pipes. My sin in their eyes was greater by far than his. I protected an outsider over my flesh and blood. For that, I was dead in my mother's eyes, dead in my brother's. I was a rotting, festering carcass that everyone turned their noses away from, but no one knew just quite how to get rid of.

Chapter 26

Comings and Goings
1941

Sarah and I spent more and more time together. Mr. Schultz had granted his blessing for our courting and it was only a matter of time before I asked for another blessing from him, her hand in marriage. We had talked many times about our future together. We made grand plans, designing the house we would live in, the kids we would have. We even selected names for them. There was never any doubt between us. We were in love, we would always be in love, and we would always defend each other.

The attack by my father against Sarah had not left physical scars; but it had left emotional ones. Those wounds ran deep in her. She refused to come around the farm for many weeks after. When I did convince her it was safe, she still took trepid footsteps and her head whipped around as she did so. Even though she had seen first-hand his death, what I had done to him, his burial; she did not feel safe here anymore.

"He's gone, love," I said sweetly as we walked past the barn taking hold of her hand.

She gripped me tightly and forced a smile across her face. Even when she was terrified; I found her beautiful.

"I know," she replied half-heartedly.

Sarah had felt guilty about what had happened. She had apologized a dozen times to me about what had happened that night.

"I'm sorry about . . . ." she began.

It was always how she began, but the end never came for her. Sarah could not yet frame the words to describe all that we had endured together.

The Outhouse

It was several months after my father's funeral when Sarah finally confronted me about what she had seen. She had avoided me for more than a week and I was growing concerned and a bit desperate to see her. We always met at the Sweet Spot and I went every day hoping she would be there. When the day finally came that she was there, I had no idea what to say or do. She sat in the grass with her arms wrapped around her legs and her knees tucked under her chin. I approached quietly and sat about a foot away from her. I wasn't sure if I was still welcome any closer than that. Sarah did not acknowledge my presence; rather, she stared blankly at the sun shimmering on the pond. She was stunning even in silence, like a painting of a medieval princess waiting in vain for the return of a lover lost in battle. I thought of the Lady of the Lake from Arthurian legend. The sun glinted and I half expected an arm to raise from the waters, sword in hand. Yet, I knew it would not be for me. Unlike Arthur, I was a man with no honor and even less courage. I decided to wait, not wanting to, or maybe, fearing to break the silence. I had a sudden pang of remorse. I was losing her and there seemed nothing I could do about it.

Suddenly, Sarah spoke. "I need to understand," she said pleadingly. Instinctively, I reached for her hand but she withdrew quickly. "I need to understand," she said again, but firmer and more insistently. The combination of her statement, the withdrawal from my touch, the distance between us I felt, all combined to sit upon my chest like a steel beam.

What she was really asking was, "Why was your father hacking apart another human being?" Worse, I bet she wondered, "Why didn't you seem surprised?" I looked at her sweet face and couldn't bear it any longer. The tears rolled and built like a snowball into an avalanche of sobs. I recounted the whole story, heaving and teary-eyed as I did. Sarah stared blankly at me as I shared the agony of that first discovery, the torment of loneliness as I tried desperately to reconcile what I had seen, and how my family had reacted to that knowledge. My mother's complicity, my brother's apathy, and worst of all, my father's growing bloodlust. I shared it all. The fights, my determination to stop him and the truth of Connor's death, I left nothing out.

"I loved him and I grew to hate him!" I spat. "I just wanted to love him but I couldn't. I couldn't," I sobbed.

It was then that Sarah wrapped her arms around me and held me.

She kissed me on the nape of my neck and whispered, "I'm so sorry."

I never lied to her again. I never hid another thing from her so long as we lived.

Sarah's companionship and love was something I desperately needed. She was the dry cave in a storm, the warm fire on a cold night, the theme music of my life. Conversely, the silence in the Miller house was oppressive enough already, but lately, things were becoming outright nasty. Ma spit venom any time she saw me. She had begun a concerted effort to turn Billy against me by casting slurs and negative comments at me whenever he was present.

"Don't you grow up to be like Paul, here. He don't respect anything, 'specially his family."

Billy was eleven now, old enough to understand that something was deeply wrong between Ma and me, Jack and me, but he wasn't quite sure if it needed to be between him and me. He began to manage the tension in the house by shunning me in the presence of Ma or Jack, but mauling me with attention whenever they were not around. It was an intense difference in attitude that he struggled to reconcile with his feelings for all of us.

It was Billy I felt the worst for. He needed a father and I knew I had taken that from him. Some days, I thought that was a good thing and other days I wasn't so sure. Billy was doing horribly in school and was in trouble more days than not. It was clear he was going to drop out sooner, rather than later.

"Jack dropped out. He's doin' jus' fine," he would argue.

"Billy, do you want to stay on this farm forever? Don't you want something better out of life?" I countered.

"It's good enough for Pa! Why is it everything that he did isn't good enough for you, huh?" Billy's voice grew enraged.

"I'm just trying to encourage you to do your best," I said, trying to soften the conversation. "Billy, please. I'm just trying to help."

He leapt at me. Aggressive and full of fury he spat, "Ya ain't my Pa! Stop tryin' to be him, cause ya ain't him!"

We, Miller's, all had that quick temper. A gift from my father's family. I just hoped Billy wasn't going to inherit anything else from Pa.

Jack and I really never saw each other anymore. He dedicated himself to the farm and took the role of provider for the family quite seriously. He had already made his feelings for me clear and felt little need to elaborate on them. I did what I could to avoid him and he pretended I did not exist. It was an arrangement that seemed to work for both of us most of the time.

Sarah and I were walking out of the house and had intended on sitting on the porch when Jack came by. He was dressed in a torn flannel shirt and denim jeans with suspenders. He was dirty, sweaty, and in every way the ghost of Pa. Sarah and Jack had reached the door at the same time. I was holding the door for her as she carried out two glasses of lemonade for us. As soon as she saw him, she screamed and the two glasses thudded to the floor and shattered, spraying the liquid all around. Sarah stood frozen in the door, Jack doing nothing to assuage her fears. He seemed to get off on the idea that he was so much more like Pa than I.

"I can't . . . I can't . . ." the words slipped from Sarah's lips and she was in the barn again.

She was watching as my father butchered a man. She stood naked, defenseless once more.

I let go of the door and held her in my arms, "It's okay. Your safe with me."

Jack chortled and pushed passed us, walking right through the spilled fluid and tracking it up the stairs as he walked. As much as I needed her with me, near me, I could no longer put her through this. Something had to give.

I was nineteen, and the Second World War was just over two years old when it happened. Ma was in the kitchen in the afternoon baking an apple pie. The aroma permeated the entire house and I yearned for a piece that I knew I would never get. Ma would sooner feed it to the pigs than allow me even a single bite. I sat on the front porch reading, having given up on pulling my own weight in a household where I was seen as the walking dead. Jack and Billy were at work in the north field, and the afternoon was as peaceful a one as the new status quo afforded me. When Ma yelled my name I wasn't sure if I was hearing things. It took a second, more forceful scream before I reacted.

"Paul! Get Jack!" she yelled. "Go get Jack and Billy! We're under attack!"

I dropped my book and dashed to the fields gathering my brothers. The three of us came barreling into the house to see Ma hunched over near the radio, listening intently.

The newscaster droned on about an attack on a naval base.

Ma looked up at us and said, "They keep repeatin' this. They don't got nothin' new to report just yet."

We all listened intently to the words echoing from the Philco radio.

"Hello, NBC. Hello, NBC. This is KTU in Honolulu, Hawaii. I am speaking from the roof of the Advertiser Publishing Company Building. We have witnessed this morning the distant view a brief full

battle of Pearl Harbor and the severe bombing of Pearl Harbor by enemy planes, undoubtedly Japanese. The city of Honolulu has also been attacked and considerable damage done. This battle has been going on for nearly three hours. One of the bombs dropped within fifty feet of KTU tower. It is no joke. It is a real war. The public of Honolulu has been advised to keep in their homes and away from the Army and Navy. There has been serious fighting going on in the air and in the sea. The heavy shooting seems to be . . . We cannot estimate just how much damage has been done, but it has been a very severe attack. The Navy and Army appear now to have the air and the sea under control."

The radio remained on in perpetuity. With various parts of the newspaper spread across each of our laps we hung on each word of the radio broadcast. The headlines varied but the subject was unmistakable. "Japan U.S. at War, Japs Attack Pearl Harbor, War!" Roosevelt's speech came early the next day. He began;

"Mr. Vice President, Mr. Speaker, Members of the Senate, and of the House of Representatives:

Yesterday, December 7th, 1941 -- a date which will live in infamy -- the United States of America was suddenly and deliberately attacked by naval and air forces of the Empire of Japan.

The United States was at peace with that nation . . . "

It was hard to fathom. Ma sat with her hand over her mouth. All I could think was that peace was something we never really had. We had the illusion of it and nothing more. I tried to envision the attacks, the billowing smoke, the screams of drowning sailors and Marines, the roar of planes and the thunderous shock of bombs. It was then that I realized that despite all our trips into Oakland, I had never seen a Japanese person before. I had seen pictures but never a real live one. They were scarier now to me then they had ever been. The President had gone on to lay out the case against Japan. It was a case the newspapers had made very clear. Japan's attack against us was a surprise. It was planned long ago. It did a great deal of damage though the extent of which was still unclear. At that time, we believed the death toll was in the hundreds, not the more than two thousand four hundred souls that marked the macabre beginning of a long war for the United States.

"The attack yesterday on the Hawaiian islands has caused severe damage to American naval and military forces. I regret to tell you that very many American lives have been lost. In addition, American ships have been reported torpedoed on the high seas between San Francisco and Honolulu.

Yesterday, the Japanese government also launched an attack against Malaya.

Last night, Japanese forces attacked Hong Kong.

Last night, Japanese forces attacked Guam.

Last night, Japanese forces attacked the Philippine Islands.

Last night, the Japanese attacked Wake Island.

And this morning, the Japanese attacked Midway Island."

This information was new to all of us. It was as stunning to us as the initial attack. Yes, the papers had mentioned that Pearl Harbor was not the only American territory attacked, but the coordinated assault of so many places was shocking. FDR's voice changed a bit, became clearer, more focused as he said,

"No matter how long it may take us to overcome this premeditated invasion, the American people in their righteous might will win through to absolute victory."

He concluded with the formal request for war, but he was right. It was unnecessary because war already existed. Peace was no longer an option. No longer could the United States delude itself into believing that war was avoidable. The nation was unified; the attack on Pearl Harbor seemed to temporarily set aside the animosity we all carried for one another. My family mirrored the nation's unity if only for the briefest of moments.

Jack had stepped out onto the porch where all the important family conversations seem to occur. I followed him out a few minutes after the speech concluded.

"I'm going," I said in a somewhat matter of fact tone.

Jack smiled at me, almost proud.

"Me too," he replied. Continuing he said, "We're gonna have to make arrangements for Ma and Billy."

It was the first time in years I didn't feel Pa's presence between us, forcing us apart.

"Maybe Mr. Schultz can look in on her? We can send money home to her to hire some hands. Plus, with what Pa had stashed. . ."

My words trailed off realizing what I had just done. I had brought back the ghost, a ghastly visage ran cold between us, and the great divide between Jack and I returned. It was the briefest respite, but I had enjoyed having my brother again if only for a few seconds.

"I'll go speak ta Mr. Schulz," Jack said coolly, trying to end the conversation.

I realized suddenly that I would have to tell Sarah.

We both signed up for the Marine Corps the following day surrounded by a large flock of other eager young men. The desire to avenge those lost at Pearl Harbor was palpable. Jack made it clear to the recruiting officer that we were not to be placed in the same platoon in basic or on active duty. He wanted no part of me. Neither of us bothered to explain our choice of service to one another. I already knew he had chosen the Marines to follow in Pa's footsteps. I doubted I could have put my reasoning into words at the time. It was much later that I realized I wanted to erase him, to remove the stain of him from Marine Corps history. Though, I was the only one who knew of it, the only one who could see the offensive blot on the Corps, I felt I had to do something about it.

I told Sarah that evening. She knew it was coming and had girded herself for it.

"I'm proud of you," Sarah said.

She, at least, pretended to be supportive of my decision to go. She was scared, worried, but proud. She hated the fact that I had chosen the Marines and would always say the word through clenched teeth when she was forced to utter it. The stories of the Marine Corps were ones she had heard told by Pa many times. She understood that they were a different breed of soldier. It was a group that she did not want me to be a part of.

Jack shipped out a week before me in order to drop into a different training platoon. He left to great family fanfare and a barrage of sweet baked goods and honeyed meats. Ma cried as she hugged him. She ran up the path, waving as Mr. Schultz drove away with him in his old '26 Ford TT Truck to drop him off at the train station in Oakland. She nearly kept pace with the old black pick up style truck as it reached speeds of no more than twenty-five miles an hour on flat ground. Eventually, the truck was able to distance itself from her and she stood sobbing, watching Jack disappear over the horizon. I knew my departure would not look anything like his.

Sarah held my hand the whole time and I felt her squeeze it as Ma made a spectacle of herself.

"Walk with me," she said sweetly.

I complied. We walked together in silence, enjoying the cool, but sunny day. It took a few minutes before I realized where we were going. Sarah was guiding me to the Sweet Spot. Upon arriving, it was clear that Sarah had planned the day well. A large yellow blanket was spread out under the tree while the wind lifted the corners. An overflowing picnic basket held one of the corners down denying the wind from stealing the scene. Sarah did not say anything. She did not take me to the blanket but rather to Anne's grave. Sarah had picked some flowers and adorned the simple stone with a rainbow of beauty.

"This was once a happy place for you," she whispered as she wrapped her arms around my waist. "I want to make you happy. I love you." She pulled me tighter and kissed me. "Come," she said tugging me towards the blanket.

I sat on the blanket and Sarah opened the basket. She had outdone herself. We ate fried chicken and fresh biscuits. She cut up an apple and we fed pieces of it to each other. I ate like a king and she served my every need, not letting me do anything myself. I lay on the blanket, the sun kissing my cheeks while the wind cooled them off. Sarah nuzzled next to me, resting her head on my chest. Flecks of her golden hair tickled at my chin.

"Thank you," I whispered. "I love you."

Without a word she rolled onto me and placed her hands on my shoulders forcing me to remain lying as I was. She smiled at me and took her hands from my shoulders and brought them to her hips. Crossing her arms she grabbed hold of her soft blue sweater and tugged it over her head, revealing her off white lacey scalloped brazier. She tossed the sweater to the side and removed her undergarment. She took hold of my hands and gently raised them, placing them on her breasts. We spent the afternoon making love under the old gnarly tree, lost in each other's embrace.

I left early in the morning the following week for the station. Mr. Schultz and Sarah came to the house just after dawn. Sarah's blonde hair was tossed and hastily stuffed into a ponytail.

"Dad tried to leave without me," she muttered a bit frustrated.

Mr. Schultz tapped my arm smiling playfully, "Didn't wanna see her sobbing like your Ma."

He had always known something had happened in my family around the time Pa died. Sarah never told him anything, nobody did, and he never asked. He knew my family had blamed me somehow for the death of their father and husband, his friend, but he never joined them. He picked up my bag and walked out the door.

"I'll give you two a minute," he said without turning.

Sarah was already covered in tears.

"I love you and I'm coming home," I promised.

I held her tightly for as long as I could and then kissed her forehead. Sarah rifled her lips to mine, pressing them hard. She kissed me in a desperate race against the inevitable, as if it were our last seconds of existence. When it was time, I extricated myself from her grasp and blew her a kiss from the door. "See you soon, okay?"

She nodded her head in consent then scurried across the room and forced something into my hand. I walked out the door and she followed a moment later, never allowing her eyes to stray from me. She greedily soaked up the few precious seconds we had left together. Neither of us said goodbye. We didn't say anything at all. No words could encompass what we felt at that moment.

As the car pulled out of sight and the vision of Sarah was obscured by the horizon, I turned to settle in for the ride. Opening my hand I looked for the first time at what she had given me. A small piece of golden yellow ribbon, the one she wore the day we buried Anne, lay curled in my palm. I brought it tenderly to my nose and took her scent deeply into my core. My eyes began to well with tears.

"You sure love one another, don't ya?" Mr. Schultz said simply.

Remembering myself, I lowered my hands and wrestled against my emotions to regain some semblance of composure. I looked at him a moment and responded in the only way I could. "Yes sir," I replied hoping the conversation would not continue too much further. My mind strayed to the events of last week and I tried to press down the guilty smile forming across my face. Mr. Schultz did not take his eyes from the road when he spoke.

"Come home. Marry my daughter and give me grandchildren."

I saw the gleam of teeth out of the corner of his mouth as Mr. Schultz gave a wide smile.

"I want lots of grandkids I can bounce on my knee before I'm too old to do it."

He was such a warm, loving man. I doubted he knew how much of a gift he had just given me. How much his blessing meant, especially since I had not had to ask for it. He gave it freely and it meant the world to me.

"I will, sir. I promise." I said. Then, he gave me one final present. One I loved him for his whole life.

"Please, call me dad."

Chapter 27

A Legend Returns

Jack was the first to make his return to the farm. He was gone from the farm for just over a year before his wounds allowed him a permanent trip home. We were both assigned to the First Marine Division. Jack was a member of Second Battalion, Fifth Marines under the First Marine Division while I was assigned to Third Battalion, Fifth Marines. It was not lost on me that I was assigned to a Marine unit that fought gallantly at Belleau Wood, my father among them. For our part, we would not see the fields of Europe but the sands of the Pacific. Instead of the Argonne Forest, we were sent to New Zealand and then on into Guadalcanal.

I excelled in training, and I was already a corporal by the time D-day on Guadalcanal came. It was August 7, 1942, when we landed in the Solomon Islands. I did what I could to keep track of Jack during the war, and I knew he was involved in the action but I did not know where or how. Japanese resistance on the island was initially light, and my platoon did not fire a single shot until we reached the outskirts of the airfield the Japanese were building. This was our primary objective.

The Japanese defense of the airfield was the first real engagement for my platoon. For many of us, it represented the first time we had taken another human life. Not for me, though. I was already destined for Hell if there was such a place. I had already seen the results of previous engagements between Marines and the Japanese. I swore I would keep my promise to Sarah. I was going to make it out of here alive. Though, not a crack shot by any means, I did my work and I did it well. I had no mercy or pity in my heart for the enemy. It's shocking how many men freeze in battle. How many actually never even fire their weapon. When the field was finally ours, I was nearly out of ammunition and overwhelmed with exhaustion. The fatigue was unlike any I had ever known.

After we took the airfield, the decision was made to christen it Henderson Field after a Marine killed during the Battle of Midway. I was resting with my men against a half-destroyed wall when I saw him. It was Jack with his platoon. He saw me as well; I was sure of it. He ignored my wave and moved away. He was thinner than I had remembered. Training had made him a bit gaunt, but I had no doubt about his identity. Clearly, Pa's memory had traveled with us halfway across the world. We hunkered down to defend the field we had just worked so hard to take.

It was here that my actions won me my first Navy Cross, and the beginnings of a very unhappy relationship with the press began. The official title of the efforts in the Solomon Islands was Operation Watchtower. We were poorly supplied, poorly armed, and fresh from boot camp. Some cranky Marine had coined the term Operation Shoestring and it spread like wildfire through the division. The term really did fit. We were restricted to two meals a day, our ammunition was thin, and we were armed with old bolt-action rifles. In short, the operation was run on a shoestring budget, but to some, we were merely holding on by a shoestring. Either way you looked at it, the name was perfect. It was the second time the Japanese had attempted to retake the field when I lost my mind. Three Marines were wounded and lay out in the open on the hardscrabble airfield. A corpsman had dashed into the open to dress their wounds when, he too, was shot as the Japanese deliberately targeted medics. I ran along the jagged line of trees and organized a fire-team to lay covering fire, and then made four trips onto the strip to gather the Marines and bring them to safety. Apparently, someone was watching and decided to make a big deal of it. I was interviewed, the story was printed widely in the press and the Captain put me in for a commendation. I was never comfortable with it. I was just doing what any of us would have done. The idea of erasing my father's sins had not really risen to my consciousness yet.

Throughout it all, I had not realized that one of the men I had thrown over my shoulder and run with had been Jack. They were all Marines to me. The Navy Corpsman, although officially Navy, was still Marine to us. Jack's wounds were severe and enough to end his career in the Marines. He had been hit in the leg and twice in the left shoulder. I went to see him in the makeshift infirmary. Drugged heavily, he wasn't conscious for my visit. I sat at his bedside and talked to him, wishing he would forgive me, wishing he would be my brother again. I held his hand for a few moments and then kissed his forehead before I left. I would not see him again for more than two years.

My career in the Corps continued while Jack made his way home. I wrote Ma and told her how brave and strong he was, never mentioning my role in the affair. I told her to take care of him and write me with updates on his condition. Ma did care for him but she never wrote me. Luckily, I had Sarah. Sarah wrote me every day. Sometimes, because of the intermittent and highly inconsistent mail service, I got twenty letters at a time. She kept me abreast of every detail of even the minutest event back home. After Jack had been released from the hospital, Sarah had been kind enough to check in on him for me. I knew how difficult that must have been for her, and I swore I would find a way to thank her for her efforts. She told me of his recovery and always stayed positive in her letters. In all the years I was gone, she only sent a single letter that had contained bad news.

My Dearest Paul,

My father passed away yesterday. He collapsed while working on the old Ford and Jane found him lying on the ground. I am terribly sorry to burden you with this news but I thought you should know.

I miss you and love you. How I wish you were here now with me to hold me close. Please, come home safely. I live in fear of not feeling your warmth again. Know that I love you always.

Sarah

It was the shortest letter I had ever received from her and the most difficult of the entire war. I cried for her. I cried for him. I cursed God for his cruelty. Finally, though, I had not done it since Anne had died, I prayed for him. I was so sorry that he would never be able to bounce his grandchildren on his knee. I wanted to be home, holding her and wiping her tears away. Of all that I had to endure during the war, this was by far, the worst of it.

The first time I thought I might not honor my promise to make it home to Sarah came in 1944 on Peleliu, in the South Pacific, just east of the Philippine Islands. We had reached our objectives within the first two days on the island. The airfield was entirely U.S. Marines but the same could not be said for the island itself. As the next few days unfolded it seemed that the island continued to give birth to Japanese soldiers. Like the emergence of a nest of spiders they appeared without warning in numbers large and small and were difficult to stamp out before they disappeared again. We used man portable and even LVT flamethrowers, satchel charges, mortars, artillery, and air support to unearth the enemy but nothing worked better than human targets to draw them from the earth. My memories of that unholy place are of fire and brimstone, blood and death. If Hell could rise and find a home on Earth, it was Peleliu.

The Japanese used the caves as perfect defensive positions. Two Marines had been cut down right in front of me by enfilade fire that swept across the entire company. A cave mouth had been shelled by our mortars but they had little effect. A dozen Japanese rifles cracked repeatedly from various positions keeping us pinned down. When a second set of rounds began flying at us from our left I knew we were in trouble. We must have missed a Japanese position because we were now almost surrounded with no avenue of escape.

"Hand me that satchel charge, would you?" I said to Corporal Martinez, the Marine next to me. "Cover me," I blurted as I dashed from the small rock I had taken refuge behind. I made my way above the cave mouth and tossed the satchel charge in and covered my head. The explosion dropped rock and dirt enough to bury the opening while spitting me into the air. I landed a few feet away, my ears ringing as I met the earth. Before I could get up, Martinez and the rest of the men were up and firing wildly, hoping to make up ground. I did that three times that day. By the third I could barely hear. I was exhausted. All of us, utterly drained, but none had a choice, we had to push on. Moving further inland and up the ridge; I was near collapse when we came under assault again. I did not have the speed to get out of my own way, much less the enemies. I took a round clean through my upper thigh. After being carried down the hill and dumped on a stretcher, I fell asleep. I woke up with my head light and my leg heavily bandaged and hungry enough to think anything tasted good. I was alive, and there was still hope that my promise to Sarah could remain unbroken. My mind drifted to her, feeling her presence. I dug my hand into my pocket searching for the piece of ribbon she had given me. It had grown as dirty and tattered with war as I had. My hand returned empty. The ribbon was gone, lost, buried on this horrible island with so much blood and death. I sobbed. I cried uncontrollably. No one seemed to care at all. Peleliu had taken my last physical connection to Sarah and to any semblance of a sane world. My actions earned me my second Navy Cross and my first Purple Heart along with a good scar on my right leg. My wound was not overly serious and I had thought I was lucky enough to be able to stay with my unit. After all, our next stop was to be my last of the war.

The Outhouse

We landed in strength on Okinawa's Hagushi beaches. It was by far the eeriest landing of my life. We met no opposition coming ashore. The Japanese were waiting for us to come inland, into the maze of caves. They would make us come to them and bleed us every step of the way.

We had been on the island almost a month. Fighting had been sporadic at first and growing more and more intense. Roosevelt had died shortly after we had arrived in theater and everyone was getting the general sense that the war would be over in maybe a year. It was a strange realization that this thing that had consumed so much of us might actually end. The thought of that fact actually caused many men to break. Some sobbed, others refused to leave their fighting holes, while a few charged wildly at the enemy spewing hate and bullets in equal amounts. They couldn't bear the thought of dying so close to a time when they might, just might, survive to see home. It was rather odd. The further away the war took me from home, the closer I was to getting home. The idea that I was getting closer to seeing Sarah, to honoring the promise I made her became a golden lifeboat amidst a dark abyss.

I had reached the rank of Gunnery Sergeant and was leading men to clear the caves on Strawberry Hill. We had just been informed of the surrender of Germany and the sense of euphoria spread throughout the unit as quickly as the sense of dread returned when we were ordered to clear the caves. We had cleared two caves and had killed at least fourteen Japanese soldiers before we lost our flamethrower. The enemy round hit the fuel and gave birth to a ball of flame, a small sun that sent the rest of us running for cover. We were separated and exposed. I left the cover of the rocks and tried to organize the remnants of the company when I got hit in the elbow and the gut. I never did get to see a single strawberry on that hill. I remember being carried down the hill by a young buck private bouncing on his shoulders. It hurt like hell, but at least I could still feel. I wish to this day I knew who had saved me. I would like to have been able to thank him for helping me keep my promise to Sarah. After almost three years, the war was over for me now.

I arrived at the train station in Oakland in the first week of August feeling tired and a bit sore. The trip from the bay was short, just enough time for my muscles to stiffen in the uncomfortable seats. I rose, cracking my back and stretching my arms into the sky, my cover sliding from my head as I did so. I laughed at myself as I picked it up. "Cover," I thought. "Three years ago this was a hat to me." So much had changed in me beyond this strange military language I now spoke. I was thinner than I was when I left but hard and strong. Riddled with scars and aching joints, I carried home souvenirs both obvious and invisible. I hated to admit it, but a boy had left this place and a man now returned.

I grabbed my bag and threw its weight over my shoulder. I was one of the few soldiers on the train that day and my uniform made me stick out from the crowd. Several young ladies smiled at me as I exited the door. My heart quickened. Seeing them reminded me how much I could not wait to see Sarah.

A man my father's age walked over to me, pushing out his hand for me to shake and said, "Semper Fi, Devil Dog!"

I returned the honor and we separated without further conversation.

"Hey Marine!" God, I remembered that voice. "Paul!" I heard her yell.

I looked around trying to find her. I finally saw Sarah's sister through the crowd and moved at the quick-step towards her. I nearly fell backwards as Jane rolled into me, hugging me.

"We missed you!" Jane yelled, too loud now for the distance between us. She looked a bit like her little sister, Sarah, but most of her looks came from her father's side. She had his strong chin and piercing blue eyes. Her hair was a short cropped dark brown, just as

Mr. Schultz had. It was odd that she could look so much like her father and still be attractive in her own way.

"I'm sorry about your father," I said softly. "I loved that man." I knew this moment was coming but the words hurt coming out.

"Thank you," she returned as she released her grasp. "He loved you too, you know," she said somewhat longingly. "This is my husband, John." Jane introduced a massive brick of a man who stood at least six-feet-two.

I shook his hand, "Nice to meet you."

He smiled and said, "I've been readin' 'bout you. Wow, you're a real hero!"

The words held not one hint of sarcasm. They were unabashedly genuine hero worship and I hated it.

"I did what anyone would have done," I said flatly. "Can we head home?" I said, realizing the sooner I was in Sarah's arms, the better.

We all squeezed into the front of John's pick up, a 1937 Studebaker Coupe Express. It went considerably faster than the truck that had brought me to the station three years ago, and it was much nicer, more modern. Oakland, itself, seemed more modern. Pipe City was gone. The Depression was gone. I returned to a different world. I wondered how much Sarah had changed.

"How is she?" I asked as I prodded Jane in the arm.

"You'll see in a minute," she teased.

Unnatural as it was, I was very scared to see her again.

We arrived at the Schultz place and it was surrounded by a dozen cars and trucks. A huge linen banner inscribed with green painted letters hung across the roof overhanging the front door. It read, "Welcome Home Paul." But, I wasn't really home just yet. I doubted I would be welcomed when I actually got there. I pushed the thoughts of Jack and Ma and Billy aside. Home would be wherever Sarah was I told myself. Big John pushed on the brake and the Studebaker lurched to an abrupt halt. I exited and then offered Jane my hand, helping her out. I went to grab my bag from the back, but John had already slung it over his shoulder and started walking towards the house. I needed to forgive the hero worship. He was a good guy.

I had taken a single step towards the house when Sarah hit me. She crashed into me with a force that knocked the air from my lungs. She was kissing me so hard I couldn't catch my breath. I gently placed my hands on her cheeks and tugged her away, taking a deep gasp of air as I did so. She smelled like morning flowers, fresh and full of hope.

"Miss me?" I asked with a giant smile.

She was more beautiful than I remembered. Her blonde hair was longer now, the ends bounced with perfect curls. Like a torrent of ocean waves her eyes welled with tears of joy. A green dress, much like the one she had shed before entering the barn the night my father attacked, accentuated her perfect figure. She pushed herself out of my hands and kissed me, again and again. I was home now.

The party she had planned would have been wonderful. It would have had great food that I would have enjoyed. It would have been many things. It would have been filled with friends, happy to see me, and I happy to see them. Except, something was missing. Everyone at the party knew what was missing. They had the decency not to bring up the subject and we all pretended not to notice. So, the afternoon crawled by with everyone keeping up pretenses, pretending like my family didn't exist. Sarah held my hand throughout it all, transferring strength to me as she did. I had been shocked that they did not attend at first. Then those feelings turned to hurt, sadness, and finally to anger. When the last of the guests had left Jane and Elizabeth began cleaning up. They smiled at Sarah and me as we headed up the stairs. Tonight, I would spend with Sarah making up for three lost years. Tomorrow, I would pay my family a visit.

Chapter 28

A Legend Endures
1945

I awoke with a start. Confusion reigned for a moment as I tried to get my bearings. The sheets were soft, the room was dark, and the smell was of spring flowers. It took a minute to remember the last twenty-four hours. Sarah was asleep, resting quietly. I spent a few moments looking at her taking a mental picture. She looked so content. I had not seen anyone look that happy for three years and the vision warmed me. It felt like a part of my humanity had been reseeded with her. In time, with tender care, it might grow again into some recognizable aspect of the man I was before the war. With her, I could be human again. I sat up in bed and caressed her forehead. Sarah did not move as I brushed the stray hairs from her face. I let my fingers slide down her cheek. They continued, heading down her soft shoulders and down her arms. When I reached her hand, I gently took it in mine. I had spent entire nights awake dreaming of her hand in mine. In my dreams, her hand was just as it was now; small, soft like velvet with tiny lines at the joints and little freckled specks. There was just one difference now. In my dreams her hand had a diamond ring on it. That was something I was going to fix.

After spending some time holding Sarah's hand I decided it was best to let her sleep. She had had a long day, a long year or two in fact. I dug through my sea bag and pulled out my only pair of jeans and a green t-shirt. Wearing anything but green or tan still felt odd. I wondered if that feeling was ever going to go away. I rummaged for my belt and finally felt it like a snake hiding at the bottom of the bag. I grabbed the head and yanked it upwards, spilling a few items of clothes as I did so. "Damn it!" I muttered under my breath. Sarah rolled just a bit, almost imperceptibly. I tossed the escapees back into the bag and left the room as quietly as possible.

Big John was already up and dressed. I found him on the front porch. I missed the porch, not just here at the Schultz's place, but at my own home as well. It was always the place people seemed to meet; the hub of family life, as it were. It's amazing the simple things you miss when you are away so long. You wouldn't think they mattered so much, but they always did.

"Mornin' Paul," Big John said as I walked out the door. Big John had already risen from his seat on the stairs of the porch, dusting his behind off. "Let me fetch you some coffee. How do you like it?"

He had a big hefty grin to match his big hefty frame.

"Thanks. I can get some," I said grabbing the door before it could fully shut.

"Nah. I'm grabbing some more. You enjoy the sunrise. Milk?"

Big John had grabbed me by the shoulder. It was clearly his version of a gentle tug, but I decided to let his kindness stand unobstructed for fear of being hurt.

"Please," I smiled and he headed off inside.

I sat on the porch steps near where John had been. They creaked under the strain of my weight, though, I was certain my body was a respite for them compared to the man who had just left. The old wooden stairs were just as I remembered them. I looked for the old knot I used to toy with when I was a kid and later, as a teen, when I didn't know what to say to Sarah. When I was awkward and afraid to tell her how I felt, I would needle it and dig at it nervously. It was still there but the years had not been kind to it. No longer a knot, but a full blown hole, I gently pressed my finger through it letting the memories overtake me. The sun was beginning to peek over the horizon now, and the first glimmers of the day shot rays across the sky. The rising sun held very little beauty to me anymore, only nightmares of a white flag emblazoned with red. The reminiscences of Sarah and I awkwardly trying to explain our feelings for one another was replaced with shelling and mortars, machine guns and beachheads, flamethrowers and bayonets. The screams of dying men, the smell of charred flesh and the eerie sound of human flesh being cut apart by the jabs of bayonets filled me. The recollections flooded every part of me and felt like a torrent that would soon flood the world. The rising sun was no joy to me. A red orb ascending through the innocence of the world; its arms outstretched in conquest, screaming, "Bonzai!" That was the rising sun to me. I had one of the flags in my bag, a souvenir of the war. I was going to give it to Billy. I just wasn't going to tell him how I got it.

"Here ya go," my body shivered, startled at John's reappearance.

The creaky stairs had failed to offer a warning, or my mind had drifted further than I cared to admit. I took the mug from his hand and pushed out a half smile.

"Thanks." Even my gratitude was a bit forced; although I was genuinely thankful.

Big John took up his seat on the stairs again and we sat quietly for a time. I was thankful not to be grilled about war stories. I had spent so much of yesterday dodging and evading the questions and giving half answers to stupid questions that I lacked the energy for it anymore. Was it bad? Those Japs are cowards at heart, ain't they? How many did ya kill? Bet the food was lousy, huh? Were you scared? But the answers I gave were the ones I knew they wanted to hear. Not the truth. Yes. No. Hundreds. Yes. All the time. John broke the silence eventually, but not in the manner I had expected.

"I took one in the left shoulder in the Ardennes. We were surrounded, no supplies, freezing, and the Germans laid into us. Leopard tanks and everything. Nearly got run over by the first wave. We found ourselves behind the tanks and in front of the infantry. Half of us took on the Krauts coming at us and the other half tried to blow the Leopards. I was going for the tanks when next thing I know

I'm face down in the snow and warmer than I have been in weeks. I got blood running down my side and two of the guys lift me up and throw me in a hole. Took almost a week to be evac'd. Funny, I was yellin' I wanted to stay when they put me on a truck."

He paused, shaking his head slowly from side to side, "What kinda mook begs to stay in shit like that?"

I didn't answer. The question was rhetorical, one that every soldier had asked of themselves at least once. John never looked beyond the rim of his coffee mug as he recounted the story. When he had concluded, he moved his left shoulder and it crunched audibly as he did so.

"It's a train wreck in there still. Can't do much with it."

I waited patiently to see if he had intentions of continuing.

When I felt it was safe I queried, "You with the 101st?"

John looked at me and answered proudly. "Volunteered to jump outta airplanes from the start. Hell, no one believed I could do it. Said no parachute could stop me from dropping like a rock." He gave a sly chuckle and said, "It's nice to be home, but it ain't easy being home, ya know?"

His words were a lightning strike to me. That was exactly it. I just had no idea how to express it until Big John said it. I had felt strange, out of place and time, like I did not belong here and the war no longer wanted me there. So much of being home was nice but I missed the war somehow. I didn't like it, didn't want to go back; but still, felt oddly connected to it and the men I had left behind.

"Ain't that the truth," I replied.

We returned to our silent vigil on the steps watching the sun rise. Words were not necessary between us, then. We were brothers in arms. As soon as I asked Sarah to marry me we would be in laws. For the rest of our lives, we never needed words between us. We just looked after one another in the way that brothers always do.

After the sun had made its full appearance I placed my mug on the stairs and got up.

"Gotta start the morning routine," I said. "Shit, shower, and shave."

John gave a hearty laugh and leaned back on the stairs and they moaned an audible strain under his weight. "God knows you Miller boys know how to take a dump! Never smelt a shitter quite like the one at your place. Do me a favor and don't stink up ours too bad."

I froze. My body felt as if it had just run headlong into a brick wall. I heard it, but it wasn't what he really said that was it.

"What?" I squeaked out.

"Sorry," John said, "Your brothers can stink up an outhouse better'n anyone I ever met. Swear somethin' crawled up them boys and died before they crapped it out, ya know."

No. Please no. It couldn't be true. I had to know. Had to be sure.

"Tell Sarah I went home and I'll be back later, okay?" John looked confused.

"Sure. I was just kiddin', you know. You're more than welcome to use the outhouse."

I never answered. I never turned around. I had to find out.

The house seemed cold and quiet when I arrived. No signs of human life emanated from it. I did not enter. Jack was probably out in the fields already. As to Billy and Ma, I had no guesses. I went, instead, to the barn and grabbed a lantern from a table. Though the sun had been up for a bit the day was still a bit gray and I needed light where I was going. A flashlight would be easier, but I would have to go into the house to get that and I wanted answers before I did that. As I walked away from the slab, I turned back quickly. The thought had come to me to look here for signs. This was where my father had been when he was at his gruesome work. I was drawn back to the table. I gave it a once over. Satisfied that there were no signs of slaughter I breathed a sigh of relief. "It's nothing. You're just tired and crazy," I thought, chastising myself. I wanted to believe the best; still, I was inexorably drawn to the outhouse.

It had not changed at all since I last saw it. It was still a pathetic looking thing. A wooden shanty assembled from an eclectic assortment of old wood, aged and neglected. If anything, it leaned further to one side than it had before I left. The gap between the door and the frame afforded little privacy any longer as it had spread further over the years. Like a fault line rupturing, a chasm had opened on one side and the door hung limply on the opposing frame. The smell remained. A smell I had grown accustomed to in the last few years.

The outhouse was currently occupied. A pair of feet could be seen through the crevice and they swung lazily to and fro. I put the lantern down and waited for Billy to be done. When he swung the door open he nearly fell back into the shack as the shock of seeing me hit him.

"Holy Crap!" he yelled.

"Don't cuss," I responded quickly then said curtly, "You missed my welcome home party."

Billy looked at his feet and did not respond. I felt bad for saying what I did. I knew it wasn't a decision he had made.

"You've grown," I added trying to make him forget the last comment. "You look good." He looked a bit like Ma, few hints of my father or Jack in him.

Billy raised his eyes a bit but still did not meet my gaze, "Thanks. You look thin. Did they not feed you over there or was the food just that bad?" Clearly he wanted to lighten the mood, too. I hugged him and he returned the gesture with force.

When he finally released me there was an awkward moment; neither of us knew what to say or do.

"You want me to go in my pants or what?" I quipped.

"Oh, sorry," Billy blurted as he moved out of the way.

"Wait for me and we'll go into the house together," I said picking up the lantern from the corner and heading into the outhouse.

I closed the door behind me and held the lantern above the wooden seat. Creeping closer to the hole I saw the ditch filled with lime and Billy's most recent deposit. I reached my hand in and felt around. Swishing my hand back and forth through the muck and filth I moved much of the lime to one side. Using my other arm I brought the lantern close. Big John was right. Half an arm was dried and decaying slowly in the pit of excrement. The remains could not be more than a few months old. I fell to my knees and gasped for air. I couldn't breathe.

"Why?" I whispered into the foul air.

I brought my hand, full of waste and death to my face, then, realized that I could not. I slammed my fist down and leapt to my feet, feces splattering from my filthy hand in a wide swath.

I dragged Billy to the barn in a fit of rage. Slamming him into the wall over his protests I kept my voice low but the seething fury could not be contained.

"Did you know?" I yelled repeatedly.

Billy protested about his treatment ignoring my question.

"Are you insane? What's your problem?"

I put my hand on his throat and he grabbed my arm in a futile attempt at escape.

He choked for air and I asked again, "Did you know?" He tried to shake his head no but I tightened my grip. "Did you know?" I roared.

Billy began to cry and his body shook with fear. Realizing how terrifying I must have been to him, I eased the vice on his neck and let him go. I took a few steps back and found a seat on a stool. Billy crumpled down the wall collapsing into a ball of tears.

I gathered myself and tried to assert some control over my emotions.

"Billy," I said as softly as I could manage, "Did you know what Jack was doing?" The question hung in the air. I rose and walked to him. Sliding down the wall I sat next to my brother. Wrapping my clean arm around him I said, "Billy, you have to tell me." When his words came, and they took a long time to do so, they were unsteady and weak.

"I'm scared," was all he could say. He kept repeating the words over and over before his sobs would no longer allow them to escape.

"Billy, I can help," I said trying to provide some measure of comfort now. He had grown tall. He was nearly a man in his own right, but not quite yet. At that moment, he was my baby brother, and he needed help.

"I wanted to tell someone, anyone but I couldn't. Ma knows. She doesn't even care. She knows. She knew all along," he said intermittently through tears and heavy breathing. I thought of myself. How alone I felt. The sense of betrayal was oppressive and inescapable. Memories of my experiences flooded the mind's eye. They were the very same things he was now enduring. I had Connor, for a time. I had Stephen, too. Then, when I needed him most, I had Tim. Yet still, I had always felt alone, that there was no one to help me escape, no one to stop it. I was just a boy then, young, and innocent. Naïve. I stood up and offered my hand to him.

"Come with me," I commanded.

Chapter 29

The Station

I stood outside the Sheriff's office and stared at the door. The building was a simple concrete exterior, gray with age. Two large double doors of dark wood were adorned with a large sign declaring it to be the Alameda Sheriff's Department. The single window was filled with various posters and public service announcements. One poster showed the flag raising on Iwo Jima, "All Together Now!" written at the bottom. The war bond effort continued just as the war did. It struck me as odd that my part in all of it had ended.

I was less than seven feet from the doorknob. A few steps, an extension of my arm, a slight turn of the wrist and I would be inside. If it were only that easy I would have done it sooner. What was I going to say? "I killed my father who was killing migrants because he tried to kill my girlfriend and now my brother is killing migrants too; but, I didn't tell anyone until now because . . ." the thoughts rambled on in my head. There was no way I could tell the story now without risking myself in some way. What about Billy? Would he be implicated? What would happen to Ma? I had to do something but I didn't know what that something was? I felt myself take a step back from the door. "Not yet, I have to think this through," I thought.

I was suddenly sent forward, the slap on my shoulder pulling me out of my mired thoughts.

"Hell, they could put you on one o' those posters, dontcha think?" A tall tan-skinned man said as he took up position next to me. He gazed at the poster thinking that was my focus. "Be over soon, I reckon," he mused, waiting for me to enter the conversation. I recognized the face but the name escaped me. I think he was in

Jack's class, several years ahead of me. Clearly, he knew me and had read the accounts of my time in the service.

"Hope so," was all I could muster.

"Japs can't withstand the bombin' forever," he said, putting his hand on my shoulder again. The gesture was overly friendly and familiar, and I did not welcome it. "Think we'll need to invade?" he asked. Not one moment was left for a response. He answered his own question. "I think we'll have to do it. Find every last one o' those rats hiding in their holes."

I glared at him and tried to keep my composure. It was always easier to talk about a thing than to do it. He spoke casually about what might become of hundreds of thousands, if not millions, of lives.

"I should be going," I muttered.

He looked put off but excused himself, "Sorry to keep you. Say hello to Jack and your family for me."

Family. The word hit home for me. Did I even have a family anymore? Did I have a home? I had dropped Billy at Sarah's ostensibly to buy time. I didn't know what to do for him. Billy didn't need a babysitter, he was far too old for that and there was no real reason for me to ask Sarah to let him stay there awhile. I would have to tell her what I had discovered. Was I just avoiding it? I had cleaned myself up in the kitchen sink and changed my shirt, though, I was stuck with the same pants I had on. Sarah didn't ask what was wrong but I know she sensed something. She had agreed to take Billy in without a single question. She knew I would tell her what was going on in my own time.

"When will you be back?" she had asked me as I was leaving.

"I don't know," I said as I soaked in the warmth of her presence like the sun on a beach.

"I love you," she said as I left.

I should have said it back. I wanted to make a family with her. I wanted to make a life with her. The thought of not being with Sarah was wedged between me and the door of the Sheriff's Department. It proved an insurmountable barrier to the truth.

I walked away from the building with Sarah foremost on my mind. I was in Oakland already, so I might as well make the most of the trip. There were a number of jewelry shops within a few blocks. I didn't have a family anymore but I could make my own. I loved her and she loved me. I would ask her to marry me, and we could leave and never look back. We could finally escape everything. Maybe we could forget everything, too.

The first shop I had entered had nearly dashed any hope I had of an engagement. The prices were far beyond me, some of them with numbers higher than I had ever seen on any product in my life. I found the ring in the second shop I went in. It was simple and elegant, and best of all, in a soldier's price range. The girl at the counter was sweet and wished me luck.

"Go get her, tiger!" she yelled as I walked out.

She seemed genuinely excited for me and that helped embolden me. I was ready. Now, all I had to do was actually do it.

I took Sarah to dinner that night. I was dressed in a button down shirt and slacks that I had dug out of my dresser back home. The shirt hung limply on my shoulders and I fought a constant tug of war with my trousers to keep them from collapsing to the ground. They remained the nicest clothes I had that even came close to fitting me by this point. The ring was in my shirt pocket and I checked on it like a mother would worry over a sick child. Sarah had donned her lilac dress and a simple white sweater for the cool night air. Her hair was tied off slightly to one side with duel ribbons of white and purple. I thought of the yellow ribbon she had given me. How the loss of that little moldy piece of cloth had almost broken me. I clutched at my chest promising never to lose it, never to lose her. We went all the way over to San Francisco Bay. By the time we got there, I was a nervous wreck and had begun to sweat profusely. I parked and helped Sarah out of the truck. She took my hand and smiled playfully at me.

"Why so nervous?" she asked. She knew. I knew she knew. She was going to say yes. I knew it. She knew it. Yet, I was still terrified and nervous. It wasn't just an engagement she would hear tonight. I had to tell her what I knew about Jack.

"Just hot is all," I croaked and it came out almost an octave too high.

We were seated at a table overlooking the bay. The restaurant was more than I could really afford, but it didn't matter. Sarah asked to leave three times after seeing the place and then, when she saw the menu she demanded to leave.

"Sarah," I whispered.

"We don't belong here. This place isn't for us," she stated loudly so that other patrons could hear.

"Sarah, please," I begged keeping my voice low.

"No, Paul. We should go. It's beautiful, but it's too much."

She was right but that wasn't going to get me to bend on the issue. The waitress appeared almost out of thin air and asked for our orders. I ordered lamb for Sarah and a steak for myself, and she folded her arms and pouted as I did.

"Please don't be mad at me," I said reaching for her hand as I did.

She sulked for a few seconds and then accepted my hand. Resigned to the fact that she was here to stay, Sarah began to enjoy the sights. The salty ocean air mixed with half a dozen other smells in the restaurant and filled the air with an indescribable aroma. We ate and laughed. We poked fun at the prices in order to avoid crying over them. Sometimes, we just sat and stared at the waves that crashed rhythmically against the shore. The sound was peaceful, like lying in the field and resting my head on her chest and listening to her heart beat.

"Sarah," I started.

She was quick on the draw and blurted out "Yes," anticipating my proposal before I had even said another word.

There was something I need to get out of the way before I asked her. I needed her to know what Jack was before she took me too deeply into her own future.

"Sarah, what my father did," I paused and she squeezed my hand.

"It's in the past and it isn't your fault," she pronounced with certainty. But I knew. It wasn't in the past.

"Jack is doing the same thing."

Sarah looked confused. I wondered if she thought that Jack was going to propose to a girl tonight, too. She couldn't ask that since I had not proposed yet, so, she sat and stared at me with a quizzical look.

"Jack has been killing people while I was gone. He's just like Pa was."

Sarah's face went white. Her cheeks blended with her sweater and the waitress nearly tripped over a chair coming to see if she was alright.

"Fine. I'm fine, thank you," Sarah murmured. She waited a moment for the waitress to leave before she asked, "How do you know this?" Her voice was quivering and her body was rigid, as if she was willing herself not to shake.

I explained all that I knew and how. She took it all in and seemed to handle it well, never interrupting or stopping me for clarification. I remembered that night. The night he was going to kill her. I know it must have been on her mind, too.

"Do you remember . . ." I asked.

She cut me off. Holding one hand in front of her like a stop sign she spoke firmly.

"Not tonight. Don't let your family ruin tonight." Her hand remained in the air as if it were a totem, warding off evil.

"I thought they already had," I replied.

"No night is ruined when we are together," she smiled so sweetly as she said it.

I knew it was forced. I knew there was a tumult of emotion underneath it, but it meant so much to me.

There, in the moonlight under the stars, with the ocean breeze pushing me forward I made it official, "Will you marry me?"

The drive home was full of dreams and wishes. Sarah barely even paused between words, much less sentences as she plotted every phase of our life together. It was as if the proposal had opened the flood gates and the rush of ideas was impossible to hold back. We pulled in front of the house and I walked her to the door. It was time I asked the more difficult question of the evening.

"I can't leave Billy behind," I said flatly as if it was a condition of the proposal.

It wasn't but I knew I would fight to bring him if I had, too. Luckily, Sarah didn't even hesitate. In fact, she never even made me ask.

"I know," she said still beaming with happiness. "He'll live with us as long as he wants. He'll always be welcome in our home."

If it was possible, her smile widened further at the words, "Our home." I took her in my arms and kissed her gently on the lips.

"Thank you," I said.

The moment was cemented a second later when we both spoke simultaneously, "I love you."

Sarah rose onto her tip-toes and held my hands in hers, hesitating to let it go. "You're already packed," she whispered, "but I have work to do," she kissed me softly, tugging at my bottom lip as she moved away and then headed to the stairs. I watched her walk away happy in the thought that I could watch her walk away and return the rest of my life.

After Sarah disappeared from view I headed outside to find Billy. I assumed he'd be pretty stir crazy being stuck at the Schultz residence for a while. He was out back using a stick to hit rocks. As I approached he was unaware of my presence, and I heard him imagining his future as a baseball great.

"The Yankee clip comes to the plate, a hush falls over the crowd," he said in a mock announcer voice. Billy tossed the rock into the air and smacked it with the stick. The rock sailed off to the left and Billy dropped his bat. "It's deep! It's far! It's gone!" Billy followed it up with mock crowd noises and cheers. I smiled at the innocent play.

"You know, he doesn't hit many homers at Yankee stadium," I said sarcastically announcing my presence. Billy turned with a start and went red-faced with embarrassment.

I smiled at him and playfully chided him, "A Yankee, really? How could you cheer for a Yankee?"

Billy came to Joe DiMaggio's defense immediately. "He's from San Francisco, ya know," he blurted.

"I know," I responded evenly.

"He played ball for the San Francisco Seals too," Billy added, layering his defense.

"I know," I said again, smiling at his efforts.

"He . . ." Billy started but I never gave him the chance to finish.

"Is the best player in baseball, hands down," I conceded.

"He's a patriot, too. Joined the Air Force," Billy added.

I kept my comments about cushy, safe assignments to myself and picked up a rock as I walked in front of him. He picked up his stick and got in his stance.

"You're coming with us," I said. "Sarah and I are leaving tonight and you'll live with us."

Billy didn't ask any questions, he simply said, "Thanks, Paul."

I tossed the pitch towards him and he swung and missed. "Come on," I laughed, "you need to pack."

Sarah's goodbye with her sisters was equal parts excitement and mourning. I suspected Jane understood more than Elizabeth did. The youngest of the Schultz girls cried, never unclenched her fists, and refused to speak to me. I hugged her anyway and held no ill will towards her. I understood that I was ripping her sister out of her life and I already knew what lengths I would go to if someone had tried to take Sarah from me. I left Jane with a robust hug and earnest gratitude for all that she had done for Sarah in my absence. Sarah's brother-in-law, and my very fast friend, John had dropped us off in front of the bus station after our hurried farewells.

"Gonna miss you," he said with more emotion than he wanted to.

"We'll write you when we get settled," I responded trying to seem put together and under control when my stomach sloshed around and felt like a rowboat lost in the middle of the Pacific.

John gave Sarah a great big hug while Billy and I looked on. When he was done with Sarah he took the two of us into his arms and hugged us, as well. Billy squirmed under his might, but I couldn't help but return it. John had been good to Sarah and her sisters and for that I owed him a debt that could never be repaid. When he released us, I walked away silently to buy our tickets. I returned to the group a few moments later and none of them had even spoken. The air hung stagnantly and everyone seemed to feel as if it was the last time we would see each other. Sarah's eyes were pink and she fought to hold back tears. Billy fidgeted awkwardly and John held his head low, worrying his chin into his chest like a dog would a bone. Then, it happened; I just laughed. The whole scene was so farcical I simply had to laugh or I would have cried. They all looked at me as if I had just danced on a person's grave.

"We're going to be fine. We're going to see each other again. We're going to be happy!" I declared and slapped John on the back.

The jolt knocked his head up and he forced a smile. Another hug was exchanged and John took his silent leave of us.

The Outhouse

While we waited we took up temporary residence on a set of black wooden benches situated in the corner of the station. We had forty-five minutes to burn and little to do but wait. So, we were happy enough to people watch as others entered and exited the station. A little boy no older than ten burst through the station doors and our attention shifted to his frantic motions. In his arms he carried a stack of newspapers. The U.S. had dropped the bomb. Hiroshima had been vaporized and the war would be over in days. By the time we reached New York and settled in, there would be peace. I sat back against the wall, my shoulders relaxed for the first time in years and I let loose a broad smile. It was finally over.

So, we got on that bus and we never went back. I tried never to look back, never to think back to those days. Your Uncle Bill died when you were little and I almost broke then. I promised myself that if I outlived Jack, I would tell the story. I won't be around much longer and he's gone now. I'm sorry I never told you or Jason, but I couldn't bear it. Please forgive me.

Chapter 30

Legacies
Upstate New York, 1988

My Dad had passed away on December 9, 1987. He had been diagnosed with stage three brain cancer a year earlier and had told no one of it. It must have been that burden that caused him to make the anonymous phone call to the police department in Alameda, California. The official cause of death was cancer; but, I knew in my heart I had killed him as he had his father. His story that day had destroyed everything between us.

"You need to leave."

Those were the last words I had said to him. I had not spoken to him since the day of his confession. He left the study and unceremoniously exited the front door. Lisa and the kids wondered why he had left without saying goodbye. They wondered what had happened in the study that day. They still don't have the answers to those questions. I could not begin to discuss it; to discuss what I could not fathom, what I could not accept.

In the days and weeks that followed the weight of the story was more than I could bear. I lashed out at those around me; especially, those I loved most. Odd, how we can save the worst tortures for those we most cherish. I screamed at my son for leaving his baseball mitt at the foot of the stairs, and two days later, he was berated for the trip to and from the field when I was forced to take him to recover his forgotten bat. My daughter got the brunt of my venom for simply asking me if I would fix the shelf in her room. Lisa, though, she got the full force of all that I felt but was powerless to say.

It started with, "Jeff, I'm here if you need to talk." When nothing came of it, she would carefully maneuver and try to probe deeper. "Your father called today. He won't tell me what's going on either. Please talk to me." God, she had not lost any of that siren's song she had. Her voice called to me and tugged at the story; pulling it towards the shore, but the storm never allowed it to reach port. Her patience was deep and far more than I deserved. It did have its limits, though.

After almost two months of lashing out at my family without warning Lisa's patience was about to find its limits. I had little more to offer my family those days other than the silent treatment they were enduring. I had spent most days in the study sunk into one of the armchairs as I listened to my father's voice crackle out of the tape recorder I had used to record his story. His confession. I had begun drinking again. Something I had stopped before we even got married. I was not a good drunk, never have been. Booze, particularly vodka, helped me to get through the sessions I spent in the study. When I emerged from the dark room I carried with me all the rage and sense of betrayal I couldn't drown with a bottle of Gordon's. I let it fly at whoever dared to be in my path. As drunk as I was, as soon as I hit her, I knew I had lost her.

From my drunken haze, I remember that Lisa had tried to confront me. She had had enough of my self-deprecating misery, especially, since she had no idea what the cause was. I gave her no hint and so I gave her no reason to be understanding. When I opened the door to the study she was there forcing me back in. She sat, in the same chair he had told his tale, and crossed her arms. Her face was pale and showing the first signs of age, but still enchantingly pretty despite the stern expression she wore.

"This has gone on far too long, you know." It was something like that she said. I cannot be certain because I followed the statement with curses and slurs and frustration and drunken idiocy. She tried to walk away from me and I grabbed her. When she pulled away I threw the first punch I had thrown since leaving Viet Nam. I fell to my knees and begged her forgiveness. I cried. She left.

Lisa had nowhere to turn and so went to my mother and father's house with the kids. My mother called and told me they were safe. She told me that Lisa was ok but bruising quickly. I cried again and begged to speak to her, to hear her sweet voice again, but, nothing I could say or do would ever change what I had done. She would never forgive me for it.

My mother said, "You and your father have to talk. I know this is between the two of you, but understand he made choices and he's lived with them. You don't have the right to judge what he's done."

I managed to get out, "Thank you for taking care of them," before I slammed the phone down. I thought, "No right. Who was she to speak of it when she was as culpable as he in hiding it all? A serial killer in the family that they protected. Who was she to tell me I needed to forgive and forget?" I would never forgive, never forget. My parents could have saved countless lives and instead chose to protect a murderer because he was blood. My father was not the man I thought him to be. Not the man he raised me to be.

I went to my son's baseball game two weeks ago, and he gave me the ending to our family's story. I stood on the third base line behind several parents and a fair distance from Lisa and our daughter, Karen, who watched from the rickety blue bleachers on the first base line. I tried not to stare but they were both so beautiful, and I missed them more than I could bear. Lisa wore her ankle length yellow dress and it made me think of Anne, the aunt I had never known, waiting for her brother to return home. I so wished that yellow dress would act as a beacon, glowing from the lighthouse to welcome me home as Anne's once did for my father. Karen stood cheering as loudly as she could for a friend that was really a boyfriend she did not want to admit she had. The mere mention of the name, Andrew, saw her cheeks flush and the denials fly. I missed it. I missed her. My son, named for me, was clad in his bright blue uniform and stood in the concrete dugout on the far end of the field. My eyes followed him as he walked up and down coxing his teammates towards victory. After a crack of the bat and a heavy roar from the gathered crowd; he turned to the field to survey the situation. He was big now. Ready for college in a year and already getting scholarship offers for his grades, as well as, his athletics. He was a natural at almost anything he tried. I was proud of him and I hoped he knew that. The thought that I wasn't sure he knew that, weighed heavily on me. As he scanned the field he saw me and averted his eyes as soon as he did. He never once looked back at me. I choked back tears and tried to stay resolute.

I watched the entire game alone with my thoughts. The severity of sadness that came from a family who was lost to me, but could be seen from afar like some distant mirage in a hopeless desert crushed me. As the mirage drew closer and Paul approached me, my throat went dry. I clamored for water, moving towards him.

"Hi. Good game." I choked out through the desert in my mouth.

"Dad." he said.

He had grown mature. His voice was deep, a powerful bass. He was becoming the man I hoped he would be.

"What you did to mom . . ." he said firmly but I cut him off.

"Should never have happened. I can't ever take it back no matter how hard I try. I'm so sorry to her, to you guys."

He stared at me defiantly with disappointment in his eyes.

I started to cry again. I spent so much time crying these days. I fell to my knees and sat back on my haunches in the middle of the town park with soccer moms and their kids passing by and I cried. Sobbing and broken, I realized all that had transpired. The epiphany hit me and sat atop me like a house and I, the wicked witch of the east. My father had idolized his father and was crushed by what he had done. He idolized his big brother and could not betray him. He could not reconcile what he was with the idealized version he built in his mind. I, too, had idolized all I thought my father was. I loved the idea, not the man, when I should have loved the man. My grandfather was not perfect. My father was not perfect. I carried on in that infamous family tradition now. My grandfather had disappointed his son, my father disappointed his, and now, I again honored the family line with my actions. Sitting in the mud, crushed by the weight of it all; I realized I had done my father a great wrong. I should have loved the man, not the idea. With all his flaws and wrongs, he was a good man and a bad man. He was not perfect but he was a good father. When I felt the gentle brush of my son's hand on my sobbing shoulder as he leaned down to hug me, I knew. I looked up, eyes swollen and foggy to see a bright warm sun standing sentinel on the horizon. Lisa and Karen were standing in front of me, the sun at their backs. Lisa's yellow dressed flickered in the gentle breeze and her hand laid gently over her mouth, tears streaming down her cheeks. Karen seemed to hold her up, a beaming smile on her face as she stared proudly at her brother. I knew at that moment, I had the greatest gift in the world. He was a better son than I. Maybe, he would finally break the family curse.

"I love you, Dad" Paul whispered.

With his arms wrapped around me, I, too late, finally forgave my father.

Epilogue

After a week-long healing process that included a long session in the study in which my entire family sat in shock as they listened to me read my father's confession, I decided it was time to end this for good. I called the police in Alameda and explained the story to them. It took three detectives before someone would actually believe I was authentic. Once, over that hump, things moved quickly.

The press dubbed the murders the Outhouse Murders. It did not take long for a "reliable source" inside the police department to release my name under condition of anonymity. The talentless Carl Erzt had risen to fame on this story. I prayed he would only get ten minutes of fame and go away, but alas, he never did. Soon, I had two dozen reporters and photographers camping on the street in front of my house seeking exclusive interviews, photos, and the gory little details they had yet to put together on their own. The phone rang constantly. Detectives that I came to know by first name, reporters that I came to know by other names not fit for print, publishers, and even some Hollywood directors all wanting the story. I was often exhausted at the end of each day and Lisa began fielding the calls for me, running interference as it were.

Despite threats to come and arrest her for obstruction of justice unless she woke me, she stood firm, "He's told you everything he can. He needs to sleep. Please, he'll call you in the morning." That siren's call that had served her so well in life, that had hooked me and brought me home was employed and before long, we had established times where each detective would call to have a fresh set of questions answered.

The reporters never stopped, but at least we now knew when we could take the phone off the hook.

Several publishing firms had called offering book deals for the rights to the story. I had already sent the manuscript based on my father's story to my publisher and interest in the story was exceptionally high. I had talked it over with Lisa and we had agreed that any proceeds from the story needed to go to the families of the victims if they could be found, and if any remained alive. Otherwise, the profits would go into a victims' fund, helping victims of violent crime. I couldn't bear to see the Miller family profit again from these people's deaths. Yet, no matter how many times I told the story; one fact never surfaced. I left my mother's knowledge out of it and so carried on a bit of the family legacy in protecting her. After all, some secrets are best left buried.

The next thrilling novel by David W. Gordon

AN ABSENCE OF FAITH

Coming in 2015